Praise for *When Sa...*

'They say don't get mad, get ev...
this excellent revenge thrille...
The Tinder Swindler meets *Sweetpea*. I'll have
what Lucy Roth is having.'
L.M. Chilton, author of *Don't Swipe Right*

'Dark, funny and thought-provoking'
Jackie Kabler, author of *The Murder List*

'Incredibly pacy, funny, oh-so-dark, devious and
dare I say, relatable . . . Who hasn't thought about getting
back at someone who's hurt you, right?
I loved everything about it!'
Noelle Holton, author of *His Truth Her Truth*

'A bold and clever coming-of-rage story that gives a razor
sharp twist on the classic romcom'
Victoria Hawthorne, author of *The Darkest Night*

'Wow! I loved it. Devoured it in two days. It was dark,
delicious and deadly. Provocative and thought-provoking
too. Layered, with depth and utterly addictive.'
Louise Swanson, author of *End of Story*

'This is how I like my romcoms – not too much rom, a
good amount of com, but most of all a wicked amount
of imagination when it comes to revenge – a book of
tremendous energy, delightful malice and menace.'
Robin Ince, author and comedian

Readers love *When Sally Killed Harry*

'Found family, found salvation and found mission – plus a few surprises along the way. And yep, you will root for all of them.'

'Sally is a compelling anti-heroine who reminds me of Jason Dean – Christian Slater's character from *Heathers*. She's unhinged . . . and watching her unravel is part of the glee.'

'A darkly funny and unhinged wish fulfilment tale about women pushed to the edge to get justice in a patriarchal society.'

'If you're looking for a rom-com that's anything but conventional *When Sally Killed Harry* will have you laughing, gasping and rooting for Sally and her crew every step of the way.'

'Sardonic and sharply written . . . a fun, fast-paced read'

'A bold, unapologetic and raw exploration of frustration, fury, and the simmering rage women feel when the world constantly asks them to tiptoe around their own pain'

'Hilariously witty, sharp and unfiltered'

'A book that tackles toxic masculinity head-on, not with kid gloves, but with a sledgehammer'

'It's about amplifying the voices that have been silenced and empowering women to claim their space, their stories and their anger.'

WHEN SALLY KILLED HARRY

Lucy Roth is the pseudonym for author Lucy Nichol – a writer with a love of flawed characters and tales from the darker side of life. She has a passion for mental health awareness, music and nostalgia. Her first work of fiction, a dark comedy called *The Twenty Seven Club*, explores music fandom, mental health and media sensationalism. Her second novel, *Parklife* (the sequel to *The Twenty Seven Club*), delves into addiction, recovery, friendship and hope, and is set against a backdrop of Northern life and 90s Brit Pop. Lucy's third novel, a feminist comedy entitled *No Worries If Not!* was published in summer 2023 by Harper North. *When Sally Killed Harry* is her debut thriller novel.

LUCY ROTH

WHEN SALLY *KILLED* HARRY

avon.

Published by AVON
A division of HarperCollins*Publishers*
1 London Bridge Street
London SE1 9GF

www.harpercollins.co.uk

HarperCollins*Publishers*
Macken House, 39/40 Mayor Street Upper
Dublin 1, D01 C9W8, Ireland

A Paperback Original 2025

1

First published in Great Britain by HarperCollins*Publishers* 2025

Copyright © Lucy Nichol 2025

Lucy Nichol asserts the moral right to be identified as the author of this work.

A catalogue copy of this book is available from the British Library.

ISBN: 978-0-00-874029-0

This novel is entirely a work of fiction. The names, characters and incidents portrayed in it are the work of the author's imagination. Any resemblance to actual persons, living or dead, events or localities is entirely coincidental.

Set in Sabon LT Std by HarperCollins*Publishers* India

Printed and bound in the UK using 100%
Renewable Electricity at CPI Group (UK) Ltd

All rights reserved. No part of this text may be reproduced, transmitted, downloaded, decompiled, reverse engineered, or stored in or introduced into any information storage and retrieval system, in any form or by any means, whether electronic or mechanical, without the express written permission of the publishers.

Without limiting the author's and publisher's exclusive rights, any unauthorised use of this publication to train generative artificial intelligence (AI) technologies is expressly prohibited. HarperCollins also exercise their rights under Article 4(3) of the Digital Single Market Directive 2019/790 and expressly reserve this publication from the text and data mining exception.

MIX
Paper | Supporting responsible forestry
FSC
www.fsc.org
FSC™ C007454

This book contains FSC™ certified paper and other controlled sources to ensure responsible forest management.

For more information visit: www.harpercollins.co.uk/green

To my husband Chris, mainly because I love him but also to reassure him that, despite the questionable Google searches carried out while writing this book, I plan to commit no crimes whatsoever against him, except perhaps stealing his chocolate from the fridge from time to time.

Prologue

My body switches on suddenly like an arcade game lighting up, every feature activated. He leans in close and his scent overpowers me. A blast of warmth spreads from my torso, getting bigger and stronger like a volcanic cloud – and just as dangerous. It's not his aftershave that gets me. It's him. It's just him. His pheromones or something, I don't know. Maybe he's born with it . . . maybe . . . I mentally shake my head ruefully. Whatever *it* is, it takes me back to the moment we first met. The park, the energy, the desperation. I've never wanted anyone like I wanted him.

Like I *want* him.

'This is wrong,' I say, as he kisses me slowly, his lips just brushing mine before he presses them closer, harder, knocking an ecstatic gasp into the back of my throat.

I feel more alive than ever. I know this is his way of numbing me from reality. This is a distraction technique. A well-worn, overused and oh-so-classic distraction. In the moment, I don't care.

But he is a bad man. And I am a hypocrite.

I kiss him back, my stomach giving Simone Biles a run for her money. His lips hover again, teasing me. I feel drunk, woozy, euphoric. I move my head to the side so I can look at him, drink in his eyes, those sharp cheekbones, that luscious mouth.

'But you're never going to stop,' I say, my hot breath in his ear. He moves his mouth back to mine.

'Neither are you,' he says gently, his voice broken as though he's as lost in it all as I am. He kisses me fully this time, pulling me into him, and I feel myself crumbling, bit by bit, like a cave falling in on itself. If he gets me completely, if I lose myself in him again, I know I'll never get back out.

I have to do something. Now.

I move my hand to the side of me, find my bag and push my fingers inside, feeling around until I find it between key rings and compacts and perfume bottles. 'No,' I whisper back to him, still kissing him. 'I'm *never* going to stop.'

He pulls away, looking at me, fear in his eyes. Real fear. God, this is the real him. I'm finally getting to meet him – no mask, no veil. This is the real him. For the first and last time.

He can barely speak, but he's trying. 'You . . .'

'I know,' I say. 'I'm sorry.'

I'm glad I wore my new waterproof mascara today.

I kiss his forehead gently. 'Goodbye, Harry,' I say.

Chapter 1

Dating used to be fun. Or at least, I thought it was. Maybe I'm simply feeling nostalgic and it's always been like this. It's . . . boring. A slog. I've travelled all the way from London to New York; I've tried blind dates, been set up, used all the apps. And nothing's really changed. Men are still so predictable. They still want to explain to you why your opinions and tastes are incorrect.

Sorry – let me back up a moment. You're probably wondering how I ended up killing Harry. Because I did kill Harry. Sweet, dangerous Harry. Not that it's a major spoiler or anything. I mean, it kind of says it on the tin. But I guess the answer to how it all went so very wrong begins with my disastrous dating career. So, here we are, a few months earlier, in a restaurant called Cerutti's, sitting across from the most boring man in Manhattan . . .

'I can't believe you've never been to Osaka.' My date, this one's called Dan, is smirking at me. 'It's literally the only place worth going if you're going to try it.'

I groan inwardly, but my face seems to be set in a mask of polite interest. I am well versed in masking.

'*I* go every time I visit Japan.' He holds a glass of red in his hand, swilling it theatrically in circles as he eyeballs it. The eddying red liquid seems to taunt me. And *he* seems completely oblivious to how close to the edge I am. Boredom and simmering rage are strange bedfellows. No matter how many times I am subjected to this torture it never gets any easier.

Mansplaining really fucking stings.

'They serve it as sashimi,' he continues, shovelling a morsel of prawn into his overactive mouth with his greasy fingers. He pauses to look at me. 'That's raw fish, by the way.' He winks at me as he says it. He is speaking slowly, as if my tiny brain couldn't possibly keep up with him. He has already explained the concept of sushi to me. This was after I'd told him it was probably my favourite food. There is (happily for me) an abundance of sushi restaurants in Manhattan. I frequent them a lot. But when I informed him that I usually eat it at least a couple of times a week, he responded with: 'Ah, but you're probably not eating *traditional* Japanese sushi.'

I push down a sigh.

This date is a prime example of '*I should've known better*'.

I've found far too many reasons *not* to date lately, that I recently decided to just put myself out there, just in case. FOMO, you know?

This one's profile proudly showed a photograph of him on a yacht (desperate) and the *"About Me"* text mentioned a couple of his favourite designer labels (cringe). Sure, he's clearly got the cash. The oversized TAG Heuer sapphire watch and Hugo Boss suit demonstrate that (I told him he looked good, he replied with the name of the label). But his charm needs a helluva lot of work.

'Honestly, Sal. It's a risky business eating pufferfish,' he says, and I wince at his shortening of my name. I don't know the man. At what point exactly did he decide he was part of my inner circle? He continues in earnest with his tale of extreme pufferfish bravery – something, it appears, he's done precisely once. 'Fifty years ago, it killed hundreds of diners, but it's just three a year in Japan now. If that.' He confidently breaks off another prawn tail but makes a mess of it. His fingers are shiny with squished pink meat and oil. I look down at his plate. There's prawn meat everywhere. Each discarded head and tail still stuffed with the expensive meal. I'm amazed this man has ever tried pufferfish when he can't even shell a basic prawn.

He picks his glass of wine back up without wiping his fingers, and I dread to think what his bedroom etiquette is like. His glass is now smeared in seafood juice.

'And eating it, well . . . it's not something I suggest *you* should try. I wouldn't want to feel responsible.' He winks at me again. One of those slight, quick little winks that make my skin crawl. 'But what can I say – me, personally, I like living on the edge.' He sits back in his seat at this point, as if he's waiting for me to jump up and down with delight and awe.

Instead I nod solemnly in response to his little tale, wishing he'd had the misfortune of trying this potentially toxic dish at one of Japan's *less* specialist establishments. I've had enough.

'So you're a fugu connoisseur?' I ask. His face drops momentarily and he lets out a nervous laugh before nodding and attempting to change the subject. He holds his wine glass between us.

'This is a nice red,' he says. 'Good. But if *I* had chosen I probably would have gone for the grenache.'

I size him up. The Japanese word for pufferfish seems to have bamboozled him. I have to wonder if he's ever even been to a fugu restaurant, never mind actually eaten the creature.

But I'm not prepared to continue being mansplained at any longer.

'The real test of fugu – that's pufferfish, by the way,' I add, imitating his previous tone. 'The real test is preparing and eating it yourself.' Another nervous laugh emanates from him. 'Seriously,' I say, in a stage whisper. 'It's all hype. In reality it's really difficult to get it wrong; it's actually hard to ingest tetrodotoxin.' I take a sip of my wine and hope I've planted a seed. It's a lie of course. Real fugu chefs take years of training to learn how to do it right. It can easily kill you if you get it wrong. But if he's egotistical enough to try prepping it himself, which I think he just might be, and if he even slightly fucks it up, at least another woman will have been saved from having to sit through his nauseating wankfest. I pick up my glass by the stem.

'Did you know that, not only is tetrodotoxin found in the liver of the pufferfish, it's found in the ovaries, too. Which means . . .' I pause and proceed to speak *very* slowly indeed, swirling the purplish liquid delicately '. . . that the female of the species is more deadly than the male . . .'

I wink at him. He is now fidgeting with his napkin and I think I can detect his knee jostling. 'God, I used to love that song,' I say, and hum the melody of the Nineties tune 'Female of the Species', which my little tale has reminded me of. 'My mum played that one in the car when I was a kid. It's always stuck with me.'

The restaurant is brightly lit, with comfy cushioned chairs and strains of unambitious jazz playing in the background.

My date has gone kind of quiet. I pour myself another glass of red, down it in one and stand up from my seat. The chair screeches over the hard floor.

'Would you excuse me,' I say with a beaming smile. I attract the attention of most of the diners. Their gaze lingers on me longer than they should, thanks to my bright pink-and-turquoise stripy ra-ra dress.

'They're at the back.' It takes the briefest moment for me to realise that he assumes I'm simply going to the restroom. I am not. I pick up my handbag, tilt my head to the side and waggle my fingers playfully at him. Oh yes, we Brits can't deny we love a bit of sarcasm. Then I walk away from the table and out through the exit.

We'd made it as far as the starters. Which I guess is better than my date last week, where I didn't make it past ordering drinks. Perhaps my immunity to dickhead behaviour is waning, I muse. But I simply couldn't sit through any more of his guff.

He needn't know that I've never been to Japan or indeed eaten fugu. I'd just picked up a lot of information from the *Lonely Planet Guide to Japan*. Mum and I could never afford to visit in real life, though we often spent hours there in our heads. Ditto New York, which is kind of why I'm here now. Compensation money, as painful as it is, can also make your dreams come true. Plus, even though my current job doesn't demand much brainpower, I came to Manhattan with two and a half years of a biochemistry degree under my belt. So I kind of understand how poison works. Dropping out of uni is by no means a measure of intelligence.

It's an indication of the crap hand life has dealt you.

The problem is, if you have exceptional taste in fashion, as I'm often told I do, you're written off as one-dimensional.

People literally think you're stupid. Such as Dan, who immediately assumed my bright and bold sartorial choices meant I had the brainpower of a small animal and would be easy pickings. Much of the time, being underestimated tells you more about them than it does about yourself. It can work in your favour. Exposing Dan as a lazy-minded blowhard was vindicating. Swings and roundabouts and all that.

The June evening air is just the right amount of fresh and breezy, so I decide to walk home. I'm wearing my low cork wedges with hot pink crochet straps, which are always a safe bet for a stroll. Nicely worn in but not shabby enough to be retired to the back of the wardrobe just yet.

The sound of sirens and car horns intermingles with horses' hooves clip-clopping on tarmac as they trot around the edge of Central Park, pulling tourists in fancy carriages. It's still light outside, the tree shadows dappling the pavement and every shade of green cushioning the horizon in the distance.

I love summer nights in Manhattan, so walking from the Upper West Side to Midtown isn't a chore – no matter how crazy the locals must think me when I can just as easily save my legs by hopping into a cab. To be fair, it is a long walk. I just need the air, sometimes. You know, like a reset.

Recalibration is so important.

I've spent a fair bit of time in this neighbourhood lately. On bad dates mostly. It's greener and more affluent than where I live on 43rd, bordering on Hell's Kitchen. But I love where I live. I love the late-night diners, Irish bars, theatres and bric-a-brac shops that are all on my doorstep. Not to mention the alluring lights of Times Square. Sure, I sometimes head north to breathe in the air of the park, just like I did back home with Hampstead Heath, but I wouldn't change it. To be fair, I *couldn't* change it – the prices up here would stretch me way beyond my means. And I haven't even been able to get a job in a field that I am (partly) trained for so I'm resigned to working in some mediocre position in an office block where I spend all day fielding queries about corporate spaces and tenancies. It wasn't exactly my dream job per se, but needs must.

And I *needed* to leave London. I had no choice about that.

The walk home is like a patchwork map of dating disasters. The cosy little Italian on the corner of 62nd and Central Park West where Megabucks Mark informed me over spaghetti arrabbiata that he was looking for a live-in nanny. Well, those weren't his exact words, and he didn't have kids that needed looking after, but how else would you describe the relationship dynamic where you're doing everything for them except wiping their arse?

I left before dessert. I've struggled to forgive Lily for that one. Surely it's a friend's obligation to identify at least some common ground before matchmaking? Perhaps conduct an audit of their pros and cons? I think she just enjoys having some influence. She works in PR after all.

Then there's the basement sports bar that was kind of nice to look at, as was my date: Russ. But given all he was interested in was watching the ice hockey on the big screen (and shouting stuff I didn't understand at it) I, once again, bowed out early.

But the worst date I've had since moving to New York was actually with a British guy who insisted on showing me all the 'hidden gems' that I might not otherwise find by myself. Mansplaining by tourist trail. He didn't know any, and instead proceeded to give me a tour of the Rockefeller Center (lovely, of course, but hardly 'hidden'), Trump Tower (I know!) and Hooters. Now don't get me wrong, I have nothing against Hooters. In fact, the wings were pretty awesome and the waitstaff were lovely. It's how some men interact with Hooters – or what they think Hooters is or should be – that's the problem. And when your date decides it's perfectly acceptable to whack his palm twice across one of the women's arses, well . . . Let me put it this way, the only thing that ended up on his lap was the remainder of my meal. The only bone he had in his crotch came from the barbecue chicken wings that I threw over him. The sticky residue seeping slowly through his jeans wasn't the kind of outcome he was hoping for. I walked out of there so full of rage I had to neck an extra propranolol from my handbag stash to stop myself from going back in and chucking the rest of my drink on him too.

I'm not sure how many more disappointments I can take. It's getting boring now. And I don't like getting wound up. In fact, being in Manhattan was supposed to be my antidote to that. My calming lifestyle change. Yeah, I came to Manhattan for calm. *Go figure!* as they say in these parts.

Like I said – recalibration.

I'm close to home now and walking towards the fruit and veg store that's situated near the bottom of our building. Its wares spill out onto the sidewalk, wooden crates packed with fruits and veggies of every shape, size and colour. Rows of radishes, carrots, chilli peppers and tomatoes line the pathway into the shop.

It's one of those places that never seems to have consistent opening hours but this evening the lights are still on and I'm glad it's open – I never made it through the planned three-course meal and I fancy treating myself to something sweet and sour.

I grab a little green carton already filled to the brim with shiny red morello cherries. Then I grab a brown paper bag and chuck a few lychee nuts inside, hearing them thud against the paper as they hit the bottom of the bag. I scoop a few pistachios into another bag and take my haul to the counter where I swear the woman audibly huffs at me.

I don't know if it's an aversion to Brits or just me in particular, but she seems to have taken an instant disliking of me since I moved here. With my housemate Priya, she's all rainbows and sunshine, asking her how her day was, calling her ma'am. And then I rock up, and she turns up her nose as if she suddenly needs to fumigate the shop.

She silently weighs my lychee nuts and pistachios, punching numbers into the till. I make a show of how miserable she is by practically singing 'byeee' in as strong a British accent as I can muster as I leave. Think Julie Andrews.

She remains characteristically mute.

I head inside our apartment block, smiling at the concierge who sits behind a shiny slate-grey desk before I jump into a waiting lift. I hit number 37 and am quickly transported upwards towards my apartment.

This has been my home for the last few months and a place I'm beginning to fall in love with – despite the terrible men I've had the misfortune of meeting here.

This place feels a world away from London and my old life. Although I did, for a while at least, feel as though I was possibly getting my life back on track. I almost had it all figured out, enrolling onto part-time study, and finding a new job with better prospects. I was finding an equilibrium.

Until he showed up again.

Chapter 2

I'm woken by the loud whirring of the Nutribullet, pulsing on and off and on again. Priya's making banana waffles – which is my cue to get out of bed and perch my bum on one of the stools at our high table that juts out into the centre of the kitchen.

I saunter through to the kitchen area in my silky sunflower pyjamas.

'Morning.' I suppress a yawn as I stretch my arms behind my head.

'Hey, girl!' Priya drawls in her native New York accent. She is the picture of health with impossibly glossy black hair and glowing, flawless skin. She's dressed for a workout – which is her standard out-of-office uniform. 'Banana waffles?' she asks.

'Why else would I be up this early?'

Priya glances at the clock, a subtle reminder that what feels early to me is late to her.

'Spill then!' she orders, as she decants the contents of the Nutribullet into the waffle maker.

'Well, I woke up here alone, so . . .'

'So what was he this time? Misogynist? Mansplainer? Dick?'

'Try all three,' I say, as if it's no surprise.

'Seriously, girl. Your luck is the pits. I swear to God there are decent men in Manhattan you know. Heaps of them. You just need to come out with Steve's buddies. He's got some great friends. Eligible, decent-looking.'

'Oh, so my best match is just decent-looking, then?'

'You know what I mean.' She sighs.

Steve is Priya's boyfriend. I never see him, but she's always running off downtown to hang out with him. Quiet bloke, by all accounts. I was never sure how he ended up with such a big circle of friends.

Priya picks up the lid of the waffle maker to check on its progress. I'm hit with the warm scent of banana and cinnamon and suddenly all is well in the world. I inhale deeply, a lazy smile spreading across my face – until I'm reminded of her less tempting offer . . .

'The thing is,' I say. 'Steve and his friends . . .'

'I know, *I know*. But we don't *always* talk psych stuff. We do have fun.'

Priya trained as a psychotherapist. And so did Steve. As did a bunch of his mates. At least, lots of them have the word 'psych' in common – psychotherapist, psychologist, psychiatrist. There's even a psychopharmacologist, which is a mouthful even without all the prescription drugs they give you numbing your brain. They've all been mates since college, as they call it, with a shared love of how the human mind works.

Priya and Steve met a couple of years after graduating at some conference and bonded over a shared love of contemporary therapeutic models and coconut water. It's deeply irritating to live with someone who can scrutinise me as well as Priya can, but in many ways her profession is a good thing for me. Not only do I get to rent a small room in a nice apartment for literally pennies, I also get free therapy. I get to talk about myself for hours on end with complimentary banana and cinnamon waffles thrown in for good measure.

And while I certainly don't need saving from the world, I do sometimes need saving from myself.

I watch Priya expertly transfer the now golden waffles onto two plates. Their warm scent fills the air as she squeezes lemon juice over them, adds a few spoonfuls of Greek yoghurt and tops them with sliced banana and a sprinkle of cinnamon. She slides one plate over the table to me.

'Thanks,' I say, grabbing the plate before it reaches the edge. I pick up a fork and tuck in immediately.

She watches me eat. 'So what's your problem then?'

'So, obviously, I'm not after getting wed or anything.'

'Of course.'

'But there is zero substance. I mean, even pure sexual attraction needs more than just good looks. I need . . .'

'Someone intellectually challenging?'

'Yes!'

'Exciting?'

'Yes!'

'Caring?'

I shudder at the word. I *know* that's what I want. Need, even. Someone to rub my feet after a crappy day at work. Someone to tell me I'm not a bad person. Someone who I respect enough that I can be vulnerable with. Just a little bit, of course. It's kind of hard to admit that when you've been so fiercely independent your entire life. It's even harder to find. Deep inside, I know that's what I'm looking for.

I pretend otherwise, of course.

'Bollocks.'

Priya starts giggling, setting me off at the same time. She still can't get over some of my British imports. The word 'bollocks'. Endless cups of English breakfast tea. Jilly Cooper's *Rivals*.

I hold my hand over my face in an attempt to finish my mouthful with a little more decorum before I speak again, but she gets in there first.

'Look,' she says. 'I think you're holding back. You're emotionally unavailable. And I think you're choosing the wrong ones because you don't believe that Mr Right can possibly exist. I mean, after what happened to your mom – of course you're scared of being vulnerable. So, rather than looking for the duke from Bridgerton . . . you've been looking for . . .'

'Decent banter, a few nice drinks and a decent shag,' I say, almost setting her off again. 'But why shouldn't I enjoy charm and intelligence? Even if only momentarily. I need stimulation, Priya. I get bored easily. You know that.'

She raises her eyebrows, finally sitting down opposite me with her own plate of waffles. I think she sees my 'complex personality' (as I once overheard her describing it) as a prime psychotherapy case study. She knew when she met me that I had 'baggage'. But she accepted me, helped me orientate myself in this strange town. Through meeting Priya, I ended up meeting everyone else – the girls she's known since she was young. Which is handy, because she spends far more time with Steve these days than she does with them, but she does care about them in her own way. It's almost as if she's thrown me in with them to ease the guilt. I'm her stand-in when she's too busy. I had little and no one else in Manhattan anyway, landing here all alone with a small carry-on suitcase and nothing else.

Don't feel bad for me though – I kind of like it that way.

'Anyway,' Priya says, continuing her assessment of me, 'your learned behaviour when it comes to dating apps will soon expose the real problem. And either you'll keep trying to get that dopamine hit, going on more and more shitty dates, or you'll stop, you'll change tack.'

I roll my eyes. 'Come on, Freud. Pretend I'm not a psychology expert. Plain English please.'

'You're Pavlov's dogs.'

'Thanks,' I say, clearly offended even though I'm not totally sure where she's going with this.

'You know Pavlov's dogs: he rang a bell every time he fed them red meat.'

I recognise the story from one of the biomedical ethics classes I took while I was still at uni. 'And? They became conditioned to associate the bell with food.'

'And you've been conditioned to think that swiping right results in meat.' Priya smirks at me. 'Or in sex. You've been salivating like a dog each time . . . so you keep doing it.'

'Well, I wouldn't say . . .'

'Your early online dating successes made you believe that you were going to hit the jackpot every time. But it's just not happening anymore.'

'My early successes?'

'You "shagged" them, didn't you?' She says this in my accent. Albeit badly.

'Shagging is only the jackpot if it's good,' I say. 'And sometimes you need to do it before you can really know if there's anything else to them. If there actually is a good match. I don't think any of them were successes, not really. Besides, I wasn't exactly myself when I first came here.'

'Yeah, well,' she says, scooping up a piece of banana,

depositing it in her mouth and waving her empty fork in my face, 'I guarantee you're already getting bored of it. You're becoming unconditioned. You're not getting the meat – the emotional connection – in return. You're no longer salivating. Soon you'll stop swiping right. Eventually, you'll stop using the apps altogether. And you'll have to go out and find people in real life.'

I frown at her, feeling even more perplexed. This is why I don't think I want to be introduced to Steve's mates again. It'll be this times a hundred.

'Whatever.' I sigh.

Priya doesn't back down. 'Girl, you need to find another way. Because you're probably making yourself even more emotionally unavailable thanks to all the disappointment. You're upping the defence mechanisms.'

She's right. I know she's right. But the alternative is tough. 'Do you know how much effort you have to put in when you do it the traditional way? I'm not looking for a husband. I just want . . .'

'A decent shag!' we both repeat in unison and fall about laughing again.

'No, really,' I say, composing myself. 'I do admit it. I want more than a shag. Of course I do. But I haven't the time or the inclination to run a full audit of each potential candidate during a night out. You can't filter out the chaff so easily in real life.'

'But that's my point. You're *not* filtering them out. Either the dating app algorithm is fucked, or you're just terrible at it.'

'Oh please,' I say. 'I'm not terrible at anything.'

She shakes her head, smiling at my confidence. I think that's why we get on so well. There's no real power imbalance. Not really. Priya entertains me because she doesn't tiptoe around me. I find her stimulating.

She finds me curious. And British.

I can't help but wonder if psychology pros like Priya can filter out the dating chaff on autopilot based on small details. You know like, if a potential romantic partner eats the core of an apple they're clearly a psychopath. Or if they relentlessly fiddle with their tie while talking to you they're obviously not as important as they like to think they are.

'I thought our girlfriends did it for you anyway,' Priya says. 'You know, they're like "Sally, meet John. He's an influencer with 2.3m Instagram followers and a sponsorship deal with Michael Kors."'

'That's half the problem,' I say. 'It's all superficial bullshit.'

'True,' she says resigned. 'Much as I love them, they're a bit . . .' We both look up at the ceiling before taking another mouthful of banana waffle in unison, thus stopping ourselves from saying anything that we might later feel guilty about.

Priya is my only proper friend here. The only one who sees the real me. And I mean, sure, we have the others. They're the people I go out with. Sometimes with Priya, often without. Lily, Tamara and Amanda, Priya's friends who she has clearly grown apart from but feels a sense of loyalty towards. They're nice enough, sweet even. Aside from Amanda who can be wicked. But they're surface-level friends. They help me get into new restaurant launches and club VIP nights. It's entertaining and fun – at least, the environment is. When it comes to the substance . . . the quality of conversation . . . it's often rather lacking. In fact, I'm not even sure we speak to each other. There's lots of chat, for sure, but I'm not sure it's responsive. It's just a bunch of people on broadcast about themselves. Perhaps we are all playing at creating boundaries?

I'm not sure Priya even bothers to psychoanalyse them anymore.

'All right, I'm calling it!' Priya suddenly announces. 'You've got one last chance. And then that's it. I'm introducing you to someone the old-fashioned way.'

'One chance? What do you mean?'

'Have a real go at finding someone at least half decent. Vet them somehow, I don't know. But one more person from that godawful app and then, if they're garbage, that's it.'

'But that's going to be . . .'

'*Exactly*. So choose wisely. One last-ditch digital attempt at finding your perfect love match for . . .' she holds her fingers up as quotation marks '. . . *bantz, drinks and shags*.'

'You're mocking me again,' I say. I hop down from my stool and go to put my empty plate in the dishwasher. I open it to find it sparkling clean and empty. Priya always beats me to it. Or do I let her? I briefly wonder what that means about our dynamic.

She continues. 'And that's it. That's your last chance. So choose wisely, girl. Because we're making a pact here. If the next man you date from that app has no potential for making it to date number two, then I'm taking you out with Steve's friends and you're meeting your next one cold. In real life. With no filter button.'

'OK,' I say, contemplating the idea. 'So what are the parameters?' My question surprises even myself. I guess I'm taking this seriously.

'You need to find someone you'd happily – and you *know* I can tell when you're lying so don't even try – someone you'd *happily* share at least three dates with.' She looks pleased with herself. 'If he's a mansplaining misogynistic fuckwit, you will commit to dating the old-fashioned way.'

Of course, Priya can't force me to do anything. She knows that. But she also knows I can't resist a challenge. I can't resist the opportunity to prove her wrong.

'Challenge accepted,' I say, picking up my iPhone. 'My last digital dating chance.'

Chapter 3

Shopping for a date should be fun. In some ways, you're trying before you buy. You get to find out what they look like, what music they listen to, how they spend their spare time.

But as we all know in this age of social media, filters and catfishing, much of it is total bollocks.

How will I know which one to take a chance on? How will I know who's genuine?

It's lunchtime at the office. The air con is doing its best to keep us awake, but the cool air is drying my eyes. I blink at my phone screen, feeling overwhelmed by profile after profile. I need some air.

I chuck my iPhone in my lime green vintage shoulder bag and make my way out of the office, walking past the boss David's desk. I notice him look at the clock. It's 11.55. I'm just five minutes early for lunch, David. Give it a rest! I roll my eyes at nobody.

I jump in the lift and in moments I walk out into the sunshine. It's a scorcher today, and the streets are heaving, so I pull my cat-eye sunglasses from my bag, shield my eyes and head directly to one of my favourite lunch spots for kimchi scallops and peach iced tea.

I stroll back to the office swinging my little paper bag of lunch and step into the central outdoor atrium on the ground floor. I perch on a chunky wooden bench and remove the little tray and chopsticks from the bag. Around me are exotic plants and, rather inexplicably, a raised outdoor koi pond that gleams in the sunlight.

I decide to tweak my own profile before matching with any new potentials.

I pull out my phone to look at the photos I've chosen. It's one from last year, with my brown shoulder-length hair cascading like silk, red lips perfectly stained, eyeliner sharp, and I'm laughing. What was I laughing at? Maybe it was staged? Whatever, it looks good. It's staying.

I take a mouthful of my scallop and chew, slowly and mindfully, taking a brief break from my search. I'm in no hurry – the world is hardly going to burn down if I'm not back at my desk promptly taking calls from rich people wanting to look around properties. The sun, however, does feel particularly hot on my pale cheeks today and I regret not purchasing the SPF 50 when I stocked up last week.

The second picture on my profile is similarly acceptable. It's from a party we all went to not long after I arrived in Manhattan. I was dressed in a red polka-dot 1950s skirt and black top, red lips, flawless eyeliner. Yes, I have *a look*. Except for the skirt. That's not part of it. It was Halloween, and I went for a sweet and sexy Minnie Mouse vibe.

And the third photo was also satisfactory. A black-and-white close-up of my face. Priya took it one morning without me knowing to prove that I was, indeed, a grouchy cow. I was hungover as hell. But it actually looks like a sexy bed-head shot. And the mono tones really accentuate my high cheekbones and angular jawline.

They're all staying.

Name: *Sally*, age: *29*, location: *Manhattan*, all staying.

What's next? The prompts. I can change those up. Currently I have *What I would do first in a zombie apocalypse*. That can go. I always lied on that one anyway. There's no way I'd kiss a zombie to see if it turned into a prince. Who'd bother with that when you've been given the prime opportunity to live out your fantasy of slicing up baddies like Michonne in *The Walking Dead*.

Perhaps I should go for something more . . . classic. Pros and cons, maybe?

I look up towards the sky for inspiration. White fluffy clouds drifting across a perfect square of blue and framed by tall exterior walls greet me. The faint sound of traffic feels almost drowned out by the peaceful view above. The sun is still blazing, making me squint slightly behind my sunglasses, but a sudden slight breeze lessens its intensity. It's like being in an open-topped bubble here. Like I can tune out of the chaos beyond these walls. Which is good, because I'm on an important mission to have a meaningful date and that needs all my concentration.

Right then, what are my pros?

I place another piece of scallop in my mouth, finish it slowly and take a sip of my ice-cold peach tea.

OK. I'm proud of my confidence, my style and intellect. But I'm not sure that's going to cut it. Will it scare men off? So many men are intimidated by the thought of a strong woman. But then I think back to what Priya said. Perhaps I *do* need to add a bit more of the *real* me to this dating game. Just a touch.

OK. Pros.

Fearless. Stylish. Loves a good debate.

That should scare off the mansplainers at least.
Cons.
What are my negatives? I have to be careful here. Too much honesty and I'll get zero interest. I mean, do I really need to tell the world about my overactive fight-or-flight responses and intrusive thoughts? At least, I always thought that's what they were, but Priya says otherwise. She says intrusive thoughts rarely result in action in most people she sees. She says I, on the other hand, just get bad ideas and act impulsively.

Ah, but being impulsive. That's a good *and* a bad thing. So if I put it in cons, it kind of helps my cause, adds to my appeal and mystery. Oh, as does being British. Americans seem to find my London accent cute and interesting. So putting it in cons is another tick in the box.

Impulsive. British. Very particular when it comes to tea and gin.

That'll do.

What's next? Relationship preference. Mine is currently set to 'short term' so maybe this is what I need to change. I click on *Still working it out*.

Update.

Now it's time to shop.

There are *so* many men to choose from. It's like being bombarded with Netflix choices. No, not just Netflix choices. It's like having one of those streaming boxes with every app – Netflix, Disney, Peacock, Hulu – and then within those, you've got every genre imaginable. Genres you've never even heard of. You can categorise men by location, or by interest or by relationship preference. And then you can subcategorise – again and again. And there are *still* too many to choose from. It's a never-ending catalogue. I simply don't know where to start.

The possibilities feel even more overwhelming now that Priya's challenged me to find a decent date on my very next attempt. I have to go on at least three dates with him – not begrudgingly – in order to win the challenge. Why am I so bloody-minded?

I can't pretend I don't know what she's doing though. She knows I won't wholeheartedly admit to wanting a 'boyfriend'. Ew, it sounds so twee. But I *do* think it's time to move on. To let the guard down a bit. To, you know, find something a bit more *meaningful*.

Yeah, I would like that, actually.

And somehow, it's so much easier to do it as a challenge. It's something I can win at – even if, after three dates, it all goes tits up, as it probably will, because then I save face. Then I can make out that I wasn't actually aiming for the long-term romance, I just wanted to win the challenge.

OK . . . so what *am* I looking for?

Confidence is a must, but arrogance is a no.

He should care about how he looks, without serving as a living breathing ad campaign for designer labels.

And of course, there needs to be that . . . certain something. A charge of good old-fashioned chemistry.

I scroll past men holding fish, men with their tops off and men who are overwhelmingly patriotic – in all the wrong ways (that's another steadfast rule – no UK or US flags in profile pics – it's too disconcerting). Sadly, there's no way to automatically filter these ones out.

Then, something catches my eye.

I'm disregarding so many men so quickly that I almost miss him. I scroll backwards to the flash of what initially stopped me in my tracks. No, I wasn't imagining it.

Harry Collins. Dirty blonde hair. Styled, but not overly

so. A crisp-looking plain white shirt, unbuttoned just the right amount. Teeth that are white and straight but not too straight. And those eyes . . . eyes that . . .

Fuck me, Harry Collins.

I mean, if that really *is* you in that photo, please, go ahead. Fuck me.

I open his profile, fully expecting to find something terrifying in there. But there are no references to making America great again. There are no slimy fish being held aloft. There are no crass comments about his favourite designer labels or how much cash he has.

Harry Collins is thirty-two. He lives in Manhattan. His pros: *Charming, requires little sleep, impulsive.*

Cons: *As above.*

I am acutely and momentarily in love.

Chapter 4

Two days later, the realisation that I am running low on propranolol stops me in my tracks. I'll no doubt be late for work now. And that makes me want my meds even more.

I check every make-up bag, toiletries bag, bathroom cabinet and bedside drawer, but nothing.

There are three left in my open blister pack. Three. What the fuck am I going to do with three? I usually double drop as it is. Spreading the effects of three is . . . like taking paracetamol when what you really need is morphine. I'm going to have to save them. For particularly difficult occasions.

They prescribed them for me back in London. I was adamant, at first, that I didn't need them. I was quite capable of managing my own mind, thank you very much. But then I realised they were actually quite useful. A slowing of the heart rate. A slowing of my reactions. Not my *critical* reactions. I mean, I was one hundred per cent assured that my reflexes wouldn't be slowed. But my *emotional* reactions. I could think before reacting. I could rationalise before giving in to feeling physically sick at the sound and smell of food frying in the takeaway. I could think before my heart raced and my blood rushed. I could stop fucking up and doing stupid things.

Well, maybe they didn't *quite* stop me from being stupid. But they definitely helped a bit.

Anyway, my doctor in London thought I was a little . . . I don't know . . . pissed off.

She also suggested I might have PTSD because of what happened when I was a kid. I've medical records detailing my time in a children's psychiatric ward after what happened to my mum. And social services records detailing my time in care before I was adopted. But aside from a brief period of catatonia, as the professionals called it, I think I handled the traumas of my childhood pretty well. In large part, I'd argue, because I rejected their various diagnoses.

Catatonia? I was much more comfortable looking back on all that as an extended game of sleeping lions.

I'd dealt with it all on my own for years. In my own way, of course. The compensation money I got when I was eighteen definitely helped. As did the years of self-medication as a teenager – booze, drugs and oblivion. Parties and fun and being whoever I wanted to be that glossed over my history, helping me to forget. I'm amazed I managed to save any money at all to be honest.

But then *he* turned up last year. And I knew I needed to get out of England. To find a safe space to convalesce and get myself back to me. Whoever 'me' really is.

So propranolol turned out to be a good call after all. A calming influence in a hostile world that I was increasingly losing my shit in. It's served me well and I've stayed pretty chill in the main. But now . . . three fucking pills. How the hell have I run out like this?

Priya's already told me she can't write me a script.

Psychology not psychiatry, she keeps saying. Plus, she thinks I'm dependent and that I'm not dealing with the core issue, just covering it up. She reckons, if I took up more exercise and vented more often, I wouldn't need them anyway. I mean, how often do we hear that?

Go for a run. Relax in a bubble bath. *Talk*.

Please! That's got to be about as effective as treating lung disease with breathing. But maybe she has a point. Maybe I do need to try life without them.

I place the leftover pills in my knicker drawer, and settle back down in front of my dressing table mirror to finish my make-up – my daily routine that was so rudely interrupted by panicked thoughts of a medication draught.

My room is like a Tracey Emin artwork. Clothes are flung everywhere. Wardrobe doors hang open bursting with an array of colours and patterns and textures. Empty glasses sit on top of my dresser – from wine glasses with red dregs to half-drunk tumblers of water and mugs of tea or coffee. Everything in it is glorious but messy. Kind of like my head.

I paint my lips red, flick strong flirty wings of eyeliner up towards the edges of my subtly nano-bladed brows, and coat my lashes in black mascara. My hair is down and flowing over my shoulders in luscious waves that I've artificially created. I'm ready for work.

As I head out of the building I see the grumpy old cow outside the fruit and veg shop. She is shuffling around in her tired old cardigan and mum jeans, rearranging crates of tropical fruit. I gear myself up for another sour exchange with her but, as I get closer, I notice something is different. She isn't looking grumpy this time. Instead, she glances at me without a trace of her usual disdain, then instantly looks away.

Weird.

She doesn't look happy. More, I don't know. Sad?

She heads back inside. I'm intrigued by this change in character and decide to pop in for an apple. I browse the selection, running my fingertips over the shiny balls of greens and reds and pinks.

I pick up a Liberty apple and walk over to the woman. She is sitting, head down, on the little stool behind the counter, turning up the volume on the TV that perches high in the corner opposite her. It's usually from this position that she glares with her judgy eyes. But today she is just staring down at her puzzle books.

'Just this please,' I chime, grabbing my iPhone from my bag and holding the apple in front of me.

She doesn't look at me. She doesn't speak, she just punches the numbers on the old-fashioned till. She's turned her face from me again. Her hair is scraped back into a plain ponytail, a fringe falling in her eyes. Little flecks of grey hair poke through her parting as if she's run Tippex through it.

'Hello,' I say, knocking impatiently on the countertop, 'customer care not a thing here?'

She looks up at me, catching my eye. And although she hangs her head quickly back down again I see it. Yellows and purples pooling under her flesh. A bloom of blood breaking through her thin, tired skin.

'A dollar ten,' she says. Her voice is quiet and wispy – not how it usually sounds.

I put the apple down and without thinking move my hand forward towards her chin. She winces, shrugging away from me. I do it again more gently this time and carefully turn her head so she's facing me. She gives in, submitting to the fact that I've clearly seen the damage.

'Jeez. What's happened here?' I say, as softly as I can. Her skin is so pale it shows up every pore and broken thread vein. And the bruising around her eye is fresh and puffy.

Suddenly, the strong Italian-American voice I know is back. 'None of your business, lady.'

She winces again and holds out her hand to demand the cash. She clearly wants this transaction over with. To be fair, since I've lived here, she's wanted every transaction of ours over with as quickly as possible.

I genuinely don't know why we never hit it off. She's always made a show of being ultra nice to Priya – even more so when I'm around. Makes shunning me even more dramatic I suppose. I've never particularly cared. But today I feel different.

'Who did that to you?' I ask.

'I said it's none of your damn business,' she snaps. We hold each other's gaze momentarily. Her eyes look weary. I hand over the cash and she automatically puts the change in the charity box without asking me. It's a thing she's always done with me. I kind of respect her for that, if I'm honest.

'Look. I know we're hardly friends.'

She lets out a 'hah' at that. I carry on. 'I know we're hardly friends. But you know. If you want to ta—'

'Talk? With you? I'd rather he punched me in the face again.'

I let out an involuntary giggle. I stop it immediately, realising that this isn't the time or place to laugh, even though I genuinely appreciate her abrasive comeback. But then she joins in too. She laughs with me. Briefly. And then our faces drop at the realisation of the situation. There's an understanding between us that there are some secrets that shouldn't be kept. And we both know who she is talking about here. Her husband. He's in here on and off through the week. He usually locks things up. When he's here, the shop shuts early. When it's just her, it tends to stay open much later.

I notice tears forming in her eyes, building like puddles about to overflow. One finally wobbles over the bottom rim of her left eye and traces its way slowly down her cheek, like a raindrop winding down a bus window.

I check the clock on my phone. I've got plenty of time before my boss is due in. Not that it would make any difference; I'd stay anyway. 'Hey, why don't I take that other empty seat behind the counter, and you can make a cuppa?'

'A cuppa?'

I forget my Britishness sometimes. I roll my eyes and let out a fake sigh. 'Boil the kettle? Make some tea? Coffee, whatever?'

She still looks a little puzzled but she stands regardless and offers me the stool next to the one she was sitting on. 'Will you watch the shop?' she asks. I nod, then she heads off to her tiny kitchenette. There's something about showing your true colours with someone that means you know you can trust them. I guess the continued lack of pleasantries between us means we both know what we're getting from each other and she can trust me not to mess up her shop. It's refreshing.

I swing my legs on the stool, holding my feet out in front of me and admiring my red summer sandals. They're far too fancy for office wear, but I guess that's why I love them.

On the counter in front of me is an old-school calculator, a dusty little glass holding a few pens and pencils, the odd elastic band and paper clip discarded amongst them, and an open puzzle book. I shift it to one side and, underneath it is a gossip magazine. This woman's daily world feels particularly limited to me.

I look around at the shop in front of me at the bright displays of plums, pears and apples – some neatly portioned into little green tubs, some loose and begging to be plucked from the crowd. There are more exotic displays too – mangoes sit next to persimmon fruit on one side, and dragon fruit on the other. She cares about this place. It's exquisite, when you properly take it in. I wonder why she doesn't take as much care of herself. But then I've probably just discovered the answer to that.

She returns moments later with two black coffees, handing one to me. I don't say anything. It's not the time to whine about incorrect beverages.

'I don't even know your name,' I say.

'Marie.'

'Hi Marie. I'm Sally.' I hold out my hand. She shakes it.

'I know your name,' she says. 'You're always with that pleasant girl. Priya. The one who smiles.'

'I smile,' I say, frowning.

'You don't smile. Not with your eyes.'

'Harsh,' I say. I take a sip of coffee. 'So. This bruise . . .' I hold up my iPhone and take a photo of her face. She immediately puts up her hands to cover herself.

'What the hell are you doing?' she snaps.

'You need evidence.'

'Tsk,' she says. 'For all the difference it'll make.'

'Tell me what happened,' I say.

She lets out a sigh and picks up her mug of coffee, her hand shaking gently. 'Last night.' She pauses, taking a sip as though she needs to assess what she should and shouldn't say to me. 'He was . . . tense. Stressed.'

'What with?' I say, even though I know whatever the answer it won't be justification.

'The shop. Takings are down. The rent is going up. And he'd had a drink.'

'And that's your fault how?' I ask, wishing I'd have been old enough to say this to my mum all those years ago. She definitely blamed herself.

'I'd bought a new lipstick. I was trying it on in the bathroom and he saw me. He doesn't like me in make-up as it is. But last night, he said I was wasting his money on trash . . .' She winces at the memory of what came next and I let her breathe. I hold her space. And then it just pours out. It's like I've opened Pandora's box. Once she starts, she doesn't want to stop. It's clear she's never told a soul about this before. About what he does. The way he treats her. She has a sister, but if she told her, she'd kill him she says. And she does love him. That's a fact.

'Might not be a bad thing to let your sister loose on him,' I say. 'Get in there first.'

She flinches. 'Be serious.'

'But this is serious,' I add, gesturing to her face. '*This* is bad enough. But how far will he go?'

'He's done worse,' she says, as if this is some kind of endorsement that what's staring me in the face right now isn't so bad.

'Then you know what he's capable of,' I say gently. Memories from my childhood wash over me, making my heart pump angrily. I'm keeping my voice calm and my body loose. It's taking all my energy, but I've been practising this exterior stillness for decades now.

Marie tells me it happens mostly on weekends. When he's had a beer too many. Which, from what I can gather, is one beer.

'There's a look in his eye,' she tells me, 'and I just know. It's like he's gone. It's weird to say it, but it's as though the lights are out and there's nobody home, and yet, he's completely bursting with rage at the same time. Gone, but raging.'

I know this look. I've seen it before.

She says sometimes it's a swift punch. Sometimes she pretends to pass out with the pain, to get him to lay off. Sometimes he carries on regardless. Sometimes, he doesn't punch her. He holds her. Sits on her. Paralyses her.

When he loses control of himself, he controls her.

And on hearing all this, my unmedicated heart races in anger.

A customer walks into the shop and Marie nods, as if asking me to stand, to leave it there, to keep it between us. I nod in response and move away from the counter. The customer is a businessman in a suit grabbing some fruit. While he is distracted by the choice of bananas, I place my hand gently on Marie's.

'I'll call in again soon. But listen, any time you want to chat. *Any time*,' I say, and I grab a pen from the dusty little glass and scribble my number on a brown paper bag.

Chapter 5

'Sally?' he asks, approaching me with a smile.

'Harry,' I say. And we both laugh at our rom-com movie names. He kisses me on the cheek, confidently, and it makes me tingle all over. He smells of expensive aftershave, nothing too overpowering. A fresh zing that gives me butterflies.

I am so immediately into him.

'You're not going to fake-orgasm loudly in the middle of the park are you?' he asks, a spark of something cheeky in his eye, and I wonder if he can actually read my mind. Then I bring myself back to reality and realise he is referring to my movie namesake.

'Ha! Who knows,' I say. 'We'll just have to see how it goes.'

Immediate flirting. Like, *immediate*. I can't help myself. And his confidence is just the right mix of self-assured and cute.

He looks as good as his photo. That's a rarity. There's usually an initial bout of disappointment when you realise the photos have been carefully selected to highlight the best of their features and everything else is either unremarkable or off-putting. Not in this case.

His dirty blonde hair has a slight wave to it and a few kinks dance around his eyes. He is tall – but not too tall. About six feet. And he is wearing a slightly fitted white T-shirt with dark blue jeans and smart trainers.

I chose my mint green gingham dress, tied across the front with bows, showing off glimpses of porcelain skin. I paired it with my beige LK Bennett espadrilles that tie high up my legs, and a pair of off-white vintage-style sunglasses.

I've basically dressed myself as a present to him. One that he may or may not get to unwrap.

We walk and talk, winding our way through the twisting paths of the park, the New York skyline towering high above the trees.

'You're a native New Yorker then?' I ask him, genuinely interested to learn more about him.

He smiles. 'This place has been my playground since I was about three. You're clearly . . .'

'British. Yes. Whatever gave it away.' I smirk at him and he lets out a small chuckle, dimples appearing in his cheeks.

'OK, I want to guess London,' he says, 'but I imagine everyone just guesses London. I sometimes think we forget there's a whole country beyond the capital.'

'Well, you're actually right,' I say. 'London born and bred. I'm from the East End, originally, which is why you can probably detect a slight hint of Eliza Doolittle if you listen closely.' I laugh. 'But I moved across to Bushy when I was in my early teens.'

'Shepherd's Bush?' he says. 'The other side of Kensington?'

'You know it?'

'I visited a couple of times. Over Christmas as a kid. My mom loved London. Did the classic tourist stuff. But we always stayed outside the centre.' He takes a beat. 'Your red buses, they're like our yellow cabs. They're *everywhere*. They're what I think of first when I think of London.'

'Ha,' I laugh. 'Why do we always think of cars and buses when we think of London and New York. Those double-deckers though, they look kind of regal but stink of piss and fustiness if you sit up top.'

'Yeah. So typically British. I mean, not the smell, obviously . . .' He clears his throat, realising what he's just inferred. He changes the subject. 'So what brought you to my town then?'

My town. Hm. Assured. But slightly nervous at the same time. I wonder, could that mean he's a confident bloke who also really fancies me? I hope so. Because that's a seriously good mix. Although I know it could also pose a challenge.

Clearly, I don't tell him the truth. I never tell anyone the truth. But I have a well-rehearsed line.

'I grew up fascinated by New York. The books, the movies. My mum left me when I was young and we'd always talked about New York together. I guess it was a bit of a dream. So eventually, I did it.'

'Your mom still in England?'

'She's, um. No longer . . .'

'Ah. I'm so sorry,' he says. 'I get it. I lost mine too.'

A moment passes between us. A silent gap that neither of us feels the need to urgently fill with anything. As if we are both processing something, a connection, perhaps.

'And your dad?' he asks.

'Never knew him. My mum was my everything. You?'

'Same,' he says, but I detect a glint of sadness in his eye, and he looks up at the sun thoughtfully, squinting a little in the light. I decide to change the subject. I can probe another time.

'Ice cream?' I ask, as we approach a seller. He smiles. 'These are on me.'

It's vanilla or nothing at this basic but traditional stand. But it's deliciously classic. Just like him.

We sit on the grass, the evening sun beaming down on us, and I stretch my long legs out in front of me, my decorated feet clearly on display for him. I can feel his eyes on me and it feels wonderful. This is not like any of the other dates. I mean, I'm no hopeless romantic or anything. It just feels, relaxed. Nice. An oriole flies tantalisingly close to us.

'We don't get orioles in England,' I say. 'I love seeing them here.'

'Impressive. You don't strike me as a birdwatcher?' He laughs.

'So what do I strike you as?' I ask.

'Intriguing, certainly.'

'Well, you probably won't find me out here with a pair of binoculars and a bag of bird seed. But I know a few of the common ones.'

Birds. Ice cream. Trees. God this is sickeningly romantic – but I'm liking it.

What the fuck is going on with you, Sally Parker?

I'm not into the traditional romantic gestures. I mean, thank God he didn't turn up with flowers like my first Manhattan date. Cut flowers are a no. I like things that grow, not things that wither away silently and die. Plants are way more dynamic. Evolving.

Cut flowers are for gravestones.

'So, what do you do? Tell me about yourself,' I ask, as I nibble on the corner of the cone.

'This is going to sound awful,' he says. 'But I don't actually work. Well, not in the nine-to-five kind of way. I have a couple of properties that bring in a good income. My dad was kind of a big deal in the ad industry. Made some waves back in the Eighties and Nineties. Those arty perfume and aftershave adverts were his specialty.' He takes a mouthful of vanilla ice cream.

I hate those arty perfume and aftershave ads. Models and film stars looking either pissed off or forcibly sexy. To be honest, I hate ads full stop. They sell lies, self-doubt and convenience. At least Harry isn't continuing his dad's legacy. Even if he is living off the profits.

He finishes his mouthful of ice cream. 'I hated those adverts,' he says – and I laugh with relief. But he doesn't question me, he just smiles.

'So you didn't want to follow in his footsteps?'

'I didn't want to follow him anywhere to be honest.' He laughs, awkwardly. There's a moment when his mood shifts slightly and he looks down to the ground, picking at blades of grass with his fingers. He looks up, squinting at the sun then back at me, his slate-grey eyes lighting up again. 'Anyway. What about you? How do you spend your time?'

'I'd love to tell you something exciting. But the truth is, I work in a minimalist air-conditioned office filtering phone calls about property. Ha – maybe we have yours on our books?'

'Which firm?'

'Catterick and Cornell.'

'Ah I do know of them. But sadly, no. Lloyds and Son pipped you to the post. You're not managing mine, I'm afraid.' He pauses a moment. 'But I guess that means, if I turn out to be a total bore or a serial killer, you'll find it easier to shake me off.'

I look at him and a moment hangs in the air, making my insides flip like a pancake.

'I'm not ready to shake you off just yet,' I say eventually. And I mean it.

'That's good.' He finishes the rest of his sugar cone. 'Because I'm kind of enjoying myself.'

Chapter 6

The Nutribullet whirs and pulses, stirring me from a satisfied sleep. But I am not getting out of bed for Priya's banana waffles today.

I open my eyes and turn my head. He is already awake and smiling.

'Morning,' I say, my voice lazy with spent hormones.

'Morning,' he says, still looking up at my ceiling, the back of his head sinking into my pillow. Then he turns his head towards me and kisses me slowly. The Nutribullet is silenced and I can hear nothing but the gentle rustle of linen bedsheets as we re-entangle our bodies.

I matched with Harry Collins. I went on a date with Harry Collins.

I fucked Harry Collins.

Whether the stars aligned, the universe heard my call, or whether simply tampering with my profile reset the algorithm, I do not know. But whatever happened, it worked out pretty well. Because Harry Collins knows how to play this dating game. He knows exactly (*exactly*) what buttons to press. And he just so happens to be a good laugh as well. As much as I try to deny it, I feel like I'm dancing on pink clouds in heaven.

I took on Priya's challenge and I won. Well, I need to get three dates out of him first to truly claim victory. But the most important thing is that I actually *want* three dates with him. More, maybe. I've done enough shallow sex and crap first dates to enjoy a little bit of sickly-sweet surely? I feel high. After last night's date, last night's absolutely phenomenal sex . . .

I'm almost girly with giddiness. A stranger to my own personality. What has this man done to me?

His fingers idly trace my spine and he runs them up to my neck, reaching around gently to feel my collarbone and the bumpy scarred skin under my tattoo. He pulls his head backwards to take in its design.

'That's beautiful,' he says.

'Thank you.' I smile.

He continues stroking the floral artwork that sits underneath my collarbone. 'So unusual . . .' he muses.

'What? A floral tattoo? I mean, it's a unique design, of course.' I laugh. 'But I hardly think I'm the first to get cherry blossom tattooed.'

'No I mean . . . its position.' He smiles, looking me directly in the eye, while continuing to trace his fingers over it. He's clearly digging for information. Why did I choose to have a tattoo that sits off-centre beneath my collarbone? Why is it bumpy? I mean, I really quite like this dude but I don't need to explain myself – or my scars – to him. I smile back, saying nothing. Reminding myself not to take past anger out on this gorgeous man.

Harry is . . . unusual. I mean, the whole experience has been unusual. He let me take the lead, but not always. And it felt . . . I don't know. It felt . . . nice. The morning after the night before. A quick fuck between two bodies that had already met. But it felt like more. Even the sex, it felt . . .

Comfortable. Satisfyingly so. Wonderfully so. This is a foreign land and I am happy to stay here with him.

For a while.

Chapter 7

I close the front door behind him and find myself falling back into it with a cheesy smile creeping across my face. A satisfied sigh escapes my lips. Last night, this morning, it was . . .

Fuck's sake, Sally. Don't be *that* girl.

The date has been achingly wonderful. The best. But, as much as I know I absolutely want to date someone I really like – like, a lot – I'm also a little freaked out by it. I feel less . . . in control. With crap dates, even if there's a bit of attraction and a bit of sex, it's easy to just move on. Simple. Uncomplicated. You can have a seriously good orgasm but not look at them in the same light outside of the bedroom. It's just technique. You know. Pushing buttons. But Harry is something more than that. He's . . .

That's it. I can't see him again. Not if this is the aftermath of one date. Absolutely not.

I trail into the kitchen and perch myself at the breakfast bar. Priya is clearing her plate and cup away, pristine white jogging gear on. She looks the picture of wellbeing. I mean, I love her and all, but it'd serve her right if a double-decker bus drove past splashing her Lycra with dirty rainwater. Who goes running in the middle of a city in bright whites?

'Well I don't need to ask if you had a good night,' she says. I shrug.

'Go on then,' she says. 'I know you're desperate to tell me all about his sexual prowess. Not that you left much to the imagination. These walls aren't exactly sound-proofed.'

'Yeah. He was *definitely* worth working up a sweat for,' I say, idly picking a cherry from the glass bowl on the breakfast bar. It's full of Priya's mostly yellow fruit – melons, bananas, mango – and my bright red morello cherries. We buy a weekly haul from the fruit and veg shop – the one where I now know that Marie is struggling with something pretty fucking monumental. It's wild to think that just days ago, I thought she was simply the woman who sneers at me.

I feel bad. I've been on a date, had good sex . . . I almost forgot about her. But I guess that's kind of the point. I'm trying to reframe my own relationship with men by finding a good one. I need to compartmentalise the good and the bad, otherwise it'll never work.

'His name?' Priya demands, bringing me back into the room.

'Oh, um, Harry.'

'Harry. Wait. Hang on . . . like the film?'

I hold up my hand. 'Old news. We've already covered that one.'

'Fine, whatever.' Priya is clutching a sheet of kitchen roll between her hands, watching me carefully as I take another cherry from the bowl. I bite it in half and it dribbles on the white surface. She dives over and wipes away the apparently offensive sour juice, as I sit back in my seat, making room for her like a child picking up their legs when their mum's vacuuming the carpet. 'So,' she says. 'Are you seeing him again?'

'Don't think so.'

'Sorry what? You don't *think* so? Jesus, Sally, what are you even looking for in a man if multiple orgasms aren't enough? Besides, the challenge . . .'

'Yeah, but. The dynamic. It was a bit . . . off.'

'You mean you like him?'

I huff. It irritates me that Priya knows me almost as well as I know myself.

She sighs. 'Sally. You get no enjoyment being rutted by arrogant, talentless assholes. You get no enjoyment making out with sycophantic lapdogs. What the fuck are you even looking for here? Do you even know?'

I ponder her question a moment as Priya leans her elbows onto the table, her eyes boring into mine. Ding! It's therapy time.

It's become a bit of a habit this. Free therapy over the breakfast bar. I always know when she's about to go in for the kill because of her stance. Getting in closer. It's a little trick of hers. Make me feel as though I can't escape. As though my only option is to open up to her.

Sometimes, I toy with her. I let her think she's got me. I reel her in with tales of emotional woe, traumatic encounters by the water cooler in the office that have for whatever reason triggered some false childhood memory. She starts spouting all the theory – you know, transactional analysis, exposure therapy, extinction. And then I laugh and she storms off in a huff. But today I'll play along properly. I'm intrigued by her question – and I'd quite like to find the answer to it.

What *do* I want in a man?

'I guess I just want last night, but on a roll. You know, someone to click with, but that first time over and over. And no man can offer that.'

'Don't we all, girl.'

'And clearly I haven't the time or the inclination to wade through the chaff to find the perfect sexual partner over and over again so . . .'

'So back to Harry . . .'

'Back to Harry,' I say. She raises an eyebrow. It's a probing look that roughly translates as: *Stop bullshitting and get to the point.*

'Harry.' I sigh. 'We . . . OK, so. The sex. It tells you a lot about how the relationship might work out, right?'

Her eyebrow remains in its arched position.

'There's no need for cynicism,' I say. '*You* told me that. Anyway, I climbed on top. Took control. He rolled me over. I rolled him back again. It was like . . . two horny crocodiles death-rolling their pray.'

'But less scaly.'

'Precisely.' I absent-mindedly trace my fingers along my tattooed collarbone. The bumpy, *scaly* skin below reminding me of the purpose of my ink. He asked about that and I couldn't tell him. Phew – I've not completely given myself up to him after one fucking date then.

'Sounded a bit more fun than death-rolling from where I was standing.'

'Yeah. But . . .' I trail off, struggling to articulate the problem. 'It's date number one. I don't want to set a precedent. I mean, sorry, Harry, but you're not going to get to take control every time.'

'It's seriously fucked up that you see this as a problem. Most women would kill for sex like that. We both know what the real problem is, Sally. And you can't let it dominate you.'

'What's that then?'

'You have a dismissive-avoidant attachment style.'

'So you keep telling me.'

'Which may present as dismissive and nonchalant. But in reality . . .'

'Don't you dare tell me I'm scared,' I snap.

'Well, not scared of him. But scared of yourself, certainly. You've met your match,' she says. 'You completely let go. Your body – your mind, even for a minute – succumbed to him. You really, *really* like him. And now you hate yourself for it and feel frightened of losing control . . .'

'Frightened! Please . . .'

'You feel *frightened* of losing control. Because, Sally, like it or not, it was more than just lust at first sight.'

'Fuck off.'

'And you know what that means?'

'What?' I say picking up another cherry defiantly. Priya grabs another sheet of kitchen roll and eyes me determinedly.

'That means there's a chance for more than sex here. There's a chance, Sally Parker, of love.' She swoons dramatically, taunting me.

'It's been one date,' I say, splitting the cherry in half, juice bursting in all directions onto the breakfast bar.

'Yeah, one date, and you're already worried about falling for him.'

I sigh theatrically, picking up my phone.

'You doing it then?' she asks, still standing there impatiently, her face emanating fifty shades of smug. 'You texting him?'

'Only to prove you wrong.'

She raises her eyebrows at me, says nothing, then wipes up the cherry juice.

Chapter 8

I preface our second date with a cocktail or two at the newly opened Traffik – a bar with a terrible name but a hotly anticipated drinks range and a really cool outdoor space. I order a bramble cocktail, paying homage to my homeland. I have to explain to them how to make it, like an off-brand 007 – dry gin, lemon juice and a hint of blackberry liqueur, shaken not stirred – but what they come back with isn't at all bad. I suggest they add it to their menu.

I join Priya and the rest of the group at the table.

'He's not even coming tonight. Can you believe it? I mean, that's so cool, right?' Lily is fawning over the absentee owner of the bar, who, according to her, has decided to eschew his own party for reasons she believes make him incredibly cool and interesting. Her hair is tied back into the smoothest of blonde ponytails, and it swishes theatrically behind her the more animated she gets.

'Do you not think it's, like, super weird? Not coming to your own party. I mean, does he even exist. What if Jonathan Rubin's like, AI or something?' This is Tamara. Tamara is, rather unfairly in my opinion, made fun of for being the 'stupid' one. And so of course everyone laughs as she shares her theory. She's not stupid. She just questions *everything*. I jump to her defence.

'I think Tam's got a point,' I say, noticing her shoulders relax and her smile spread as I speak up for her. Priya flashes me a look – one that is clearly asking me to make sure I play nice. Tamara, meanwhile, shuffles around smugly in her seat, and I wonder how her legs are faring on that hot plastic chair. For a new bar launch in the middle of summer, they really haven't considered bare skin. Tam's legs have got to smart. 'There's every chance he doesn't exist at all,' I add.

'But like the perfect man,' Priya says laughing, 'it doesn't stop us looking for him.' She glances at me when she's said it.

'Please.' It's Amanda now – the uber-bitch of the group. I'd call her the princess but she's not even *that* bitch. She's the rich bitch, but she's also the fiercely independent bitch. She's hard to disrespect, but impossible to like. She sits with her legs crossed, her huge gold-rimmed aviators catching the sun, and her martini held high as she remonstrates her disdain of Tamara. She's never liked Tamara. And she doesn't hide it. 'Someone's got to own it,' she says. 'And he's probably here, watching from a distance. This whole mystery owner thing is so contrived.'

The group, bar Priya and I, predictably all look around them, twisting their necks and being far too obvious. They'd never make detectives.

'Why are we so paranoid about AI anyway?' Amanda adds. 'It's *progressive*.' She uses this word pointedly, facing off Tamara and feeling pleased with herself. I make a note to anonymously AI the fuck out of her photos when I'm at a loose end. Nothing too intrusive. Something obviously deep fake and minimally damaging. There's an app for that.

'Anyway,' Lily butts in, clearly bored of the mysterious bar owner. 'I have a *scenario*.'

Everyone leans in, eyebrows pinched as tightly as the Botox will allow. (Yes, they are still mostly in their twenties. I don't understand it either.) They hold their drinks aloft to the side of their bodies to make way for serious conversation. We play 'scenario' often. It's a *thing*. According to Priya it all started because they wanted her professional advice on relationship problems when she started practising as a psychotherapist. But, as she made very clear, she wasn't some cheap magazine agony aunt, and she certainly wasn't providing her services for free. So it became a thing that everyone joined in with – and Priya usually listened quietly from the sidelines – chucking in the occasional snipe or witty observation for fun.

'Go on,' Amanda says, shuffling her bum in her seat as if to prepare for the relational conundrum of the millennium. It's as though she feels she has to give permission for the others to speak sometimes.

'OK. So. There's a guy at work. Handsy Ethan.'

Just to provide a little context here. Lily works for a boutique PR agency that's *very* fussy about the clients it takes on. She's actually seething she's not behind this bar launch. It's kind of her speciality. Hence all our free drinks and VIP invites. She continues. 'He's up for the same promotion as I am. Interviews are happening soon. But – and here's the thing – I know for a *fact* he's been enjoying a bump or two before pitches . . .'

Amanda dives in. 'It's PR, darling. Who doesn't. And besides, you can't—'

'I *get* that,' Lily interrupts defensively. 'But that's not all. He's been feeding it to the twenty-year-old junior on his team.'

There's a collective 'whoa' as everyone leans back and shakes their heads. Lily doesn't have to tell us the twenty-year-old junior is a young woman. We know what's coming. It's all, sadly, far too predictable.

'And, is she, like, is he—' Tamara asks.

'No. She's *so* not into it. You can tell. Think Peggy Olson in *Mad Men*. She's probably hitting the confessional in church the moment she clocks off.'

Another disgusted shake of the head.

'So,' Lily says, 'do I out him as a manipulative, misogynistic pig who's probably trying to take advantage of her *and* land her with a coke habit? I mean, there's a risk my own extracurricular activities might come out in the process, but I could end up securing the promotion for myself, and, by default, take out the trash.'

Tamara squirms in her seat. 'But wouldn't you do it anyway? I mean, if it wasn't for the promotion?'

Amanda jumps on this one, backing up Tamara in a rare display of loyalty. In reality, she's just seen an excuse to give Lily grief. 'Interesting point. Lily – do you actually care about the sisterhood – or are you in it for yourself?'

I cringe at 'sisterhood'. It doesn't suit Amanda. She's never been a woman lifting up other women. Stomping on them on her way up, maybe.

'Yeah. Like *totally*. I'm all for that,' Lily says. But I notice something uncertain in her reply.

'But how long have you known about it?' Amanda challenges her again.

'Personally,' I say, stepping in before Lily can answer, 'I'd give him a taste of his own medicine.'

'But isn't that what I'm—'

'No. I mean more *literally*. Just maybe, I don't know,

cut his coke with something vile. Give him the shits.' They almost balk at that. I don't know why. It's kind of mild. 'Or send him deep into a K-hole before the interview. Can you imagine? He'll be on delay before answering each question, and even then he'll answer it with something entirely random about space or pizza or whatever.'

I clock Lily's expression. She's clearly tempted. But I doubt she has the gumption to switch his baggie with ket. 'God. No. I can't do that.' She pauses for a few seconds. 'Can I?'

'Think of the twenty-year-old,' I say. 'I mean. If you know about the coke, what else is he doing with her? What else is he doing with the other young women in the agency? What is he capable of?'

As I say this Lily looks to her feet and I can sense she's hiding something from us. There's something more personal going on here.

I ponder sharing my own scenario. Marie from the fruit and veg shop. I've been burning with rage ever since she opened up to me. And my gut says I must do something. How could I not? But I fear my friends will not understand the lengths which we have to go to in order to deal with men like that. But first I have something else on my mind.

'I have a date.'

'A date?' they all say in unison. Tamara is beaming, while Lily fakes a half-smile. Amanda merely lifts an eyebrow.

'Date number two, in fact,' Priya adds with a smile. 'And yes, she's already tried him out. I had to endure the soundtrack on full volume the other day.'

'Don't pretend you didn't enjoy it,' I mock. She shakes her head and rolls her eyes.

I knock back the rest of my drink and place it on the

glass table. They all gawp at me. 'It's a second date with a man. Not an orangutan. No need to look so shocked.'

'Babe,' Amanda pipes up. 'That's precisely why we *are* so shocked. Date number two. With a man? You've usually sacked them off by the time the main course arrives.'

I smile. 'Yeah, well that's certainly the case when any of you lot try to set me up.' I cast my eyes in Lily's direction.

'I've already apologised for Mr I-Want-a-Live-in-Nanny,' she complains.

'Anyway. I'm taking a chance on this one. When a man makes you come three times in less than twelve hours I'd say he's worth a second outing.' I pretend it's all about the sex. I'm especially conscious of not letting my guard down after that first date. Not with anyone.

Amanda nods, her mouth arching upwards from its centre in clear approval. Tamara and Lily sip their drinks silently.

'Later, losers,' I say, in my faux NY accent.

'I expect a full report on WhatsApp please,' Lily calls after me.

I raise my hand behind me. 'We'll see.'

Chapter 9

After dinner, Harry comes back to my apartment. Priya's doing some boring thing with Steve's family (again) so we have the place to ourselves.

I pour two glasses of cold wine in the kitchen and walk over to where he sits in the living room. I like the view of him on our sofa, shoes off, making himself comfortable. He's wearing a soft, ribbed khaki Henley-style T-shirt and I can see the contours of his arm muscles through it. Even his clothes seem right for the moment. Relaxed. Casual. I really can't believe how relaxed all this is. I pass him a glass. 'Thanks,' he says, taking it and having a sip. He puts it down on the table, making sure to grab a coaster. God, seriously good-looking, and considerate too. I slouch back on the sofa with him and giggle.

'What?' he says, eyes all sparky. He grins and makes those gorgeous cheek dimples appear again. I lean over to him, touch the slight stubble on his chin and kiss him on the lips slowly, softly. I pull away, eyes still shut for a second longer.

'Nothing,' I say. 'I just like having you here.' I realise I am close to sharing Priya's challenge with him, the fact that he's just one date away from me winning my bet. But I'm not sure how he'd take that – even though the bet, in its own right, was designed to make me find someone I actually, *genuinely* like. 'You realise, until I met you, I've not had a single date in this town that I've properly enjoyed since I've been here,' I say. 'It's been almost nine months now.'

'Then I'm honoured.' He leans over and kisses me again, fully this time, and we fall into each other, making out like teenagers. We pause, admiring each other's faces for a moment, and then snuggle in together.

'We should do a cheesy date next time. Like a drive-in movie,' he says. 'Something stereotypically American. I can show you what high school dating over here would have been like. Movies, bowling, pizza . . .'

I laugh. 'Ha, yeah, we never did much of that in London.'

'So what was dating like in London? I bet you were popular.'

'Moderately so. I did OK in the dating stakes, I guess.' I decide not to tell him how some of the boys in school hated me. How I would cheat on them with their best mate in front of everyone. I decide not to tell him that because I know that wasn't what I really wanted. It was just what I felt I had to do to protect myself. To do it to them before they did it to me.

'Any big romances?' he asks.

I think back to my teenage years and imagine that they are nothing like the stereotypical American dream. 'I'll be honest, it was less about movies and bowling and more about how much vodka we could nick from our parents' drinks cabinet. Although prom became a bit of a thing when I was leaving school. But yeah, Phil and Cassie ended up putting a lock on their drinks cabinet after me and my first boyfriend puked up all over their bedroom carpet.'

Harry laughs. 'So, Phil and Cassie are . . . ?'

'Oh, my adoptive parents. You know, cos Mum died when I was eight.'

He looks into my eyes, and I look away. I'm not sure how much I'm ready to tell him. But there's something about him that compels me to open up to him.

'My mom died too,' he says. 'I mean, I wasn't as young as you. But it's tough, isn't it? Especially when you don't have a good relationship with your dad.'

'I didn't have *any* relationship with him, to be honest. I never met him. Not my real dad. There were various "stand-in" dads when I was a kid. But they were never any good. My mum had *pretty* bad taste in men. It's why I'm so picky.' I smile at him, trying to think of a way to move the conversation away from my past and onto him and us and now. I've never really talked about my mum to anyone over here other than Priya. But it felt good. It felt like she said it would. Like a connection. And we've got something in common there. Not like having the same taste in music or movies in common. It's a *big* thing in common.

Harry strokes my hair from my forehead, his fingers tickling my skin gently. I close my eyes and feel like I'm melting into him. 'I guess I'm pretty privileged to get to be in your bed then?' he says.

'Of course.'

It's a lie. It's nothing special to be in my bed. Sex has always been just that. An act. A form of exercise, a release. A way of feeling better about myself without giving too much away. But Harry *is* privileged. Because for some weird reason completely unknown to me, I *am* giving myself away to him. My true self. The bits of me inside. And I know I shouldn't, but I can't stop it.

'I don't trust many men,' I blurt out, immediately wishing I hadn't.

'Bad relationship?'

'It's because of the bad stepdads mainly. All of them. None of them treated my mum with anything like respect. I think that's why I went off the rails a little in my teens. Rebelled against Cassie and Phil. And it wasn't fair on them, not really. They were the kindest people. They gave me everything I could possibly want. But I had to take all my hostility out on someone. And they were just . . . there.' I feel a pang of guilt shoot through me.

'We all do it. And you can't blame yourself for the way you behaved as a teen. You were a kid. And you've obviously been through a lot.' It's like he can read my mind.

'What about you?' I ask.

'Mom and I were close, too. She passed away a few years back. My dad a few years earlier than that. But it was just me and Mom mainly. Even when they were together, my dad was always away on business.' He holds his fingers up to create speech marks when he says the word 'business'.

'Sounds like we've both had shit dads then.'

'Yeah. In different ways. But yeah. My father had zero respect for my mom. And he was never interested in me. That's why I had no hesitation in taking my inheritance. It was the least he could do.'

'Same here,' I say absently, even though compensation and inheritance are two entirely different things. But I can't go into detail about being wrongly accused as a kid. Not now. Not while everything is so . . . perfect.

I need to remember to compartmentalise.

Harry grabs another sip of wine and places the glass carefully back on the coffee table. Then he leans into me, moving on top of me. Before I know it we are having sex. Slow, lazy sex. Half-dressed sex. And he is looking me in the eyes the whole time. And we are breathing each other's breath. In and out. It's so intense it makes me dizzy. We never take our eyes off each other. And then we are spent, and his full body weight collapses into mine. He rolls us over slightly onto our sides so as not to crush me.

And as we fall asleep just there, I realise I haven't slept in someone's arms like this since that night with my mum.

Chapter 10

I'm sweating profusely and panting like an exhausted dog. Surely the whole point of sweating is to stop us panting like exhausted dogs in the first place? Obvious design flaw.

Priya and I are running along the Hudson River – her suggestion to help me release my excess energy. I told her this morning about Marie. About the anger and palpitations I felt after chatting to her. I needed to calm down to get a handle on my rage – before it got a handle on me, Priya said. Before it triggered bad memories. And, more worryingly, she had said, negative actions.

'Harry's helping though,' I say.

'Good. That's really good.'

I'm enjoying this run, in spite of the heat. And I wonder if maybe I should keep this up. Get my fitness levels back to their peak. Maybe propranolol isn't the be-all and end-all after all. Maybe running and Harry are just the tonic.

The air is sticky, but the view is refreshing. A welcome break from the towering structures and brick buildings of the city. The water is gently rippling beside us, and the Manhattan skyline feels like a picture to be admired from afar – rather than a claustrophobic reality. Runners, cyclists and skaters disappear behind us as we push forward, feeling the burn. It's a hive of health and wellbeing.

'So where . . . are you . . . going tonight?' Priya asks me, her words escaping her mouth in between quick intakes of oxygen. We've been going for ten kilometres now. She knew I could run, but I think she was expecting me to be more out of practice. The thing is, when you grow up experiencing some of the situations I have, there are three things in life you always have to have at your disposal: the ability to run, the ability to fight, and the ability to intellectualise your way out of a situation.

Hence running clubs, Thai boxing classes and an almost obsessive focus on my university studies in my late teens and early twenties. Until I became distracted with the kind of comforting oblivion that booze could bring.

'That new place up on Madison for dinner. You know, the Cuban one.'

'The rooftop . . . one? . . . Nice . . . Good reviews.' Priya is still not speaking in full sentences. She's running out of steam. We stop for a breather by the grassy area where an outdoor fitness class is moving in perfect synchronisation. We both automatically grab our soft flasks from our running belts and drink deeply.

'How are you not out of breath?' she says, clearly annoyed. 'You haven't worked out in ages.'

'You know why. I'm over-energised. Seriously, Priya. It's not a good state to be in. There's no need for jealousy.'

'Fuck off! Jealousy?' she says, glugging from her soft flask until it's as deflated as a spent cock. I chuckle at the image as it crosses my mind. She ignores me. She never asks me what I'm randomly giggling at since she never likes the answer. 'Anyway. I'm staying with Steve's family tonight so you can release more of your negative energy with Harry. He's obviously having a good effect on you.'

'Jesus. You're there again? Fuck's sake, Priya. It's not like you're even married.'

'Yeah, but there are certain expectations in his family. You know that.'

We carry on walking, heading from the riverside and back across to midtown and our sky-high apartment. Neither of us speaks as we regain our composure and I use the time to reflect on the last two weeks. They have gone by in a blur of monotonous work, fun nights out and dates. Three delectable, delicious dates with Harry Collins. I'd already given Priya the low-down. The very detailed debrief of dates two and three.

Date number two was the meal followed by the most intense, almost tantric and most emotional sex I've ever had.

Date number three was pretty special, too. Movies With a View at Brooklyn Bridge Park. The movie chosen that night was cult classic *True Romance*. Not exactly romantic, but who needs traditional romance. We sat on a picnic blanket with a bottle of wine and a pizza, the evening breeze in our hair and the Manhattan skyline twinkling behind the big screen. And Harry made me stealth-come in public. A long flowing maxi-skirt, dimmed lighting, a blanket and a picnic basket to hide behind can make all your dreams come true it seems. It was as close to perfect as it possibly could be.

And tonight is date number four.

This is the longest I've dated anyone in, like . . . wow. I can't even remember. Probably since Eddie from freshers week back home. I did promise myself that I'd limit it to three dates with Harry. To make sure I don't trap myself in some kind of addictive love fest that I can't get out of without setting myself back fifteen years. But my excuse is that having another date with Harry will prove that I can in fact get into someone without getting too into someone. I *am* into him, sure, I'm not going to pretend otherwise. But I'm not falling in love with him. That's the difference. I could walk away if I wanted to.

It's just that I don't want to yet.

We wander back to the apartment, runners peacocking by us. Bad choice of words – some look more like those dancing horses. Straight backs, swishing ponytails, bouncy trainers that they lift higher off the ground than they need to. An expenditure of energy purely for aesthetic purposes. They'll not get far.

We stop at the fruit and veg shop for refills for the fruit bowl. I just hope Priya doesn't let on that she knows anything. I promised Marie I'd keep it to myself. But I've always told Priya everything.

However, no amount of running fatigue can quell my anger when I see him. The way he has treated Marie. Just who does he think he is?

When she's on her own, she's fiery as hell. I should know, I've been on the receiving end of it. But today she looks small again. Mousy.

Suddenly, I'm filled with a memory of my mum and me dancing in the kitchen to that Sugababes song. 'Hole in the Head'. She got me up out of my chair when I finished my soup, and I copied all her moves. She was pulling pouty faces and I copied those too. She was dancing to it like it was an action song and we laughed and laughed until my cheeks burned. And then he came in through the back door and turned it off. And she said nothing, picking my bowl up off the table and taking it to the sink to wash up. I sat silently too. He made us both dull and silent.

Marie's now also sitting silently. Her husband, Frankie, meanwhile, face like thunder, is ordering her to go home.

Priya and I pretend we aren't completely aware of the tense atmosphere, and instead look as though we're seriously pondering over our fruit selection. But I can hear what he is saying.

'You look ridiculous,' I hear him spit. 'Only a whore wears that much make-up. A filthy fucking whore.'

He moves away from her, busying himself by picking up a crate of veg, and then he clocks us and smiles across, his face changing in an instant.

I look back at him and force a smile to keep up the pretence. Before I knew what he was like I might have described him as kind-looking. Not a man of many words, sure, but there was a softness to his weathered face.

Now when I look at him, those bushy granddad brows remind me of grey wiry pubes running wild across his forehead, and his smile, which I once took as genuine, gives off the vibes of a modern-day Ted Bundy. It's a leering, knowing smile. How did I not see it before?

I look over to Marie who is doing her best to focus on anything but me. She's clearly tried to cover up her bruises, but there isn't enough concealer in the world to disguise his handiwork.

The door opens again and a man walks into the shop and picks up a paper bag, selecting a few pieces of citrus fruit before grabbing a bottle of sparkling water from the shelf above. He walks to the counter, places everything on the countertop and I watch as Marie smiles blankly at him. Her hand trembles as she takes his money.

The moment the man leaves Frankie is back by her side, picking up another crate, hissing at her under his breath again. As Priya continues putting fruit into paper bags I strain to listen.

'Think a man like that'd be interested in an ugly old broad like you?'

Marie shudders.

'Right then!' Priya says brightly, seemingly oblivious to the continuing drama. Or perhaps she's just a better actor than I am. 'We done?'

We walk over to the counter but by this point Marie's quietly gathering her things as he ushers her out and takes her place. She walks past and momentarily locks eyes with me, looking up from under her heavy brown fringe. I go to open my mouth, to say hello, but she shakes her head imperceptibly, pleading with me not to say anything.

She scurries out of the door and my chest heaves with anger. I stand impatiently, twirling the loop of my empty soft flask around my fingers while Priya places our brown bags on the countertop.

I look at him, thinking about what he does behind closed doors as he smiles jovially at his customers, putting on his jolly-old-man persona. I simmer with hatred for him.

'That'll be twelve dollars fifty, sweetheart,' Frankie says, his eyes lighting up as Priya pays him.

But, despite the friendly words, all I can see in front of me is a rotten piece of grey meat sitting here among the colourful displays. A dangerous, disingenuous, infectious piece of male trash.

We leave the shop and I struggle to raise a smile, but I can't betray Marie, so I force another grin and say 'thank you'.

I bet she'd have left him years ago if she felt able. Under the dour cardigans and nondescript hairstyle she's got a lovely face. A *genuinely* kind face. Eyes that light up subtly when she feels free enough to smile without faking it – which I imagine is not often. Hiding his nasty side seems to come naturally to him though, the two-faced prick. You simply can't go on first impressions – not with men.

He's stolen her sparkle.

Why do so many men take our sparkle?

Chapter 11

I pour a glass of Malbec, spilling a dribble on the breakfast bar. I wipe up the small red puddle – where's Priya when I'm being the paragon of a good flatmate? – and take the glass with me into my room as I prepare for my fourth date with Harry. Priya has already set off to see Steve and then head to his parents' house for dinner. Yawn.

Priya was one of the first people I met in Manhattan. The first person I got to know properly. The first person I let into my head. To be fair, I didn't have much choice. Any psychotherapist worth their salt would try to get into my head. And Priya is worth far more than that.

I can trust her. Not one hundred per cent – but at least ninety-five per cent.

There's nobody in the world you can trust one hundred per cent, is there?

Harry has been WhatsApping me. His texts are mostly easy banter and innuendo, but occasionally he'll let something slip that makes me feel like I'm floating. And the excess excitement he is building deep within me is certainly not something I want to let fizzle out. The anticipation is as blissful as the orgasm. Almost.

My imagination is running wild. I bite my lip to hold on to the feeling, to capture it, as I read his next message.

Harry: *Apparently they encourage diners to salsa dance. Not sure how close I can be with you in public before we're asked to leave.*

I imagine our hips swaying together. Feeling him pressed against me. All eyes burning into us. I mean, damn, we make a good couple.

Couple. Fuck's sake, Sally. Snap out of it. It's just a fucking date.

I send a salsa-dancing emoji. Then I put my phone down and pick up my lipstick. I drench my lips in my favourite long-lasting red lippy (these forty-eight-hour lipsticks are a delight for waking up looking just as good as when you first arrived on your date). Then I add defined eyeliner to elongate my eyes and, this time, I go for a touch of dark green shadow. Something a little different.

I sip my wine, my taste buds dancing, and pull open my wardrobe, standing in front of it in my pink vest and white shorts combo. The brightly coloured array of patterns and bright blocky shades welcome me. But tonight I'm going for something a little more sophisticated. Something that places power over play. I feel like I need to assert myself slightly after opening up to him so much. So, I've gone with tailored black trousers, heels, a dark green bandeau top and two-tier gold necklace, the lower tier displaying a heart pendant.

I stand in front of the mirror, assessing my choices, and immediately know I've made the right ones. I swig a little more wine, confident in the knowledge that my lipstick will not budge. I grab my clutch bag and head into the lift.

As I emerge thirty-seven floors below, I walk out into a blast of heat as I leave the air-conditioned lobby for Manhattan's hot summer streets. I take a left, and, as I walk past Marie's shop, something makes me U-turn inside. I'm overwhelmed by the need to see what her husband's like when he's on his own.

As I walk in I notice Frankie lugging crates inside from the sidewalk. I smile and wave, conscious that I was in here just hours ago with Priya. 'I forgot something,' I say, shaking my head and rolling my eyes. He chuckles heartily and carries on clearing his wares from outside. It's got to be almost time for him to shut up shop by now.

My heart thumps like a racehorse's as I think about what he's done to Marie. How dare he?

I feel as though I should buy something, just to give myself justification for being here, and, of course, to see how he responds to me.

I stroll along the displays, past the cherries and mangoes we already bought today. There's an empty spot where the lychee nuts should sit. It's an excuse to speak to him, I guess.

"Scuse me!' I say brightly, calling out from the shop. 'I know you're closing up soon. But I don't suppose you've got any lychee nuts?'

'If there aren't any over there, you'll have to give me a minute,' he says, placing a crate of yams from outside onto the floor of the shop and shoving it to one side with his foot.

'OK!' I say, almost making myself nauseous at the sickly-sweet tones emanating from me.

I wait for him to come inside. He checks the empty crate.

'Fraid we got none.' He shrugs his shoulders and wipes his forehead with the back of his hand. 'But lemme check out the back.'

My mouth curls in fury as he disappears into the storeroom at the back of the shop, towards the tiny kitchenette where Marie made our drinks the other day. How can he be so nice to me and treat his own wife like shit?

I peer into the room and can just see him climbing onto a mini-footstool and groping along the top shelves.

'Nope. No lychee nuts,' he yells again as he steps backwards from the stool and back onto the floor. 'Sorry, sweeth—'

The impulse is so strong I've slammed the storeroom door shut before I've had a chance to gather my thoughts, cutting him off mid-speech. A key is sitting in the lock just waiting to be used. I frantically grasp it between my fingers, but, as I'm scrambling to turn it, he crashes wildly into the back of the door, pulling on the handle.

What *am* I doing?

'What the hell are you doing?' he shouts through the door. He prises it open a touch and my heart jumps into my mouth.

I pull back with all my might, using my weight to anchor it, but he's strong and pulling hard on the other side, issuing a stream of threats against me. I'm unsteady in my heels so I press one foot against the wall to gain some leverage, gouging a hole in the plaster, but I manage to regain some purchase. Then somehow he wedges his fingers in the gap, and the gap gets a little bigger. Shit!

'Fucking bitch,' he yells, tugging at the door. I wait a second then let it loosen just a touch, throwing him off balance. I hear him crash into the shelves behind him as I yank it as hard as I can – and the door slams shut. I turn the key with a metallic thunk, then collapse with my back against the door, attempting to get my breath back.

'Unlock this fucking door! Now!' he shouts, his fists banging against it.

I have just locked a grown man in a store cupboard.

The reality of what I've just done hits me. Talk about impulsive. I begin to giggle, collapsing onto the floor as my chest jigs up and down and my laughter becomes almost manic. The door pounds behind me, punctuating impotent threats.

Something inside me burned when Marie told me her story. The beatings, the put-downs, the total loss of confidence, of independence. The threats. The time he took her new clothes, the outfit she'd bought for her sister's wedding, and burned them in the backyard. The time he cracked her jaw so hard with his elbow when they were on vacation she locked herself in their room for three days, telling the hotel staff she had food poisoning. Her mouth was so sore she couldn't eat for days – never mind the sharp, cracked tooth that ripped her to shreds. And then there was the time he made out she was losing the plot in a long reign of gaslighting. Hiding her mail, deleting her calls. Isolating her from everyone and everything until, when she eventually confronted him about it, he didn't even bother to deny it. He just told her she was overreacting, then opened a can of beer and put the game on.

I feel rage swirl in my chest. The nerve of these men – and it's always men – who think they can just waltz into our lives and destroy us without any consequences. There's a thud next to my head and another torrent of abuse is hurled through the door. I take a deep breath and try to remember some of the techniques Priya taught me to help me to calm down. It was like Frankie was *him*. Sometimes it's like any bad man can be him.

I decide I'm glad Frankie is locked in the store cupboard. It's damage limitation.

The idea of just letting it slide, letting him get away with it for another day, I just can't do it. I did nothing too many times and I know how much I regret it. I know how regret can grow into pure rage. He's better off this way. He's better off letting me get it out my system more . . . tamely. He can consider it a warning. A way to knock him off his pedestal and let him know that he isn't as indestructible as he thinks he is.

He's still shouting. Crashing around in the cupboard. Suddenly all the adrenaline in my system seems to collide and I laugh again. Loudly. Theatrically. It's an on-purpose cartoon villain laugh because, well, you've got to have fun, haven't you?

I pocket the key and walk out, closing the shop door behind me. The banging is still audible, but only if you listen closely. His phone was on the countertop, so, of course I now have that too. Unfortunately it's locked. Otherwise I could have sent a message from it, from him, telling Marie that he wasn't coming home. Making up some reason for it. Giving her not only respite, but peace of mind, too.

Fuck. Marie. When Marie arrives tomorrow, he'll be furious. He could hurt her. What have I done? God, I'm so stupid. Why do I never think?

I look at the key, then I chuck it down a grate in the street. It's not like I'm going to go back and let him out, and Marie won't be able to let him out without it. She'll have to call a locksmith. Which means, the moment Frankie gets out, there'll be someone else there. Someone who will need to hang around to mend the door. Frankie won't hurt her in front of a witness. Bullies are cowards like that.

And I'll make sure I'm there early too. Just to be safe.

Chapter 12

Grappling with that monster of a man in the cupboard has made me a few minutes later than I'd planned for my date with Harry. Plus, I've gone for killer heels tonight, which look amazing but slow me down.

I hail a cab, which are, as ever, in abundance, and make my way to Fiesta – the rooftop restaurant we're trying out tonight.

As the cab pulls up outside the restaurant building I can see him already waiting for me. He's leaning against the wall, his legs crossed casually out in front of him. He's wearing a light blue linen shirt, slightly open at the collar, and jeans. He's more divine than ever. I thought the electricity would fizzle out a bit after a few dates, but it's just getting sparkier.

I'm in *serious* trouble. And I'm loving it.

Harry is looking the other way at first, his eyebrows knitting together in that James Dean kind of way as he looks out for me. I see him kick his heel against the wall.

Nerves, maybe? Or perhaps he's just impatient to see me? Either is good.

I open the cab door and step out feeling fabulous. He

spots me and immediately smiles, his killer cheekbones and chiselled jaw jutting out at all the right angles.

I go to kiss him, holding the back of his head, my fingers in his hair, and wish immediately that we weren't in public. He smells great.

'You smell great,' he says.

I smile, breathing in the scent of his skin. 'As do you.'

I notice he's wearing a thin gold chain around his neck, rippling over his skin and his collarbones. Every little detail is delicious.

'Shall we?' I say, stepping away and moving the evening on. I can't wait for us to go home together, to be together completely, but first, we must indulge in some Cuban cuisine and rum-based cocktails.

We head up to the rooftop in the lift, a concierge in a matching suit greeting us as we stand behind him, wishing we were alone. As the doors open we are met with salsa music and every colour imaginable is rushing before our eyes.

'Wow,' I say. 'What. A. Vibe!' I cringe at myself as the words escape me while I am distracted at the sight. I look to my right and I see he is chuckling, his head nodding and those dimples appearing in his cheeks. Fucking hell. I clear my throat.

We scan the room. There are already people dancing. Mainly in couples. The music is as bright as the decor, and the place is bouncing, with waiting staff moving at pace around the tables, bringing colourful cocktails and delicious-looking food to animated customers.

I make a note to stick to one cocktail and then revert to red wine. I know where I'm at with red wine. And I want to remember every second of this night. Our fourth date.

Fourth date!

We're shown to our seats and immediately brought the menus.

'How's the rest of your week been?' Harry asks, moving my attention away from the menu and back onto him. I put it down in front of me and lock eyes with his. I don't know if it's the lighting out here or what, but he looks even more handsome tonight. He's let that little bit of light stubble I noticed the other night spread further across his face. I imagine feeling it bristling against my skin later and I prickle in anticipation.

'It's been interesting,' I say, without going into any detail. It might be date number four but I'm not sure I'm ready to let him in on my temporary incarceration of the fruit and veg man quite yet. 'You?' I ask, changing the subject.

'Not so much. It's dragged, if I'm honest. But I've got a nice weekend planned. My brother's got a catamaran out in East Hampton.'

'Your brother? I didn't know you . . .'

'He's a couple of years younger than me. A little wild at times. But he's one of the good guys.'

'Nice,' I say, even though I immediately feel disappointed that Harry is going to be away for a few days. 'We better make the most of tonight then.' I smile. 'How long are you away for?'

'Just four nights. It's kind of a tradition. We go every July and again on Labour Day,' he explains, just as the waiter returns.

'Oops, sorry,' I say to the waiter. 'We got distracted.' I look to Harry 'Do you know what you're—'

'Cocktails? We could order those now?' Harry says.

'Sure,' I say, picking the menu back up. 'I'll go for a caipirinha, please.'

The waiter nods, making a note on his tablet. Harry smiles. 'Good choice. Make that two,' he says. The waiter nods again and leaves us.

'You know the last man I dated before you suggested I choose the drinks for us both then explained to me why my choice was incorrect.'

'Sounds like an asshole.' He laughs.

'Yeah.' I sigh. 'I've never had much luck on the apps, to be fair. I mean, before you of course.'

'Of course.'

'What's your experience been like?' I ask.

'How do you mean?'

'On the dating sites. I mean, like, common pitfalls. Dubious dates . . . You must have some tales to tell.'

'I've not dated many people to be honest. I'm too picky. Just like you.'

I raise my eyebrow suspiciously just as our drinks arrive. The waiter places them carefully in front of each of us. I take a sip. It is sour and refreshing. 'Delicious,' I say. The waiter leaves us again.

Harry takes a sip and pulls a face. 'You know, if it were me choosing, I'd have probably gone for the margarita.' He holds the caipirinha out in front of him as if it's sour milk.

I am so taken aback that I'm temporarily speechless, but then he breaks out into laughter. 'Ha. Just kidding!'

I chuck my napkin in his face. 'Twat,' I say. 'Anyway, you were telling me . . .'

'Hm?'

'About the dubious dates. The app.'

'Ohhhh yes. You were mentally accusing me of being a cliché?'

I laugh. This guy really can read my mind. 'Well . . .'

'I just mean, I don't trust those apps, so I don't bother meeting many people. Because, yep, you're right. I've had some horror-story dates.'

'Go on,' I say, sipping my drink.

'Catfished once.'

'No! I didn't know women did that as well?'

'Seriously. She actually looked fine in real life, but if she's going to lie about her looks, if she's switched her photos, what else is she going to lie about?'

'Trust issues?' I ask.

'Don't we all?' He laughs. 'I don't know. I mean, it's sad, isn't it. I don't think she was dangerous or anything. Just . . . sad. Lonely, maybe.'

The waiter heads back over to take our food order and I realise we haven't even glanced at the menus.

'Can you give us five?' I ask. He nods and quickly walks away, clearly irritated by us. 'We better make our minds up,' I say.

Harry closes his menu. 'You pick,' he says. 'I'm starting to get the feeling that you like to be in control.'

Chapter 13

My ears ring loudly with sirens, car horns and my own raging pulse. I blink to remove the Vaseline-like film that seems to be smeared across my eyeballs. It doesn't work. Everything is blurred and yet far too bright at the same time. I blink again, take a breath, and strain to read the time on my alarm clock: 10.37. Is that what it says? The red numbers are fuzzy and shake as if exploding with static energy. I don't even know if it's morning or night.

I'm as thirsty as a fish in the desert and my head is pounding. There is a full glass of water by my bed, along with a wine glass still holding the dregs of the red I was drinking as I got ready last night. I pick up the water and down it, almost choking on each gulp. I try to stand, willing myself back to life, but my legs feel as if they lack all trace of bone or muscle. I immediately slump back down onto the bed.

What the . . . ?

I must have been wasted last night. But I never get wasted. Not really. Not since . . .

It's a rule I stand by. And that was a quality bottle of Malbec. It surely couldn't be responsible for this throbbing headache, which was easily now a 10 on the Richter scale.

I look around me. Last night's clothes are folded neatly on the dressing table stool. My heels are positioned tidily underneath. I would never do that. Especially if I was this drunk. I look down at myself. I am wearing my silky sunflower pyjamas. Everything is tidy and organised. Except for my head, that is.

Did Harry bring me into the apartment? Did he do all this? My skull bangs again, making me wince, the sounds from the streets outside only adding to the chaos. Squawking, honking, beeping.

Jesus fucking Christ! I grasp my forehead in my hand, squeezing tightly at my temples.

I am thirty-seven floors above ground level. Thirty-seven entire floors! Seriously, how high do you need to climb in this city for a moment's peace. Big Apple? Big bangin' Apple more like. Normally I love it. But today I hate it.

This isn't just a hangover.

I sit up and steady myself, leaning back against the headboard. I rub my eyes harshly in the hope my vision will clear. How did I end up in this state? I feel like I'm in one of those movies. Do I even know my own bloody name?

'Sally,' I say aloud.

Yes. I know who I am. I know where I am. It is 2025. I haven't lost my mind. There's no amnesia, not proper amnesia, anyway, and yet whole chunks of last night have vanished.

I try to tease out memories that must surely be lurking somewhere in the back of my mind. I was with Harry – sexy, kind, gorgeous Harry. And then I was wasted or I must have been. But that can't be right; it doesn't add up.

I must have been spiked.

Pictures come back in flashes. His white smile as we

laughed together, rescuing the spilled contents of my bag from the sidewalk. His slate-grey eyes catching mine as he handed me my purse. My legs stumbling, crossing one in front of the other as I leant into the road to hail a yellow cab, its headlights dazzling me more than I already was.

There was only me and Harry. I'm sure of that. And I would never have got this drunk . . .

Unless . . . the cab driver? But Harry wouldn't have left me alone.

I squeeze my eyes shut and think hard. I try to imagine myself getting in, climbing out, making my way up the stairs to the building. It's too hazy. But then I remember Harry was with me in the back seat of the cab. I remember inhaling the scent of his aftershave as I nuzzled into his neck, my eyes unable to stay open.

Oh God. A sickening realisation washes over me. Someone must have slipped something into my wine when we were dancing. But I have a sudden strong vision of him whirling me around. I have a vague sense that my memory starts to collapse just before we left. After we ordered that last drink.

Wait a second. Is sweet Harry . . . not so sweet after all?

No, no, *no*!

He must have done this to me. He *must* have.

He must have slipped something in my wine. Before we left the restaurant, when I nipped to the loo, perhaps? It's the only possible explanation.

How could I not see this coming? How did I not suss him out with my (usually) highly accurate bullshit detector?

What were we even talking about before I became suddenly inebriated?

Fragments of conversation float in and out of my

consciousness. Drunken little clouds, pecking at my headache like a hungry seagull.

'You said you lost your mum too. What happened?' I had asked. He hadn't gone into any detail before, and, as he opened up about losing her, about how close they were, I immediately felt an even stronger connection to him. I couldn't believe how much we had in common.

He hung his head, his dirty blonde hair falling into his eyes. He appeared genuinely pained. This was the first time I'd seen him vulnerable; it had only taken four dates. Still waters run deep – that's what they say, right? I guess that's what I liked about him. I can't do with oversharers. But then he looked up towards the heat lamp, biting his bottom lip, trying hard not to cry. That moment marked something more between us – more than just sex. I put my hand on his and I felt my own eyes well. That was when I thought I'd found my soulmate . . .

For fuck's sake. It's finally happened. I've been fooled. Tricked. How could I be so bloody stupid?

He was looking directly at the light. Staring hard at it unblinkingly. He wasn't trying *not* to cry. He was trying *to* cry. I've pulled that stunt myself a thousand fucking times.

I hit my forehead with the base of my palm over and over and over. Stupid, stupid, stupid.

But why? What did he get out of this? Out of drugging me? What was his endgame? It can't have been about sex. We'd had sex before. More than once before and it was good. Fuck, it was always good. Of course we were going to have sex again; we both knew that. I wriggle my hips around in my bed trying to get a sense of things. No. We didn't have sex last night. I don't think.

So then why? Why drug me, Harry? I mean, it can only have been Harry. Couldn't it?

I think hard, trying to find another explanation, but I can't find one. And I know this isn't just booze. I so desperately want to find another explanation.

My ears rush harder, the sirens drowned out by the blood pumping anger to every extremity of my body. I am furious. Livid. Completely fucking raging! My heart palpitations have returned, thrashing in my chest like death metal.

I pick up last night's glass and throw it hard against the wall, screaming a ragged, guttural scream. A reddish-purple stain spatters the pure white paint, droplets racing downwards towards the skirting board, intertwined with tiny shards of glass. Priya's going to kill me when she gets back.

Things like this do not happen to me.

I've been primed to spot it. I've seen what happened to my mother. I've tried so, so hard to not fall into the same traps. But it left me lonely. Perpetually single. And the one time I decide to let go, to trust someone. Fuck!

The thought of my mother triggers something I've tried to bury deep down since I first arrived in this city. Since Priya first rescued me. Feelings I've tried to move past. But he's changed all that. He's reminded me that it's not in the past.

The danger is everywhere.

Chapter 14

With my heart trying to jump out of my chest, I race towards my drawers and pull them open, spilling out the contents as the beating gets louder and louder in my ears.

'Fuck you, Harry Collins!' I scream at the empty space.

Knickers, a bright pink menstrual cup and empty pill packets fly high into the air as I empty my top drawer, revealing its bare oak bottom. The contents fall around me like essence-of-real-woman confetti. Then, I see them, tangled in the luxurious black ribbon of my silky wrist ties.

I grab my emergency pack of cigarettes and immediately light one with the disposable green lighter tucked inside the carton.

As I inhale deeply, my heart slows and my thinking finds clarity once more. It's been a while. But my God, I need this.

The bastard spiked me. Harry. My Harry. I didn't think he could hurt a damn fly – never mind a fully grown woman with nearly three decades of feminist rage behind her. I take another drag on my cigarette. I need to recalibrate. To calm myself. To think clearly. To work out what the fuck happened last night.

How could I have been so stupid?

I wouldn't say that to another woman, would I? The thing is, I've always prided myself on having a strong nose for bad men. I've had enough practice – and it's not like I made a habit of seeking them out. They just landed on my plate alongside the beans and sausages my skint single mum served up when I was a kid as she got ready for her latest bad date. Or, as a more recent example, the smashed avocado on toast the creepy waiter served me in that awful coffee shop back home, along with his number.

I used it, but not for the reason he'd hoped. Instead I signed him up for every awkward text-mailing list I could find – Viagra, male incontinence, graphic porn. See, I'm used to dealing with self-entitled, misogynistic men. But why now, when it comes to a *truly* bad man, have I fallen for it?

I've had years of relentless exposure to all these toxic strains of man that are about as endearing as a dose of Omicron. But maybe that's the problem. Like overusing antibiotics, you eventually become immune.

Maybe my toxicity radar is fading.

Not anymore!

I reach for my phone from the bedside table, straining to focus my thoughts. I contemplate the impulse to call or text him, still uncertain of his true intentions here.

Then I see a text from my bank. Insufficient funds. My heart plummets all the way to my pedicured toes. He hasn't . . . he couldn't . . .

I click open my banking app and hold my breath as my phone captures my facial recognition and logs me in.

Come on, come on, come on . . .

My account balance pops up in front of my eyes. Oh. My. God.

$0.07.

That fucker. How has he done it? Did he have my PIN? Did he somehow stick my phone camera in front of my face to open it? But it barely recognises you when you've a pair of glasses on, let alone when you're off your face from . . . whatever the hell your con man boyfriend's slipped in your drink.

Fuck!

He's cleaned me out. Every last penny of my compensation.

The spiteful . . .

Drugging . . .

Sleazy . . .

Lying . . .

BASTARD!

I feel sick. I run towards the bathroom, my bare legs buckling underneath me, sending me sideways into a slump on the hardwood floor. My skin squeaks painfully as I haul myself onto all fours and vomit on the spot. A combination of unwanted toxins and intense disgust towards Harry purges out of me.

I look at the gloopy pinkish pool of sick in front of me and I realise I have two choices here. Either I collapse into it face first, surrendering to failure and becoming a victim. Harry's victim. Or I do something about it. I get my revenge.

Not just on him, but on every bad man who's ever tried to bring me down. The ones who exploited my mum. The ones who exploit all of us, using their power and superficial charm to secure a seat at the corporate table, making horrific advertising decisions that sprinkle insecurities like fairy dust over every girl and woman just trying to get by in life.

No. I don't need your fucking wrinkle cream or your slimming pills or your fad diet. And no, I don't need my mum to be 'looked after', if looking after means controlled and gaslighted. And great big fat no, I don't need to be duped and drugged and cleaned out by a lying, conniving reincarnation of Dirty John.

Dirty Harry. It was obvious, really.

These men have been manipulating us since the dawn of time. And they've been doing it on a global scale. But now it's personal. I guess it always has been. But I thought I could put it behind me. I thought I could move on, but I can't. He's brought it back to the fore. He's dredged up the past. And now he's going to pay.

The choice is easy.

I leap up, almost skidding in my own vomit, but nothing's going to floor me this time. This time, I am thinking clearly. This time, he is going to feel the full force of my anger. Slowly. Painfully. Embarrassingly.

And when I say slowly, I don't just mean that the final act of dying will have him begging for oblivion. I mean the anticipation will have him on his knees, too. The dreadful build-up. What's the point in just killing someone when you can enjoy making their life painful too?

He's not going to know what's hit him. I'm going to find out every last detail about that man, and I'm going to disrupt every aspect of his life until he's ready to submit.

But first, I need to find him. To track him back down. I click into my messages.

Harry Collins has left the conversation.

That's what you think, Harry Collins. Or whatever your fucking name is.

Chapter 15

There's being ghosted. Then there's being fucking poltergeisted.

He arrived with a bang, fucked with my head, smuggled me back into my apartment, stole my money and left me unconscious, having folded my clothes into a neat little pile. And now here I am surrounded by broken glass, dregs of red wine and my own vomit.

I pick up my phone to call him, even though I've no idea what I'll say to him. But I can't. I no longer have his number because whatever he's done on WhatsApp has included blocking me or removing himself altogether.

I go back to the dating app but it's as though his profile never even existed. He's clearly gone beyond unmatching and blocked me, because searching for him draws a complete blank.

I try typing *"Harry Collins" Manhattan* into Google but it just feels futile. No con man worth his salt is going to carry on conning women using the exact same name. He *has* to be using different names. Even if it's just a different surname, because there are loads of Harrys in New York. Fuck, there're loads of Harry Collinses in New York. But none of the ones coming up look like him, and some of them are featured in the obituaries section of the New York papers, so . . .

I wonder if he's even a Harry at all? He could be called Keith, for all I know. I could have been fucking a Keith. Or a Colin. Or a *Donald*. And I wouldn't have consented to it in the first place.

I swore I'd never date a Keith, never mind shag his brains out in my own bed.

Maybe he used the obituaries to come up with his name? Maybe he defrauds dead people as well as women. Come to think of it . . . did I ever see a credit card? Any form of ID? I guess it was only four dates, but he must have carried something. He was flashing plastic – not cash – so there has to be a trace of him somewhere.

I look back at WhatsApp. Where his photo once sat in the little circle at the top, there is now just a grey circle with a white head-and-shoulders outline.

I think of the image that was on his profile. It was a close-up of his face. I remember screen-grabbing it so I could zoom in and look at his face.

Don't call me obsessive – we all do it!

But I did the same with his dating app photos. I screen-grabbed them too . . . and sent them to Priya when we first matched.

I go into my photo library and find a few scattered around in there. I open the WhatsApp pic and zoom in. Unfortunately, I can't see anything. I stare into his eyes on screen.

Fuck – why is he so hot? Why do I want to fuck him and kill him all at the same time? This is why men like him are so dangerous. They shouldn't be allowed to exist.

I flick through a few more pics, the ones from his former dating profile, but then something needles its way into my brain . . .

Marie – shit!

It's almost lunchtime. I've been so preoccupied by my current situation that I entirely forgot about the man I locked in the store cupboard.

And his poor wife who has no doubt had to deal with his wrath this morning. I was meant to be there when they were opening it up and letting him out.

I stand far too quickly from the sofa and have to sit back down again. Crumpled. I am still too wobbly. But I need to check she's OK. I need to check he hasn't taken it out on her.

Fuck, fuck, fuck! What the hell was I thinking?

I grab some joggers and stuff my feet inside my running shoes. I throw a hoodie on over my bra, and head out of the apartment.

The movement of the lift is playing havoc with my scrambled brain. We hit the ground floor with an unwelcome thud and I stagger outside and into the streets. Jesus, what exactly did he put in my drink last night? I know if it was GHB or Rohypnol it would stay in my system for a few hours at least. But this is lingering on uncomfortably. It's like the world's worst hangover.

It's far too warm for a hoodie, especially with the sweat pouring out of my body jettisoning the poison. Lurching along the edge of the sidewalk, I feel as though I'm out at sea or something. The ground seems to be moving beneath my feet. Cars and yellow cabs whoosh by, horns blaring, and my senses are struggling to keep up.

I stumble into the fruit and veg store, steadying myself on the edge of stacked crates, overflowing with berries.

They wobble slightly, making me jump. A single strawberry tumbles onto the floor, but I know that if I bend over to pick it up I might never get up. Shit, I'm not sure I can hold it together right now.

'Watch yourself!' Marie's voice carries in the air. I turn to look at her.

'Marie! Thank God!' I say, making an effort to walk towards her.

'It was you, wasn't it?' she snaps angrily. But she doesn't seem as shaky as she did yesterday, and her voice is stronger. I'm desperate to know what happened to him.

'Where is he? Did he hurt you?'

'No. No thanks to you.'

'I just wanted to give you some peace. I wanted to teach him a lesson. It was a harmless prank.'

She raises an eyebrow, lifting her fringe slightly with the movement.

'I mean really,' I plead. 'It wasn't like dangerous or anything. I didn't plan it.'

'You always go around locking people's husbands in cupboards on a whim?'

She seems more angry with me than she has been at him.

'I was meant to be here when you opened it up but . . .'

'Shame you weren't. I'd rather you were cleaning up his stale piss instead of me.'

'I am so, *so* sorry,' I say. And I mean it. 'Where is he anyway?'

'I had to get the locksmith out, didn't I? Yet another expense we don't need. Assume you've got the key?'

I explain to her that it's currently swimming along in Manhattan's underground sewage system.

'Well, you owe me for the locksmith,' she says.

'Fine,' I say 'But where is he? What happened?'

'He was so mortified. He'd pissed all over the floor. And the locksmith had to hang around to fit a new lock, so Frankie left. I don't know where. He doesn't seem to have his phone. I take it you've got that, too?'

'I think it's at my apartment,' I say.

She shakes her head at me. 'I opened up to you. I trusted you.'

I'm confused by her tone. Yes, she seems angry with me, but she also seems back to her old self. More assertive, somehow. I can't get my head around it. If anything, surely my stupid impulse has put her in even more danger. I wince. 'God, I'm such an idiot.'

'You got that right. What the hell made you do it?'

I focus on the floating sensations in my brain and body. I take a deep breath and try to stand straight. Standing still on this flat surface feels as challenging as performing a choreographed dance on top of a narrow log of wood. I'm all over the place. But I know exactly why I was so wound up about Marie. I just don't want to fully disclose that part of my life.

Besides, the last person I opened up to in any detail was Harry and look what happened.

'What's the hell's the matter with you anyway?' Marie says, a look of pinched concern in her face.

'I know, I know, I just . . . I wanted to teach him . . .'

'Not that. I mean . . .' She gestures towards me, her hand flapping wildly. 'You look a mess.'

She's not wrong. I take another deep breath but my stomach lurches and I gulp. She must see the inevitability on my face as my throat begins to contract. 'Bathroom's out the back.' She points towards the door next to the store cupboard. 'Make sure you close the door!'

I'm already collapsed over the toilet before she finishes her sentence, the door swinging violently behind me. My guts heave nothing but a trickle of clear water into the bowl.

I am literally purging Harry Collins! But it'll take more than a bit of sick to get rid of him.

I remember how angry I am. Rage floats in and out of me, alternating with feeling desperately sorry for myself. I need the anger, the rage. I'm no good to myself if I lose that spark. And I'm certainly no good to Marie. Bad men need dealing with.

I stand up and wipe my mouth with a sheet of tissue, getting an unwanted glimpse of myself in the small mirror hanging on the wall by a chain. It's the first time I've looked in a mirror since I was getting ready to go out last night.

Jesus, it's not a pretty sight.

My eyes are bloodshot and ringed by dark circles. Mascara runs down my cheeks and winged eyeliner smudges out in every direction but the right one. My lips are still stained with a little faded red, but beneath the colour the skin is chapped. I splash my face with water in an attempt to make myself look more human, and wipe my eyes with dampened tissue. But it's going to take a lot more than that.

How did I let this happen? This isn't me.

Marie is serving a customer when I open the door, so I wait a few moments until she hands them their change and they say their goodbyes, then I step out again.

'This,' I say to Marie, gesturing to my sad appearance, 'is the result of a man.'

'Yeah, well, you need to do something about it; you'll be scaring away my customers.' She's still clearly pissed off with me. 'What man is worth getting that drunk for anyway?'

She looks back down to her sudoku puzzle book, ready to dismiss me.

'No, I mean . . .' I'm mortified. But my brain is still not working at full speed and I blurt it out regardless. 'I was fucking spiked, Marie.'

She places her pen down and looks at me, horrified. 'Spiked?'

'And he's taken all my money. He's cleaned me out.'

'What? Not my Frankie?' She stands up from her chair as if ready to deal with it.

'God no. No!'

'Who then?'

Another customer walks in. It's obvious this isn't the place for the full story. 'Do you want to meet me somewhere after I close?' she asks, as a smart woman in a pencil skirt suit and an old-fashioned up-do browses the apples and pears. 'Somewhere a bit more private? So you can tell me what's happened? And I don't just mean with your spiked date.'

Chapter 16

'That's the last time I'm listening to you.' My phone is still sitting in front of me playing terrible on-hold music on a loop.

'*I* didn't pick him,' Priya retorts. She exudes serenity, even while shovelling mango and Greek yoghurt into her mouth. I, meanwhile, am pacing the kitchen with what Priya describes as my 'elephant feet' in full marching mode. I look more like myself now, and I've managed to clean up my puddle of sick from earlier this morning. Priya, thankfully, hasn't seen the state of my room yet. The wall definitely needs repainting. I'm not convinced you can get red wine out of a matt white emulsion surface.

I'm agitated, which is not helped by the maddening on-hold music from the bank. My anxious energy is coming back as sharp electric bursts, each one zapping away what little control I've managed to hold on to.

'You suggested the stupid challenge,' I huff. 'You made me believe he was worth seeing again.'

'First, Sally, nobody makes you do or believe anything *you* don't want to. Secondly, if we're going to start blaming each other for what he's done, we're allowing misogyny to win. We're allowing it to break us.'

'I'm not fucking broken.'

'You know what I mean. Harry's the fucker. Not me, and certainly not you. Not in this instance, anyway.'

I glare at her. 'A little more compassion, Priya.' I light up a cigarette.

'Since when did you start smoking again?'

'Since I got spiked and conned.'

'Look,' Priya says more softly, opening a window and wafting the air theatrically with her arms, 'you do have my compassion. But I know you. You wouldn't thank me for the softly-softly approach anyway.'

'How do you know?'

She holds out her arms and walks towards me. 'Want a hug then?'

'Fuck off,' I say, turning my nose up and laughing.

I'd come straight back home after being presented with my ghoulish reflection in Marie's bathroom mirror. Sadly, before I was able to remove all evidence of the horror show that took place last night, Priya walked in. She dropped her bags and her jaw the moment she looked at me.

When I got the headlines out of the way, she sat at the breakfast bar as I paced up and down telling her the whole story, well, the bits I could remember anyway. Harry had, unfortunately, removed many hours of memory from my brain last night with whatever his choice of poison was, along with the entirety of my savings – bar seven cents. Suddenly, a human voice speaks through my phone's speaker. 'Hello, can I help you?'

'Hello! I've had money stolen from my account,' I say. 'It happened last night.'

'Can I just take you through security?'

I take the woman on the other end of the line through

all my details, even though I already inputted them into the phone when dialling.

'Ah yes, I can see that $43,700 has been withdrawn,' she says. 'By you.'

I exhale dramatically. 'Except it wasn't me – that's what I'm *trying* to explain. I was spiked. He must have used my face to unlock the app.'

'That's unusual,' she says. 'You can't do that without having your eyes open.'

'Well unusual or not, that's what happened. And I might have had my eyes open, but my brain had been turned to mush by whatever he gave me, so . . .'

'Have you reported it to the police?'

'Yes,' I lie. I glance over to Priya who raises an eyebrow at me. I shrug and look back towards the phone.

'Then we'll need the incident report number you'll have been given as part of the case, so my colleagues can assess whether or not they can approve any compensation.'

My stomach drops. Why did I just lie about the police? 'Sorry, I don't recall getting one,' I say. 'I was just so out of it. Look, can't you tell me at least who owns the bank account that *I* – apparently – transferred the money into?'

The woman keeps talking, listing all the potential issues that may make things difficult for me to get my money back. Shouldn't they be trained to support and comfort you in these situations? Still, she explains how these things happen. Apparently, in cases like this (which apparently isn't 'usual' but whatever) the account the money is transferred to is usually just a holding account. They then move the money from there and on to another account – or several different accounts. It's called layering. And it makes it harder to track down the real people behind the scam.

But I know who's behind the scam. I just don't know where he is or, well, who he *really* is.

I end the call, promising to try and furnish them with my non-existent crime number.

'How the hell am I going to get my savings back?' I yell at nobody.

'You can't go to the cops,' Priya says.

'You think I don't fucking know that,' I seethe, thinking back to the night we met. We'd made a deal then that I would never go to the police. 'Fucking hell, Priya, why the hell did he do this?'

'There must have been a sign?' Priya asked.

'Are you kidding me?' I snapped. 'A sign? The whole point of spiking a woman is to erase any sign. I mean, for fuck's sake, I was on my fourth date with him. Fourth! I'm not a fucking idiot.' I angrily wipe the remnants of the smudged black make-up from my eyes and chuck the dirty cotton wool pad down on the table. God if only I'd kept to my own pact. If only I'd walked away after date three.

'I never said you were. It's just, usually, you're so . . .'

'Don't you dare say careful.'

'I wasn't about to. I was about to say you're usually so ridiculously cynical and suspicious. I mean. Nobody gets past you. It's just . . . What a *bastard*.' She is furiously scraping the remains of yoghurt from her bowl. She is getting riled and saying the wrong things. Things the professional therapist in her would admonish her for. But we are syncing our rage.

She opens the dishwasher and her bowl clatters angrily into the bottom of it. 'I just can't believe how he turned out. He seemed so—'

'I know! How are you meant to let people into your

life if the only time you do—' I fight back a tear before it turns into a deluge. I feel so stupid. I've protected myself for so long and now, I let my guard drop just once and this happens to me.

'Sally, I know it's hard, and I know this has made everything a million times worse. But don't let it jeopardise your future. Don't let one lying, manipulative bastard dictate what happens next. If you don't let anyone in your entire life you'll be completely isolated. Human beings need connection. *Real* connection. We're social animals. In many ways, it's riskier to encourage people to carry on living their lives – if that's what you can call it – and not connecting with anyone. We're not like the solitary snow leopard. We aren't built to wander alone and hunt alone and just meet up once in a while for sex.'

'Sounds exquisite to me,' I say.

'Yeah well. You're not a fucking leopard. You're a woman. And you definitely weren't happy when we met, so . . .'

'Anyway, I've got you,' I say. 'Besides, you know plenty about me. Why the fuck should anyone else need to be let in on all my messy baggage?'

'You're being defensive. Self-preservation, I get it. But if you want to thrive, if you want to be really, genuinely, happy . . .'

'Ah, bollocks, I'll get a cat.'

'Not in this apartment.'

I huff.

'Anyway,' she says, brushing her palms twice. 'What are we gonna do about him?'

'I can't find the guy. He's deleted his profile. He's blocked me on WhatsApp. He might not even be called Harry. I mean, who the fuck even is he?'

'OK, so what *do* we know about him?'

'Who knows. Who knows if any of it is true.'

'He'll have slipped some kernel of truth in there. It would have been hard not to over four dates. Talk me through anything you know.'

'So, he said this weekend he was going to the Hamptons. East Hampton. Said his brother had a boat or was hiring a boat or something.'

'Right, so we can check that out. Anything else?'

'He said he had a couple of properties he rented out. Inherited from his parents or something. They aren't managed by my company, but – if they do exist – I think he said they were managed by one of the other big firms. Lloyds maybe? But then—' I look up to the ceiling '—that's why I'm so baffled. Why would he need to clear me out if he was already loaded?'

'Maybe this is *why* he's loaded. He cons unsuspecting women from their savings . . .'

'He probably wangled those properties from some other poor cow,' I say. 'I can't imagine I'm the only one he's swindled. I bet there are loads of us.'

'Well, that's probably the best place to start,' Priya says. 'There could be another victim out there.'

'Do *not* call me the "V" word,' I snap, my hand coming up in front of me.

'What I mean is there will probably be *someone else* out there, fuming, writing about this happening to them on Facebook or Reddit or something?'

I stand up from my stool. I grab my laptop from the sofa and bring it back into the kitchen. Priya stands over me as I begin my search.

'Sally, do you want to do this?' She stops me before I

even open Google. 'You know if we find him, you've got to be so, so careful.'

I laugh her comment away.

'Seriously, Sally,' she says. 'I can't have you going off again . . .'

'What shall I start with?' I interrupt her. I'm sick of her sensible warnings already. I am raging. 'Con Man Manhattan?'

She sighs. 'Sure.'

I type into Facebook's search bar and hit enter, scrolling through the posts. 'It's mostly just stuff about Donald Trump.'

'Keep scrolling . . . wait – what's that?'

I stop and go back a couple of entries. There's something from the *New York Post*. 'Yeah, here, look. Con man, but he was arrested in November 2024.' I click on the link and a picture of an older man with curly hair and a sneering mouth appears beneath a lurid headline. 'That's definitely not him. Ugh. How the fuck did that guy get away with conning anyone?'

'Maybe try amending the search a bit. Like, um, stick in the name of the dating app you were using.'

'OK.' I add *Accord* and hit enter. There's a post.

Ladies beware! There's a man operating on Accord who is a CON MAN and a CATFISH

'Catfish?' I say. 'Harry's, unfortunately, too good-looking. He doesn't need to use fake photos to lure unsuspecting women. In fact, his success rate would probably drop if he did.'

'Read the rest anyway,' Priya says, stopping me from clicking out.

He goes by the name of Richard O'Connor and he is a DANGER to women everywhere. I feel so stupid. I arranged to meet him. But the man I thought I was meeting never arrived. I should have known he was too good to be true. I sat alone in a practically empty dingy bar (that he chose) for about fifteen minutes.

When I got up to go to the restroom this awful, gross man appeared and pushed me into the wall. He had shaggy brown hair and a goatee. He smelled of stale whiskey or something. He knew my name so I knew it was him. He wrestled me into a cubicle and started touching me, but I managed to get away when what must have been the only other customer in the bar luckily walked in – he must have heard something, I don't know. Anyway it distracted him. I kneed him in the balls and got away. The other man asked if I needed any help but by that point I didn't want to be near any men. Who can you even trust anyway? He said he would call the police but then Richard, or whoever the hell he was, barged past and ran into the streets. He disappeared after that. His profile has since been deleted. But I've got no doubt he will be doing this again.

PLEASE be careful – and watch out for this man – and all the other lying bastards out there. If you're using an app and something feels off, if the place you arrange to meet doesn't feel right, then get the hell out of there.

The comments are riddled with women relaying their own horror stories.

'Oh my God. Some men are just awful,' Priya says.

'Absolute scum,' I spit. 'I mean. Fucking hell. Just because some sad twat can't get laid what the hell makes them think they deserve to take it anyway?'

'Blame incel culture,' Priya says. 'That's probably where it all comes from. The idea that women owe them something. Christ, I had one in the therapy room this one time. I mean, I was torn you know? Like, can I make a difference and stop this man from offending? Or should I just refuse to treat him?'

'What did you do?'

'I had a go. But the venom, Sally. He hated women. *All* women. I reported him as a potential danger.'

'Seriously. These fucking men. Coming to you for help when *we're* the ones who need help. *Because* of *them*.'

'Yeah. Some of my referrals . . . they're—'

'We need some kind of peer support network,' I interrupt her. 'There are women all over, like me: Marie, the woman online with the catfisher. *You*.'

'Don't drag me into it.'

'But surely it'd help you to talk about—'

'You know I don't want to go digging into my past.'

I raise an eyebrow, acknowledging the sheer irony of a psychotherapist refusing to analyse her own history. But we both know why she refuses.

'Anyway, I think nearly every single one of us has had a bad experience with men. It's time to come together and put things right. And I'm going to start with Marie.'

Chapter 17

I've probably walked past this place a million times and never actually registered it as a church. Even though, when you properly look at it instead of just sauntering past it, it's *clearly* a church.

It's small in comparison to the high-rises that flank it, and far more traditional. It has dark grey-brown bricks and an arched entrance. The higher up you look, the more intricate the design and windows, and a spire stands proud on the left side of the building. There's signage on the facade saying *Feed Your Faith* and *Let Your Light Shine On*.

I shrug. I'm not your regular churchgoer. In fact, I'm not sure I've even stepped inside one since Harvest Festival in Year 6. I feel like *such* an imposter. And on a Sunday too.

I push the door open and can see a couple of people milling around. It has that unmistakable church vibe about it – something calming and peaceful yet unnerving at the same time.

I turn when I hear the door opening again behind me and see Marie.

'Follow me.' She leads me between rows of pews and through a set of archways until we come across a small room at the side. She opens the door with a key and gestures for me to go inside, closing the door behind us.

'You're not planning on locking *me* in,' I joke uncertainly. Maybe she is.

She tuts at me and puts her bag down on one of the chairs. 'You look more human now,' she says observing me. I nod.

Scattered around us on the uneven tiled floor are rickety chairs, a few random shelves holding Bibles and a flip chart. In the corner, a battered sideboard holds several mismatched mugs, along with a silver container labelled with the word *SUGAR* in black bold letters, and there's a coffee machine in the corner that's seen better days. I still can't believe there's nowhere to get a decent cup of tea in this town.

'So why here?' I ask, still noseying around the place. A poster bearing the words *The Serenity Prayer* grabs my attention and I go to look.

'I volunteer here. I know the building.'

'You volunteer?'

'You know, fundraisers, managing the diary for support groups, that kind of thing. It's respite for me, if I'm honest.'

My ears prick up. 'Support groups?'

'One-to-ones, AA, NA meetings, that kind of thing. I help sort the space for them, manage the church diary.' I nod, realising how helpful this could be, and I sit down. Marie never struck me as the Christian type. To be honest, she never struck me as anything other than grumpy until now.

'Coffee?' she asks.

'I'm fine.' There's enough cortisol pumping through my body already and I've completely run out of my medication. I definitely don't need to poke the dragon.

Marie places a filter in the top of the machine, tops it

up with water from the tap and switches it on. It begins chugging and whirring, water trickling into the stained glass jar beneath it.

She waits, fills her cup and then walks over to me, coffee in hand. I take a breath, desperate to know what's happened and racked with guilt.

'Was he OK with you?' I ask nervously. 'Frankie?' I'm terrified I've made things worse for her. Me and my stupid impulses. It's one thing putting myself in danger, quite another putting someone else in danger.

'I haven't seen him since he left yesterday morning. The locksmith was there, a young man – very handsome, very fit – I think Frankie realised he'd be up shit creek if he behaved badly in front of him. He's probably gone on one of his benders.'

'That's good then.' I exhale, feeling at least some temporary relief.

'Yeah, and he was ashamed. Frankie was. *Deeply* ashamed. Pissing in that room. From my point of view . . . it felt good. He *should* be ashamed. About a lot of things.' She moves closer to me. 'He once locked *me* in a room you know. Overnight when he went out. I kind of forgot about it because he's done so much, but then I remembered, and now I'm sure he does too.'

'So how will things be tonight?' I ask. I'm not sure I want to know the answer. I'm still worried that I've put her in more danger. Especially if he's gone out drinking. Why do I do these things without thinking them through properly? Priya would say it's the amygdala in overdrive.

'I don't care,' Marie says, her voice solid and strong. 'I'm not going home tonight.'

'Wait – really?'

'I'm staying with my sister,' she says.

I smile at her. 'That's good.'

'Yeah. Never had the guts, before. I don't know . . . I maybe just always thought, I married the man. He had some good traits once. Lately, though, I haven't seen anything good. And having you notice the bruise and telling you everything. And then seeing him, ashamed and mortified. I suddenly saw him for what he is. A sad piece of shit. I hate him, Sally. I'm not going back to him.'

My chest rises as I breathe in, a mix of relief and pride. I haven't fucked up after all. She's leaving him. It's always a good thing, the decision to leave. But, as we know, this is just the beginning. When women leave dangerous men, the risks ramp up. It's one of the most dangerous points of an abusive relationship. I know this. I'd seen my mother try it. She *will* need help. The idea of her managing this alone – it's too risky.

'Nothing changes if nothing changes,' Marie says, nodding to another poster on the wall.

'It's true,' I say. I feel strangely connected to her. This woman from the fruit and veg shop downstairs who used to practically snarl at me for waltzing into her space in my OTT outfits. But now here we are.

'I'll need to go to the apartment tomorrow though. Rescue my cat. Get some things I need. I just hope to God he's at the bar for the game. He should be. But . . .'

'I'll come with you,' I say quickly. 'You're not going back there alone.'

'You sure? My sister's at work tomorrow, so . . . it would have been tricky.' She leans over and squeezes my arm gently. 'I really appreciate it. Thank you.'

There's a moment of silence as we both take in how difficult tomorrow could be.

'Anyway,' Marie says, 'you haven't filled me in on what happened to you.'

'I wish I could say it was a long story,' I start. 'But it isn't. Four dates with a guy who, to be fair, seemed too good to be true. Not like in a sickly way, just, he was hot and kind and. . . lovely,' I say, looking up towards the ceiling. 'But then it turns out, he was a total cunt,' I say.

'Whoa.' Marie holds her hand up. 'You're in a church, girl.'

'But some of them are, aren't they. Total cu—'

'Say that word one more time and I'll drag us both to the confessional,' Marie says. 'Anyway, what did he do? Spiked you, right?'

'Yep. The last thing I remember clearly is being in a gorgeous rooftop restaurant having fun. Then it becomes a haze of bright colours and people talking loudly. Music. Falling to the ground. And the next thing I know, I wake up, banging head, he's left WhatsApp and he's cleaned out my savings.'

'All your money?'

'He had the balls to leave me seven cents. My checking account is untouched. But he took all my savings.'

'What will you do?'

'Not sure. Don't much fancy going to the police . . .'

'Waste of time,' Marie snorts. 'So what are you going to do?'

'I'm going to track Harry down,' I say fiercely.

'You need to be careful,' Marie cautions. 'If you're going to get your own back, if you're not going to the police, you gotta be careful. No going out there all guns blazing on your own.'

'Don't worry,' I say. 'I have an idea. I just need to track the cunt down first.'

Marie draws the cross over her body. But then she looks at me curiously. 'Maybe I can help?'

Chapter 18

Marie gingerly puts her key in the lock. It unclicks and she pushes the door almost in slow motion. She's scared. Of course she's scared.

The door opens and our noses are immediately hit by a waft of fust and fried food. It hits my stomach like a battering ram, curdling bad memories and allowing them to rise to the top again. I try to swallow it back down, bury the association, but my chest flutters and images flash in the front of my head.

Slumped.

Bleeding.

Burning skin.

I exhale sharply, attempting to stay present.

As we step inside the apartment we can see pizza boxes and empty beer cans.

'I thought this was a cliché,' I say, gesturing to the mess. 'The idea that no man can be left alone for more than twenty-four hours without knocking beer into half-empty pizza boxes.' I pick up a soggy pizza box lid, stinking of yeast and pepperoni, congealed cheese forming a plastic-like sheen on top of the crust. I turn up my nose and let it flop back down onto the coffee table.

'Sugar! Sugar!' Marie is calling for the cat. She turns back to me. 'I swear, if he's done anything to her . . .'

We hear a door creak and a little tortoiseshell cat trots out, mewing incessantly. 'Ah, Sugar!' she says, picking up the fuzzball and kissing its head repeatedly. 'I bet he hasn't fed her.' She moves towards the kitchen. 'I knew it! Bowl's empty and crusty. Jackass won't have bothered since I walked out.'

She gathers up the empty bowls and shoves them quickly into a carrier bag.

'Can you check in my bedroom, Sally? For the cat carrier? It's underneath the dresser, behind the chair.'

I notice two doors. In one, I can see a sink. I move towards the door to its left and push it open.

You can see Marie's influence in here, but it's as though he's rejecting it through untidiness. She's only been gone a night! Cushions lie on the floor. One corner of the elasticated bed sheet has popped, exposing the bare mattress underneath. And the duvet is twisted and unmade.

There are ornate lamps to either side of the bed, each depicting a slim standing woman holding a bird in her hand, while a curved black pole swoops behind and above her to hold a peach glass light shade. One bedside table holds just the lamp and a book, while the other is littered with ash, an ashtray and a beer can lying on its side.

I knew he was a rancid fuck. At least my mess is aesthetically pleasing.

I spot the cat carrier and drag it out from underneath the dresser. You can tell Marie tries to keep a sense of space and calm in here, giving everything a place despite how compact the accommodation is. I can't imagine what it's like being holed up in here with him.

'I've got it!' I shout, carrying the soft material cat carrier by its handle. I walk back into the living room and find Marie frantically going through drawers.

'Aha!' She pulls out a letter and some cards, then turns around. 'Thanks,' she says, taking the carrier from me. She unzips the front and coaxes Sugar in with some cat treats. Enticed by the smell, Sugar hops in, only to turn around and yowl when she realises she's been zipped in.

'It's OK, sweetie pie,' Marie says, putting her nose up to the mesh of the cat carrier. 'Don't you worry.' Then she turns to me. 'I'll just grab a few clothes. Won't be long.'

I crouch down to Sugar, tracing my finger over the mesh. She hisses at me before letting out a low growl.

'Charming,' I mutter to myself, just as Marie returns. 'That was quick,' I say.

'Yeah,' she says, looking around her as though it might be the last time she steps foot in here. It probably is.

'You OK?' I ask.

She nods, solemnly. 'It was always in there. Always in him. I should have known before I married him.'

'Can we not do that? You should've known. I should've known. Lorena fucking Bobbitt should've known. We can't blame ourselves for what they choose to do.'

'No, you're right. You're absolutely right,' she says.

'Good to go?' I say. She nods, and we move towards the front door. But just before we reach it, we hear the clunk of a key turning in the lock.

Chapter 19

We stand in silence with bated breath as the lock clumsily turns, the repeated scraping of the key on the door an indication that he's drunk. Then, it swings open and reveals his huge mass, swaying dangerously in the hallway.

He doesn't immediately see us. He shuffles in before his brain has time to catch up with his legs, chucking a six-pack of beer on the hallway table, along with his keys. He clocks me, confusion spreading across his face. Then he sees Marie and his expression changes instantly. He scowls, while his body waves backwards uncontrollably.

'We're just leaving,' Marie pants, her breathing irregular and panicked.

'Fuck you are.' He sneers, standing in front of her, looking down on her with an additional five or six inches of height and God knows how much bulk.

She never stood a chance in this tiny apartment with this drunken monster.

I hear Marie draw a sharp intake of breath. 'Stand aside, Frankie,' she says, her voice quivering slightly. He pulls a face at her then looks across at me, realisation dawning.

'You!' he bellows. The smell of booze fills the air,

making the place seem even more claustrophobic than it did before.

'Yes,' I say flatly. 'Me.'

'What's *she* doing here?' he hisses at Marie, his body completely blocking her while he continues to stare directly at me. His eyes are not his own. He is animalistic and unpredictable. You can feel it in the air, like the onset of an electrical storm. He could go off at any moment.

Sugar yowls again and Marie pulls the cat carrier in closer to her. Frankie's eyes dart towards the helpless creature.

'You're not taking that cat.'

'You hate her. You don't even want her here,' Marie pleads, clearly panicked by his inference. She wraps her arms around the cat carrier.

Frankie laughs and puts on a mocking, childlike voice. 'But you *love* her.' He lunges forward to grab at Sugar and Marie swings round, protecting the cat.

I weigh up the situation. There are two of us. Two of us and an angry, frightened cat. But this man is big. And unpredictable. And really fucking drunk. Which also means his reflexes won't be sharp. And his legs won't be steady.

'Reckon you should do as you're told for a change,' I say. I want to rile him, to make him focus on me, give Marie a chance to slip out. The door isn't closed. She could make it.

'Fucking what? Some bitch coming into my apartment telling me . . .'

'Telling you to do as you're told for a change,' I say, as firmly and as calmly as I can, despite the memories from my childhood stomping around haphazardly in my gut. The smells of fried food are threatening to bring up all that happened on that day. The day I found my mother, helpless.

Frankie laughs and I try to ignore it but rage is building up inside of me.

Hold it together, Sally.

'Should've known you'd be in it together.' But I can see he is out of his depth. I can see he is unsure how this is going to go down. Normally, it's just him against one small woman. Now there's more to the equation. And he's not used to it.

'Then what are you waiting for?' I say. 'Come on then, big man. Do your worst.' Marie shoots me a look. Her face telling me to stop. But something's got to give. Something's got to change. It's checkmate, and we need to get the hell out of here. I wish she would just take Sugar and run, but I realise she won't leave without me.

He stands as still as his drunken waste-of-space heft will allow.

'What? Lost your nerve? Can batter one woman but can't take on two – that it?' I jeer.

Beside me, Marie's eyes are filled with fear as I goad him.

He takes a breath and shakes his head. The veins in his arms pop and his jaw tightens. He turns redder, if that's even possible. He's holding his arms out slightly bent, his fists balled tightly.

'Just let us go, Frankie,' Marie begs, her pupils wide and black. 'Just let us go.' She is almost sobbing. She's been here too many times before. She knows how it goes. But I can't stop the adrenaline that is spiking through me and charging its way outside of my body. I feel as though a force is buzzing around me like an angry aura.

'Get. Out. Of. My. Fucking. Way,' I say, teeth gritted, my own fists balling and releasing, fingers stretching as far as they will reach. With that, he brings his fist up and charges towards me.

He lunges so close to my face I smell onion and that lingering stale booze on his breath as he yells, 'I'll fucking kill you!'

He lashes at my throat. But he can't manoeuvre in the small space and he stumbles, wobbles backwards and falls on the coffee table.

We both stand watching as he tries to pull himself back up but he's even more woozy now. He turns back around to face us and takes two steps forward.

'Stop! Please!' Marie screams out as he turns his attention to her. He grabs the cat carrier from her and waves it in front of her.

'I've always hated this cat.' He is slurring worse than ever.

Sugar is yowling desperately and Marie is crying. 'Please, Frankie, I'll stay, I'll . . . please.'

I'll stay . . . please. I've heard that plea before. It rings in my ears. A haze washes over me, the smell of fried food becoming sharper and overwhelming in my nostrils. Everything looks as though it's in slow motion and I'm barely in the room.

Sizzling fat.

Him, burying his face.

Her, lying on the floor.

My heart rams into my chest. Faster, harder. Stronger. I press myself against the wall watching as Frankie swings the carrier and its yowling, terrified occupant. Marie is now collapsed on her knees, her arms held out in front of her, placatory.

'Please, Frankie, give her back. Don't hurt her,' Marie begs again, tears rolling down her cheeks.

He looks into the cat carrier, holding poor Sugar to his face, and spits into the mesh. 'I should have got rid of it the moment you brought the little rat home.'

'Please, Frankie, no.'

It feels as though I'm watching it play out through a window. I watch myself as I push backwards into the wall, lift my leg, and lurch my foot forward, connecting instantly with his stomach. He drops Sugar to the floor, she lands awkwardly, the box rocking to one side. Frankie clutches at his sternum and gasps. I've winded him.

I pull my knee back and kick out again, propelling myself hard from the wall. He slams onto the table, head first, unable to stop himself. There's a loud crack. And then he slithers sideways onto the floor, collapsing in a tangled heap.

Suddenly, I'm back in the room. Everything is silent and real again.

Chapter 20

What happens next comes back to me in fragments. Like I've been spiked all over again. Marie runs straight to Sugar. I feel relieved that she's instinctively gone there first. I seem to be frozen, even though adrenaline is pumping through me. Once she's calmed Sugar down, Marie gingerly checks Frankie's pulse. She shakes her head. Nothing.

I guess locking bad men in store cupboards isn't all I've got in my repertoire.

Then we leave.

We gather Marie's things. I carry the sports bag of clothes and Marie carries Sugar protectively. We walk as quickly as possible towards the waiting lift and walk out into the sunlight. A warm glow rushes over me. A feeling of satisfaction. A feeling of youth and a change in the wind.

Just like that time all those years ago.

Self-defence is a necessity in this world. Attack, well, that's recreational.

That feeling that all is right with the world stays with me. Through the boring meetings at work. Through Priya going through with deleting all the dating apps from my phone.

Even cocktails at another opening night, care of Lily, who seems more on edge than ever over her dickish workmate.

Now, three days later, I walk into the church to find Marie sitting on a chair in our little room, cradling a mug in her lap. This is the first time I've seen Marie since we accidentally murdered her husband. Since *I* accidentally murdered her husband. We decided she should carry on as normally as possible. There was no point pretending she hadn't left him, that they hadn't had a major falling-out and, if anything, it probably made his drinking binge even more expected. Man loses wife, gets wasted, can't stand up, falls and cracks his head. That's the line of investigation we were hoping for anyway.

I crouch down in front of her.

'How're you holding up?' I ask, putting my rucksack on the floor by the chair legs.

'OK, I think.'

We take a moment. It's hard to know what to say. I'm unsure how she must be feeling. She's lost her husband after all and that's got to be huge – not that I'd know.

I shift my bag with my foot and sit on the seat next to her, edging closer to her. There's a sharp intake of breath and I can sense the tears are on their way. I pull her in close to me, putting my arm around her and letting her head nestle into my neck.

'I'm all right,' she says, her voice breaking. 'The police came round again this morning.'

'What did they say?' I ask anxiously.

'Misadventure. That's what they're thinking, anyway. There's the coroner to go yet, bloods and stuff, but they're pretty happy that he was there alone. They asked about his drinking.'

'What did you say?'

'I told them. I just said, yeah, he's a big drinker.' She pauses to correct herself. '*Was* a big drinker.'

'Do you think they suspect anything?'

'I don't know, but I didn't get the feeling they did. They said I could move back in tomorrow. Thing is, I just don't know if I want to. And it's not because he died there. It's because I kind of did.'

'I totally get that,' I say, squeezing her hand. 'So what will you do? Stay at your sister's?'

Marie nods. 'For now, yeah. She's a bit overbearing at times, but Sugar's settled. Barb loves her – she's been spoiling her rotten. And it's not far from the shop, which I need to open back up really.'

'And how are you feeling? Seriously?' I ask.

She looks up to the ceiling for a second or two, then back at me. 'I'm free, Sally. It might sound callous, but it's how I feel. I've ignored my own feelings for so long. I owe it to myself to not waste any more tears on him.'

'That's exactly what I wanted to hear!' I squeeze her happily. I hesitate for a second, wondering how to phrase what I want to say next, but Marie takes it as an opening.

'So what are we going to do about Harry? We need to nail that guy to the wall.'

'Actually, I'm glad you asked,' I say. 'I was chatting to this woman online. She's from New Jersey. She was catfished.' Marie looks suitably outraged. She makes for an excellent audience. 'Terri, she's called, got away relatively unscathed, thank God. Anyway, it turns out she works in some kind of tech business. She said she'd take a look at my missing money. Go through my bank accounts and stuff, see if there's anything she can do. I really think,' I add, testing the waters, 'we can help each other out. I told her to come meet us.'

'But we can't tell her—'

'Don't worry. We'll keep that one between us. But I think there's something in getting us together. Like one of your support groups.'

Marie nods thoughtfully. 'You know Barb said something about her neighbour too, when I told her about what Frankie did to me. She's heard the shouting, bashing around and stuff from the apartment downstairs. It's a couple, about my age, a bit older maybe. Their daughter, Georgia, visits regularly, and often comes up to chat to Barb. She's been telling Barb all about it, wishing she could do something. Her dad's been beating her mom since she was a kid, but her mom always seems to make excuses to stay. Bit like me I guess.' Marie looks upset with herself.

'Don't be hard on yourself. I mean, I can't even imagine what it's like having to exist like that. Being controlled by a man. A much bigger, angry man.'

In some ways I can imagine it, though. I think of my own mother and the frustration I felt as I grew up without her. Wondering why she never left those awful men she was with. Wondering how she kept ending up with them in the first place. She was vulnerable, I guess. As soon as you open up to one dickhead about what another dickhead has done to you, I think they maybe see it as an opportunity to get their claws in too. To trick you and do it all over again. It becomes a never-ending cycle. It's certainly not as straightforward as my naive teenage mind thought it was. I hate myself for thinking badly of her back then.

'Do you want to ask her then?' I say.

'Hm?'

'Georgia, and her mum? To meet with us.'

'I'll speak to Barb first; she knows them. I've only said hi to Georgia and never even met her mom. But yeah, it's definitely helped me having someone to talk to. And the rest.' Marie smirks and I laugh. It all feels surreal. But I feel no guilt about what I did. It was for the best. Sometimes you have to break a few eggs, et cetera. And my God, he was a particularly bad egg.

'Anyway,' Marie says. 'It's my turn to help you. So what are we gonna do about Harry?'

'We don't have to do that now.'

'Need to keep occupied, Sally.'

I pick up my rucksack and take my laptop out, opening it up on my knee.

'So the issue with getting back at Harry is I don't even know if he's called Harry. How can I get back what was mine if I don't know his name, his number, where he lives, or in fact anything at all?'

This is a major complication. Those savings were my compensation. They meant more than just their monetary value to me. They were symbolic.

Did he know that?

I'm starting to get paranoid. I can feel my train of thought getting lost in conspiracy and rage. I don't need Priya to keep reminding me that it's a red flag. It's a risk for someone like me to get so bogged down in such obsessive thoughts. So, I have to rationalise it. I use those little CBT exercises. You know, what's the percentage probability of him knowing why that money was so important versus it simply being a coincidence that I've had the misfortune of running into an absolute bellend on a dating app. I mean, that happens all the time. All. The. Time.

Of course he couldn't know why that money is so important to me. How could he? Priya's the only person in this country who knows. But the way that he's taken it, by leaving me incapacitated and then disappearing without bothering to make sure I'm even alive, I feel like history is repeating itself. What's worse is he's left me completely without recourse. He's silenced me. He's fucking silenced me because I can't confront him. My heart races as I think about it.

'So, where do we start? You got any photos?' Marie asks.

I open the photos on my iPad and flick through the five I grabbed from his profile previously. I don't even know what I'm looking for. They're just pictures. They're hardly going to show him wearing a shirt with a name badge and address on it.

There must be something though; it's all I have.

I look more closely at the one of him wearing sunglasses, zooming in to see what's in the reflection. But all I can make out are a couple of shadows that mean absolutely nothing. God, I chide myself, there's finding clues and then there's expecting things to just fall into your lap. *Of course* I'm not going to find anything in the reflection of his sunglasses. What is this, *Murder, She Fucking Wrote*?

'Handsome,' Marie says, pinching the screen to zoom in on Harry.

'I know; that's the problem. Totally disarmed me.'

'Can you do one of those reverse image search things? Like they do on TV cop shows?'

'Maybe, but I think that's more about finding similar images rather than the same people posted online.' I try it but all we get are images of various sharp-cheekboned models in perfume ads gazing back at us. I flick to the next one and zoom in on it. It's a photo of him standing by some water, wearing khaki shorts and a black collared T-shirt.

'I wonder if this was the place he was talking about that night? I remember him saying something about a boat and the Hamptons before everything got skewed and fuzzy. His brother, he said. He was going away with his brother. On a boat. It's the one thing I mentioned to Priya.'

'Well, he's standing in front of a boat in that one,' Marie says, leaning in to study it.

We both look closely at the photo. You can just make out the edge of a white boat to the right of the photo. I pinch the screen and zoom in closer still.

'There's wording on the boat,' I say. '*Sweet Ca* . . . What could that be? Sweet what? California? Canary?'

'Aha!' Marie says. 'It's *Sweet Caroline*! It has to be.'

'Wa! Ha! Ha!' I sing in tune to the song. 'You're right. Of course!' We both fall about laughing.

'Your Harry's not going to get far with us on the case, is he?'

I laugh. 'I mean, how many boats of the same name are going to be moored at East Hampton? We've got him, Marie! We've fucking got him!'

Chapter 21

I'm lucky that my face can play host to almost any hair colour without shapeshifting me into Marilyn Manson or Draco Malfoy. As a brunette, my cheekbones can slice rock, as a blonde, my eyes shine like starry gems. You could argue it's because I'm middle of the road – just enough but not too much to be undeniably one or the other. I suspect it's because I'm a true Gemini – and so it's something I take very seriously indeed. Even a Halloween party wig needs to be meticulously selected.

Today, however, regardless of the quality of my blonde wig – bobbed with bangs (as they say this side of the pond) – and my long-held ability to concretely fool my therapists (Priya aside), I am feeling ever so slightly like I've met my match. Not that that's necessarily a bad thing. We all need a challenge. It's just that Harry . . . well . . . fuck . . . he's fooled me once.

It's a feeling that intrigues me. He is a *genuine* challenge. Not like that big sweaty wank-stain Frankie. He was easy. You don't need to spike a drunk, after all. Sometimes, they make themselves vulnerable all on their own. That's what they say about women, isn't it? That we're 'asking for it'.

If that's the case, Frankie was on his knees and begging for it.

Harry might not have the same oversized physicality as Frankie, but he makes up for it in other ways. And, if I'm honest with myself, he's honed a charm offensive that's as addictive and all-consuming as crystal meth.

But as exhilarating as that thought is, I am also seething. Seething that he got me. *Me!* I've seen the very worst of men since I was a frightened young girl. The *very* worst. Letting someone in like that – as an adult – I'm not sure if I can ever forgive myself, to be honest. It won't happen again that's for sure.

In fact, the only way I stand any chance of finding personal redemption from my utter stupidity is to beat him at his game.

My skin prickles at the thought – like ecstasy rushing through my body, making me feel simultaneously sick and electric.

But there's also something else. Something I hardly dare admit to myself. I feel like I'm grieving for something. Something that never truly existed.

Dealing with Marie's husband only further ignited my desire to hunt Harry down. It took me back to when I was a kid, the day I woke up on the kitchen floor and discovered everything had changed. When I realised I had nothing to lose. I became feral overnight.

Harry has reignited something that I thought was long gone. A hunger?

It was only partly satiated when I accidentally unalived Frankie, and now it's driving me on. Propelling me into this hunt for Harry.

I'm almost disappointed that it doesn't take much effort to find this particular boat.

We typed *"Sweet Caroline"* in quotation marks, added *boat* and *Hamptons* and hit enter. The search results come up in a split second and there were plenty of them. There are about fifteen boats with the same name connected to the Hamptons, but only one that looks like Harry's with that same swirly blue font.

Harry Collins might not exist in the digital world, but the *Sweet Caroline* boat certainly does. Marie was beside herself with excitement. It was almost as if she'd completely forgotten about that fuckwit Frankie. I could see her coming out of her darkness with every second that passed as we discussed our sleuth-like plans. And she called me later that evening full of elation to say Georgia was going to come along the next time we meet up. After feeling hopeless for so many years, she'd found purpose.

And so have I.

We decided Marie shouldn't come with me on this part of the mission though. We thought it made more sense for her to stay close to home in case the police needed to speak to her. If they found her partying in the Hamptons with me they'd probably start looking into Frankie's death as a life insurance scam or something. And we didn't need the police to know we were friends just yet.

Harry's vessel is advertised on a boat hire website – and having the name of the boat took me directly to its profile. It appeared I was scouring the equivalent of a dating site for boat nerds and upmarket hen parties.

Turns out the *Sweet Caroline* is a catamaran. It can host up to eight passengers, its rental comes with a captain, and it costs a bomb. The website also told me that it's moored at East Hampton – which is precisely where Harry said he was going with his brother this weekend.

Bingo!

It appears he was telling the truth about something after all.

I nabbed a bunch of clothes from Priya's wardrobe, chucked on my blonde wig, and here I am. At least, here 'Lisa' is.

Two can play at the name game.

I checked into the Harbor Front Hotel just after lunch. It's one of those lovely places that feels as though oxygen and rehydration are built into the very fabric of the building. Light, airy rooms, exterior white wooden panelling with hardy coastal reeds and grasses framing the view of the vast and uninterrupted ocean to the right of the building. Directly in front, of course, are the boats. And there's one boat in particular that I'm keen to keep a beady eye on. Not that it seems to be here right now . . .

I look at my reflection in the mirror and wince at how monochrome I am. Platinum blonde hair with a heavy fringe hanging in my eyes, Priya's clothes – a white linen trouser suit, wide wafting trousers and a loose-fitting summer jacket. I've teamed it with a mint green T-shirt and cork wedge shoes. I am the epitome of minimalist. And I'm itching to get changed.

I wander down to the little boathouse office on the front. I'd already discovered that you can book the *Sweet Caroline* online or in person. It's like an agency type thing. And clearly, I wasn't going to charm the information I needed out of a digital booking system simply by clicking 'I am not a robot'.

The boathouse has similar vibes to the hotel, except the panelling is powder blue this time. There are A-boards outside promising luxurious ocean experiences, and images of the sea,

Champagne glasses, bright white teeth and fancy canapés adorning the windows as both framed prints and promo posters for various boats and boat companies. It is promising a lifestyle. A mini-break for those who aspire to be *someone*.

I realise that this place is all about posturing, peacock-like. With or without the pretty feathers.

A pair of perfectly made-up women in frankly stunning Versace tea dresses from this season sashay past me in towering wedges, waving exuberantly at someone behind me. I turn in time to see them air-kissing two men in cargo shorts (cargo shorts!) and baseball caps.

I still don't get how in nature, in wildlife, it's the males who are working so hard to attract a mate. I mean, they put in the fucking graft, don't they? Bright colours, patterned feathers, unadulterated exuberance. In nature it's the boy birds going all out with their funny little displays and fancy threads. It's the boys who are preening and puffing and displaying. It's practically interpretative dance – but more transparent. We all know what the end goal is – no bird of paradise is pretending they just want a night at the movies with a milkshake, are they? There's *real* effort to get those lady birds into the sack. That's a really fucking hard balance to master. They go all out. It's ironic how we women of the human species are the ones that get called 'birds'.

When it comes to humans, however, arrogance makes the males of the species lazy.

Fuck the feathers, fuck the choreography, just stick a needle in our skin or a pill in our drink and wait for us to lose consciousness. It's so fucking base and vulgar.

And so fucking common.

The sex life of birds is still on my mind when I walk in through the door, propped open by a small white wooden wedge, and am immediately hit by the small office's cool air conditioning. Thank God. My forehead was starting to protest against the heavy bangs by producing beads of sweat.

'Hi, how are you?' Seated behind a pale wooden desk, an attentive man in his forties or fifties smiles at me. He's got to be on commission. I bet the invoice for his bleached teeth is filed under 'expenses'.

'Hi!' I say, sprightly and uncertain.

'Are you looking for a luxury ocean experience?'

I smile, but my insides are contorting with the amount of cheese he has piled into his copy-written greeting. I take a breath and remember I am not Sally today. I am Lisa. And Lisa really *does* want to be *someone* on a boat.

'I'm not sure how this all works,' I say, giggling and gesturing to the framed pictures of the boats and yachts and more white teeth that also adorn the interior walls, spaced equally and consistently in their simple white frames. 'But my parents used to hire a boat from here and I loved it.'

'Oh, really?' he says. 'Please, take a seat.'

I smile and sit.

'I'm Charlie,' he says, holding out his hand.

'Lisa,' I say, shaking it more gently than I usually do, conjuring a New York accent.

'So, Lisa. You're after a similar experience?'

'To be honest,' I say, 'I'd love to find the exact boat. It's just tricky because I can't ask them . . .' I look up at the sun shining through the window and allow my eyes to prick and my nose to fizz. 'They, died . . .'

'I'm, I'm so sorry to hear.' He quickly grabs a tissue from a powder blue cardboard box on his desk and I accept it graciously, dabbing gently at my nose.

'It's life, right?' I say, sniffing.

'It's very sad. But listen,' he says, smiling kindly. He's speaking as if he's a therapist, not a boat trip salesman. 'If you can give me your parents' names, I can look up which boat they hired?'

'Oh, but I know the name of the boat,' I say. 'It's the *Sweet Caroline*. I was hoping to charter it. If that's even the right term.' I let out a small giggle, this time looking down, faux-embarrassed.

'Oh, yes, the *Sweet Caroline*. You've certainly come to the right place. But it's out this weekend I'm afraid, so I can't show you around.'

'Oh. Really?' I say, looking up to the ceiling, disappointment scrunched into my face. 'I *knew* I should have called to book or gone online. I just wanted to talk to someone in person. I've never done it myself before, and just needed to find out what was involved.'

'Well, if you want to look at another date, we can certainly arrange that? But I have a gallery too, if you want to take a virtual tour?'

'Oh my God, could we do that? That would be great,' I say, full of sickly enthusiasm. Charlie picks up the glasses that dangle from a chain around his neck, pulls them onto his nose and types something into his laptop.

'I assume you get a captain with the booking?' I ask, waiting for him to talk about Harry's brother. 'I mean, I've never actually driven a boat.' I bring my shoulders forward slightly and look up at him through my fringe, making myself appear smaller still.

He laughs at my naivety. 'Of *course*. In fact, you don't just get the captain. You can get a small crew too if you want. Your catamaran experience can be as luxurious as you'd like it to be. The owner of this boat is always happy to arrange Champagne, canapés, music. It's very popular. I think he once even took a group snorkelling. Personally. He's very amenable. In fact, Harry – the owner – is out on the boat this weekend. He's so passionate about it.'

So it's Harry's boat, not his brother's.

'Oh really, so he's actually in town?' I'm shocked that Harry is using the same name. It seems so amateur. But then, there's no trace of Harry Collins anywhere. Maybe I am underestimating him. Maybe he is using a different surname?

'Yes. Great guy, Harry.' Charlie beams. 'I'll show you some of the testimonials he's had from happy customers.'

Harry's clearly charmed him too. I bet he's ripping him off. There's no way he's getting all the commission he's due.

'Wow,' I say. 'I'll have a think about the snorkelling then. See if it's something my friends would enjoy. I want to plan a girls' break, you see.'

'Oh you won't regret it. Harry's great. He's entertained bachelorette parties, birthday parties. His boat is his, so he's super flexible and always willing to add a personal touch to his bookings.'

'I bet he is,' I mutter absent-mindedly.

'Sorry, ma'am?'

'I . . . *good* he is,' I say, realising I sound like Yoda. I clear my throat, regaining my outward composure. 'So . . . so nice of him to add these personal touches.'

I know all about his personal touches. Harry Collins has one hell of a personal touch. In fact, that's what started all this. I swear if he hadn't made me scream like a banshee on MDMA *multiple* times I would never have fallen for his nasty little trick. Although, in retrospect, I guess the multiple explosive, mind-bending orgasms were all part of his nasty little trick in the first place.

He's played me like a fucking fiddle. In more ways than one.

Cunt.

I maintain my innocent exterior while my insides bubble with fury. Why is Harry causing me so much rage and so much unrestrained lust all at once?

'Yes. It's all in the detail,' Charlie says, and I realise I've almost forgotten where I am. He types something else into his shiny MacBook and spins it round so I can see the screen. 'You'll see he has lots of testimonials.' He points to the quotes.

I mentally shake the thoughts from my head like it's a snow globe. I clear my throat. 'I never saw these online,' I say.

'No, they're just what I gather in the post-hire customer survey.'

'Can I . . . ?' I ask, and he pushes the MacBook closer to me.

I scroll through quote after beaming, sycophantic quote. His name comes up on multiple occasions. Of course it does. Except I don't imagine the ones he's drugged and stolen from would have written a review. Unless he keeps this business separate from his other 'activities'. Yes, that would make sense. He clearly has multiple income streams.

And then I see it. His full name. Not Harry Collins. Of course, he wouldn't have been stupid enough to use his real name with me. Not when he had plans to destroy my life. And whether this name is real or not, it's another lead. It's a step closer to tracking him down.

Harry Gladstone.

Got him!

Chapter 22

I walk along the fairy-lit harbour front. The reflection of the lights ripples in the water as the sun sets, creating an orange haze. Boats of all shapes and sizes are moored up and bobbing, and the water gently smacking the harbour wall creates a relaxing soundtrack. In fact, as I look around me, everybody strolling along here looks completely at peace with the world.

I wonder why Harry chose this place. Is it all an act? Maybe this is the real Harry? I snort to myself at the thought of him taking part in yoga on the beach, stretching his legs and exhaling with a low humming sound as he releases all his pent-up anger.

He must be driven by anger – why else would he be such a twat? I wonder what it is that made him this way. I think back to what he told me of his parents – but what, if any of it, was even true?

A stylish bar with chunky wooden seating in an outdoor courtyard grabs my attention. I decide a glass of wine and a bit of investigative googling wouldn't go amiss now I've found out his real name. I take a seat, stretch my legs in front of me and am immediately served by a solicitous young man in a white shirt and chinos. I order a glass of Malbec and he leaves me to sink into my seat, taking in the breeze and the sparkling water directly in front of me.

I look at the boats and imagine being out there on the *Sweet Caroline* with Harry.

Him sitting high up on deck on a cream leather swivel chair as I lean into him, whispering in his ear. Telling him that all is forgiven. I understand. My childhood was hard too. We are soulmates, he and I.

I remove his short-sleeved shirt, letting it fall off his shoulders and onto the deck. I throw it into the water. Then I tug at his belt, pulling it from his waistband, my hand on his crotch, feeling the shape of him pulling against fabric as he writhes expectantly. I undo his button, unzip him, release him from his shorts as he kicks off his shoes, fumbles with his socks.

I put my hand between his legs and . . .

'Ma'am.'

Fuck.

'Oh, thank you,' I say to the waiter, who takes his time to place a coaster in front of me, before carefully positioning a large glass of red on top of it.

Go away already!

I'm going to have to start all over again. Building up the tension, making the most of that delicious moment when *I take my hand around behind me and grab a screwdriver from my back pocket . . .*

Oh come on, it's fantasy. *Of course* I can hide a screwdriver in my back pocket if I want to.

. . . that moment where, holding his cock tight with one hand, I use the other to drive the tip of my weapon down hard into the centre of his dick as he writhes in agony and warped pleasure.

A couple walk past me, giggling sweetly. Dammit.

Why can I not fully immerse myself in this fantasy?

I wonder if it's the distractions, or whether it's, dare I think it, because I have feelings for him. But how can I feel anything other than hatred for him after what he did?

I light a cigarette, inhale, and try to reset and calm myself. I go back to the start of the fantasy. I have to prove to myself that I can hate him. Like, truly, coldly, hate him.

My phone rings.

Fuck's sake!

Can a girl not have a violent fantasy without getting interrupted these days?

I pick my phone up and roll the loose ash from the end of my cigarette onto the edge of the table. It's Lily. I roll my eyes.

'Lily. How lovely to hear from you,' I lie.

'Sally!' she pants. She sounds strange. Manic, almost. 'That bastard. He . . .'

'Whoa, slow down. What bastard?'

'Ethan. From work. You know, I told you, the handsy guy; anyway, he's really fucking done it this time. We have to do something.'

I wonder why my friends think I'm the one to go to about this kind of thing. They have no clue as to my past; they have no clue as to my deviant fantasies. To be fair, even *I* had started to forget them until just recently. As far as my friends are concerned I'm just an everyday girl with an acid tongue. But still, here we are. And apparently, *we* have to do something.

'What's he done, Lil?'

'The account exec, Rachel, Jesus, she's only twenty. I found her crying in the toilets.'

'And I take it she wasn't crying over a typo in a press release.'

'Fucking listen to me! It was him, Sally. It's worse than I thought. She . . . she has no memory of what happened. She woke up knowing she'd had sex though. But she blames herself because she willingly had a few bumps on a night out.'

'He's her superior.' The details are starting to come back to me. 'If he's pushing coke on her . . .'

'I know, I know. I tried to tell her. Power dynamic, all that. But she doesn't feel she can say anything. All she knows . . .'

'Is that she's been violated,' I finish for her. The smell of frying meat begins to waft under my nose from the kitchen. I feel physically sick.

'Exactly. She'd had a few bumps. But that's not gonna make her pass out, is it? She remembers nothing from about 1 a.m. Just waking up feeling . . .'

'Sick. Fuck, Lil. It's fucking rape. Clearly spiked, right?' I feel my blood boil. This poor girl. I'm nearly thirty; I've seen some of the world and it was bad enough when Harry spiked me. This woman, this *girl*, is so young. Too young to have some monster of a dickhead abuse his power, to abuse *her* like this.

'Seems so. So what do we do?'

'Well,' I say 'there was that ket idea? But maybe that's . . .'

'Too far . . . ?'

'. . . not far enough!' I say, perplexed. 'We're talking about a rapist now. Not just some jumped-up sleaze with a coke habit.'

There's a beat of silence. I'm not sure what Lily was expecting me to suggest. We should hide his stapler?

Switch his sugar with salt? 'Look, Lily, I'm away in the Hamptons.'

'Ooh, Sally, you never said you were having a weekender. With gorgeous Harry?'

I realise in all the chaos I haven't even told my friends about what happened. Marie and Priya are the only ones who know. Lily has no idea that what she is talking about did indeed just happen to me. And, to be completely honest, I feel fucking ashamed. Which I know, *I know*, isn't right. But I can't help how I feel.

'No. Gorgeous Harry turned out to be . . . not so gorgeous after all.' I decide not to go any further. Not now. 'So it's a bit of a solo break. A breath of fresh air. Some R&R. But listen. Back to Rachel? Has she got help?'

'She's refusing. On account of the coke, the cocktails. She doesn't want to go to the police, much less HR.'

'OK, I might have an idea to help her . . .' I trail off, it will probably be better to explain the group in person. 'Listen, can you meet me after work tomorrow for a coffee? We can chat then. Believe me, Rachel isn't alone. We can do something to help her.'

'Sure. Meet me outside the office building?'

Lily's office is just a few short blocks downtown from mine. I can meet her there and walk us to the church. I'm meeting Marie, Terri and, possibly, Georgia at 7 p.m. I need to get these women in a room together.

'Yep, I'll see you on the corner – 6 p.m.'

We say our goodbyes and I put the phone down. I sigh and look out towards the water, realising immediately that I've missed some of the action. A boat is on its way into harbour.

I watch as it gets closer. It starts reversing into a space

not too far from me. It's beautifully lit up inside, exposing its plush interior and decking. A white catamaran that looks as though it glides on blades. I recognise it. Even though it's far more impressive than its photo in reality.

I knock back the rest of my wine excitedly and I see Harry. It's clearly him, placing a ramp onto the harbour wall. He's wearing a white shirt and shorts and I shiver, wondering if my fantasy could come true. Wondering if, tonight, I could steal him away from his brother, tell him all is forgiven and fool him into thinking he'll be treated to the twists of my tongue, rather than the stabbing of a screwdriver. I feel instantly alive and yet completely unprepared.

I have no screwdriver in my back pocket. Alas, fantasies don't take into account the boring logistics of planning the fantastical event. And they also don't involve consequences. That word makes me think of Priya. She doesn't know I'm here and I feel a stab of something in my chest. She would want me to be cautious. To think about the consequences. OK, Priya, fine. I breathe deeply. I don't need a screwdriver.

But still, there is potential. There is potential to do *something*. Surely.

Think, Sally.

I tilt my sunglasses down onto the bridge of my nose and watch him climbing off, trying out the sturdiness of the ramp, then reboarding.

He reaches out to take hold of . . .

My insides contort. The woman is tall with flowing red wavy hair, pale blue shorts and a matching halter-neck top. He is helping her off the boat, holding her hand as she navigates the ramp in her heels. Got to admire her determination there.

So . . . not out here with his brother then. Of *course* he's not. Fuck's sake.

My rage has turned green with envy. I don't want him on his boat with another woman. Why? For me? For her? I don't know. Does it matter? Does it matter if I stop another woman getting hurt purely because I don't want him to focus his attention on her? But it's not just that. Not after everything that I've seen.

He never laid a finger on me. He never raped me. He never told me he loved me and tried to control me. But he *did* con me. What's a little con?

Shut up, Sally!

For. Fuck's. Sake. He's like a drug. I'm like an addict. Oh, you can't have vodka anymore because it makes you want *to die*. But you can have a beer. You can have a wine. Because it only tickles you. It only flirts with you. So as long as you know what you're dealing with, you can dip a toe back in . . .

I shake the thoughts from my head. Why am I making excuses for him? I think about my mum. Is this what went around her head all those times?

Fuck this man. This fucking gorgeous vile specimen of a man. What is he doing to me?

What the fuck is he doing to me?!

Until now, all I had really wanted was to get my money back. For all the fantasising, *that* has been my main motivation. But now I realise it's not enough knowing his real name. It's not going to be enough getting my money back. I need to stop him. Stop his nasty, lying tricks. Starting with her. I'm going to toy with him through her. I'll fuck up all the dates that follow if I have to. And he's not gonna know. Not at first.

But when it's time to finish him. He will know it was me.

I take my eyes from her and back to him and look at him intently once more, while he stares at her as if she's the only person in the world. The way he used to look at me. I feel sick.

I stand up from my seat and watch them walk along the promenade. I grab my bag and follow them from a distance. He won't recognise me from here, not in these clothes, with this hair. But I'm a stranger to her, too.

Will she even believe me?

Chapter 23

I've started ordering the non-alcoholic Prosecco because I've been sitting here for three hours now. And I can't lose my wits.

I followed Harry and his mystery woman to their hotel. They disappeared into the lift and I watched the floor numbers shoot up to level five before stopping. They had clearly gone to have sex. What woman wouldn't after sampling his prowess? I'm surprised I can't hear the wailing from the hotel lobby if I'm honest.

But now all I can do is sit and wait. After all, this was never part of the plan. Sure, I achieved much of what I set out to do. I've tracked him down. I've found out his real name. But the woman was a surprise. And part of that surprise was how it made me feel.

I've faced much, *much* worse than Harry Gladstone. But I have to wonder if it's Harry who triggered what was already there. Or was it the ill-timed return of that bastard back home that prompted my relocation to New York. Maybe it's both. Either way, my trauma is coming back up as nausea. And if I'm not careful, it's going to violently spew over everything it touches. Just like it did once before.

I've exhausted my Google searches for Harry Gladstone. There is no social media presence, no news articles about men called Harry who have conned, spiked or attacked women, and no dating profile for him on any of the dating apps.

I check my watch again and decide I can order myself something boozy. I've been here before when it comes to Harry, albeit in the bedroom, not staking out the lobby. I know what he's like. Now they're upstairs, that could well be it for the night. I certainly wouldn't have left him alone in bed that's for sure. As infuriating as it is to admit that now.

I walk to the bar to stretch my restless legs and take a pew on one of the high stools. I nod at the barwoman to get her attention.

'Aperol spritz please.'

'Coming up.'

The bartender turns her back and I watch as she carefully polishes a glass before dunking it for a few seconds in an ice box. I'm lazily looking up at the line of bottles and optics, mesmerised by labels, when I feel a presence next to me.

I glance to my right. It's her. She's changed out of her shorts and halter top – so they've clearly had sex. She is wearing smart jeans, black T-shirt and pumps, and her hair is slightly less smooth but she's still glamorous as hell. I want to hate her. But she could be me.

'Sorry, ordered a cocktail,' I say, continuing to impersonate Priya's New York accent. 'Might take a while.' I realise I need to even more carefully disguise myself now. If what I say to her doesn't work, she'll definitely report back to Harry.

She smiles, but says nothing.

'Here for the weekend?' I ask. She looks at me, all big

brown eyes and huge eyelashes. It's very obvious why he went for her.

'Yes,' she says. 'With my boyfriend. You?' She's polite, if not exactly friendly, and clearly doesn't want to chat to a stranger. I wonder if she's about to order a bottle and a bucket of ice to take back to the room. I press on nonetheless.

The woman behind the bar is now attaching a slice of orange to the side of my glass, carefully balancing it so it perches solidly.

'Boyfriend, huh?' I say. 'How well do you know him?'

I might as well jump straight in – I realise I have very little time to tackle this matter. He could walk into the bar any second.

She turns to me, her full body facing me.

'Do I know you?' She looks wary.

'No. But I know your boyfriend.'

'Oh Jesus Christ. You're not some crazed ex-girlfriend are you? I mean, I know he has baggage, but—'

'Yes,' I say, knowing it will catch her off guard. After all, a crazy ex wouldn't admit to it.

I am handed my drink. It goes on my tab. My rather long tab.

The woman behind the bar clears her throat. 'Can I help you, ma'am?'

Harry's 'girlfriend' keeps her eyes on me and says, 'A bottle of your finest Champagne and a bucket of ice, please.' I knew that was coming.

'He's not who you think he is,' I say.

'So what, Connor dumped you?'

I nearly spit the gorgeously bitter Aperol spritz out from between my lips. 'Sorry, Connor?'

143

She says nothing but shakes her head as if to say 'what of it?'

'He's not called Connor,' I say. I pick up my phone and share the screen grabs I took of his dating profile. 'He's Harry.'

'Harry? Who the fuck is Harry? Look, lady, whatever you think you're doing, you've either got the wrong guy or you've completely lost it.'

I push the phone further under her nose. 'Wrong guy? Really?'

She sighs, rolls her eyes and snatches the phone from my hand. 'So what?'

'Look at the picture. It's the same guy.' There's a flicker in her eye that tells me she knows I'm telling the truth about that, if nothing else. I point to the name at the top of the screen grab and read it out. 'Harry. That's the name he gave me when we met. Four dates later he cleared out my bank account.'

'Bullshit,' she says, but she sounds defensive. The woman behind the bar places a bucket with a bottle protruding from it onto the bar in front of her.

'And there's more,' I say, scrolling through my measly album. 'Harry on WhatsApp. Harry on the dating app. Harry standing in front of his sweet fucking boat. Me and Harry.'

Her expression changes. She looks again and speaks more calmly. 'You must have photoshopped these. I mean, come on. Who looks like the crazy one here? Are you fucking stalking him? Us?'

The woman behind the bar places two flutes with strawberries nestled in their bowls in front of us. Harry's whatever-she-is grabs them. 'Fuck you. Connor Brightman is a good man and you're clearly deranged. I'm going upstairs now to tell him I've met his crazy bitch of an ex.'

'Yeah, you do that,' I say. 'But seriously, look at the dates on these photos. You say you're his girlfriend? How long for?'

I see a shift in her facial expression. Her muscles don't relax; if anything, they tense further. But she seems less angry with me and more . . . curious. She's starting to believe me. She's definitely not been seeing him long.

'And seriously,' I add, 'why the fuck would I come all the way out here if I just wanted to be with him? To do what? Chuck a glass of wine over his head? Try to get him into bed? Fuck that. I want my money back. And I don't want some other poor bitch waking up tomorrow morning with a banging head and a bloodstream teeming with fucking GHB.'

She looks concerned. 'GHB?'

'Yep. Either that or Rohypnol. I'm not entirely sure. But I sure as hell didn't take it voluntarily. And I sure as hell didn't spend all my savings in one fell swoop.' I scroll through the pictures in my phone and show her the screen grab of my bank account with the big transaction.

She places the glasses back on the bar, fidgets with the strap on her bag and looks up at the ceiling. 'How can I be sure you're telling me the truth?'

'How can you be sure *he* is? What do you know about him? Ever been to his apartment? Met any of his friends? He told me he was coming here with his brother.'

'He told me he's an only child,' she says, her voice growing more faint. 'He's going to be wondering where I am.'

'Well, do as you please. Go back to him; leave him lying cold and naked in bed. Just whatever you do, watch your drink. Watch your cell. And don't, under any circumstances, tell him you met me.'

'I don't even know your name.'

'Yeah, and we'll keep it that way, shall we? Because right now, I can't decide whether you're going to get the fuck out of here or make the biggest mistake of your life.' I lather it on nice and thick. Like clotted cream on an English scone. He's bad, there's no doubt about that. But if she doesn't believe he's even more dangerous than he is, she might risk telling him. And that means risking giving me up too.

Not that he'll have any idea. He won't recall dating a blonde New Yorker with bangs. Because she never existed.

Chapter 24

I look at the time: 14.03. The day is dragging like a body in a carpet.

All I've done today is type up contracts and renewals. It's a big crash back down to earth after being in the Hamptons for the weekend where I had more important shit to deal with. All that biochemistry study and for what? Inputting data into templates on screen. I can do so much more than this.

I pull open my top drawer and take out my cigarettes. I've already had a talking-to today for rocking up late after getting back into Manhattan in the early hours of this morning. I had literally two hours of beauty sleep and I was here with my face and heels on. You can't beat that for commitment. But my brain just won't rest.

I push my chair backwards on its wheels and stand up to go for a ciggie break.

The lift is ready and waiting so I dive in and press for the ground floor atrium to head into the central open-air space. As we hit the second floor, I light my cigarette in preparation. The woman on reception glares daggers at me and waves her hand furiously at the smoke the three steps it takes for me to get outside.

I stand outside, hearing the random carp splashing around in the random built-up pond. But it's not all I hear.

A woman's shrill voice breaks my moment of peace.

'So you're telling me I can't access my own money?' I look around to see a smart woman, shouting down the phone, furiously vaping as she does so.

'This is a violation of my rights. Yes, I know. I know I signed . . . But don't you see . . . Yes, I know he's my husband. So what, I signed my entire human rights away when I got married . . . ? Are you . . . ? Seriously? Thanks for nothing.' Everything is now silent, aside from the artificial sound of her vape being sucked on like her life depended on it.

I put my cigarette under the toe of my shoe and twist my heel until its extinguished and practically dust. 'You OK?'

'You'd think, in this day and age, you wouldn't be dismissed just because you're a woman.'

I raise my eyebrows.

'Banking. Soon as you mention being married and joint bank accounts they assume you're a submissive housewife with the intelligence of . . .' she glances at the pond '. . . a fish.'

I laugh. 'Do you want to talk about it?'

'Ugh. It's a long story,' she says.

'Yeah, and we've all got one of those, sadly. The world is a misogynistic cesspit,' I say, taking another cigarette from my packet and lighting up. I offer her one. She takes it.

'Thanks.'

I perch on the edge of the pond and she hovers around me. She's dressed sharply in a black trouser suit, crisp white shirt, sunglasses. She has dark brown skin and mid-length black coily hair worn half up, half down. Her chunky silver jewellery makes a statement and I can tell instantly that she's got power, confidence. Well, clearly not in all aspects of life.

'I've had a banking issue lately too,' I say. 'Sorry, I didn't mean to eavesdrop.'

'Oh, no worries. I was hardly discreet.'

'I was the same,' I say. 'A guy scammed money from my account. Bank did sweet FA. I still don't know how I'm going to get it back.'

She sits down next to me and takes a deep drag on the cigarette I just gave her, as if she hasn't had one in decades. She looks at the cigarette, smoking away between her manicured fingers. 'Ridiculous that they drive you to this,' she says.

'I just started up again. After the bastard took my cash.' I don't hold back. I remember what Priya said about 'meaningful connections' and all that. And I can tell, immediately, that this woman and I will likely have a meaningful connection.

'The ridiculous thing is, I know where my cash is.' The woman sighs. 'He's just . . . fucked around so much with the accounts I can no longer access it.'

'How do you mean?'

'Being married, it takes your rights away. You just don't think about it. You think it gives you more rights. But when you're the main breadwinner. And you trust the asshole.' She sighs again. 'I feel so fucking stupid.'

'Don't,' I say. 'We have to trust people. If we don't, we just become isolated. Like snow leopards.'

She frowns and I decide that Priya's snow leopard comparison is stupid. 'Sorry, that's something my housemate came up with. Come to think of it, I don't think any of us would have an issue with being a snow leopard,' I say.

They're majestic creatures who can rip their prey apart with their teeth. They don't need screwdrivers or knives.

Or date-rape drugs.

'She's a therapist,' I explain. 'She doesn't always get it right though.'

The woman laughs, and her breathing is starting to slow. But I can see the anger pulsing through her.

'I'm Sally,' I say.

'Shenika.' She holds out her free hand. We shake firmly, respectfully.

'Sounds like we've had a similar experience then?'

'Your husband rip you off too?'

'No. No. Not married. Some twat I met online. Stupid really. But I was trying to follow dating advice. Take the plunge. Form a "meaningful connection". Turns out he was the wrong sort to form any sort of connection to. Cleaned me out.'

'Shit. Sorry,' she says, putting her cigarette out on the flagstone and immediately puffing on her vape.

'So, your husband?'

'Honestly. I thought he was trying to help. He doesn't work as long hours, you know. We kind of made an agreement. I'm a lawyer,' she explains. 'So with me working all hours, he'd do more of the domesticated stuff. Unfortunately, my alarm bells didn't ring when he suggested managing the finances. I mean, fuck's sake. How could I have missed it? The biggest red flag.'

'We've got red flags inbuilt. Since day one. If we paid attention to them all the time we'd never hook up. Never get married.'

'I think in this case it would've been preferable to stay single.'

It's remarkable how instantly relaxed we are with each

other. Having something in common, one big awful thing in common, kind of does that.

Shenika tells me how, gradually, over the years, her husband has slowly taken over all the accounts, house deeds, all that stuff. She's been so distracted with her job – she's a senior in a law firm – that she's completely missed it. She trusted him implicitly. She's known him since they were kids. But his name, his passwords, they're now the very things controlling *her* cash. And now she's got a complicated web to unweave in order to get it all back.

'It's not impossible,' she says. 'I mean, it's difficult. But I'm pretty sure I can get it back. Eventually. But in the meantime, I'm totally frozen out. My credit card's maxed and I can't get access to the checking account. The ridiculous thing is, I've seen this happen to other people . . .'

'But when you've seen it before, you're so overly aware of how these things can shape your views, you start wondering if you're being paranoid . . .'

'Exactly,' Shenika says, then looks at her watch. 'Shit, got to go. Client meeting.'

'Hey, I know this might seem a little . . . forward. But do you want to meet me after work? I'm meeting up with some other women I know. We might be able to help.'

She raises an eyebrow. I continue to explain.

'One of them, Terri, she's a bit of a tech expert. Might be able to help you with your banking problems.'

'Really?' She seems interested.

'Yeah, and, to be honest, it could be useful to know someone with legal knowledge, so . . .'

'Where and when?' She smiles as she stands up.

'Tonight, 7 p.m. In the community centre attached to the church on 9th and 39th.'

'I'll see you there.' She nods, smiles, then rushes off.

I walk back slowly to the lift and head back into the office, feeling cautiously optimistic about where things are heading. As I approach my desk I hear David, the boss, calling over to me. He sounds stern as hell. 'Sally. A word.'

Fuck.

Chapter 25

I leave the office and walk south, picking up two takeaway coffees from a street vendor en route. A coconut latte for Lily, and a double-strength cappuccino for me. I know I'm already riled and over-energised right now, but something is telling me to tap into it. To harness it. I have a feeling I'm going to need my wits about me with everything that's going on.

I round the corner just as Lily appears on the sidewalk, looking around for me. I lift the coffee cup high and attempt to wave at her, my handbag hooked into my elbow. She spots me and smiles.

'Thanks,' she says as I hand her latte over to her. 'I thought we were going somewhere for coffee?'

'Decided on takeout. I want to introduce you to some new friends of mine,' I say.

We begin walking south, winding our way through crowds of people – from office workers who still seem to be in a hurry even though it's the end of the working day, to shoppers and couples and groups of friends. The sun is still high and bright, making me squint, and I pull my sunglasses down from the top of my head.

'New friends?' Lily asks, looking cautious.

'Yes. We've got a bad man problem, Lily. Many heads and all that.'

'But . . .' She trails off. 'I thought it would be just us.'

Lily carries on walking, her head down. Something seems to be troubling her.

'Is there something else you're not telling me?' I ask as we take a left. We pause momentarily on a corner by a newsstand. I hear her let out a huge sigh, like she's resigned to spill the beans, but then she sticks her empty coffee cup in the bin and goes to buy a bottle of water. I stand impatiently as she hands some coins over to the street seller and we start walking again.

'Come on, Lily,' I say. 'There's more to this than just Rachel, isn't there? Has he done something to you, too?'

'Not exactly,' she says, her eyes refusing to make contact with me. 'Not as bad, anyway.'

I pull Lily to the edge of the sidewalk, sheltering from the crowd under a building entrance.

'What's happened?'

I remove my sunglasses and look at her face. She looks white and unsure. Tears well in her eyes.

'I don't know what to do, Sal. It's such a mess.' Then she falls into my arms and hugs me tight, her body convulsing with sobs and breaths. I can feel her tears smudging against my blusher.

'What the hell's he done to you?' I demand.

She holds her gaze on me for a second and then it just comes out. 'He's got naked pictures of me, Sally.'

'What? How?'

'He took them. Fuck. I can't believe how royally I've messed up. I mean, I'm gonna get fired. Or worse.'

'Whoa, just go back to the beginning. Why – how – has he got naked photos of you?'

We pause a moment as two women walk past us into the building, smiling at them as if we're stood chatting about the latest collection from Miu Miu or a new brand of mascara of something. They pass, the door swings closed behind them, and the atmosphere tenses again.

'Last Christmas staff party,' Lily says. 'We totally overdid it. We all did. You know . . . there was loads of booze and coke. And . . . I never even liked him. Jesus, I don't know what I was thinking. But I somehow ended up back at his. Fucking stupid move. We fucked, it was, you know, standard, we drank more. Then I noticed he was taking photos. I can't remember tons about it – it's kind of hazy. But I just didn't even think about it. Till now.'

'Cos of the Rachel thing?'

'No. It was on my mind before I found Rachel. It's because of the job thing. The promotion. He's blackmailing me. These photos. He's sent them to me. I'm literally . . . Jesus I don't even want to say. Put it this way, I'm acting out some kind of, you know . . .' she pauses and looks over each shoulder '. . . some kind of *move*, you know. And there's coke everywhere. A little tray right behind me. You can see it. Couldn't have set it up better. What am I talking about, he probably did set it up that way. But I did my best to forget about that night until he sent me those pictures. Just as the interviews for the promotion were coming up.'

'God, Lil, I'm so so sorry. That's just awful.'

We start walking again, and I hook my arm through hers in solidarity.

'But it's the same as with Rachel,' she continues. 'I feel

the same. Guilty, I mean. I drank those drinks, I took that coke, I chose to sleep with him.'

'You never asked him to take photos. You never gave him consent to do that.'

'Yeah, probably because I was too out of it.'

'Exactly.'

'But I made myself too out of it.'

'That's ridiculous. When you mix coke with booze, it usually pulls you round more than anything, doesn't it? What if there was something else involved? Look at what happened to Rachel.'

'What do you mean?'

'Like what if he spiked you? Like Harry did to me?'

She stands bang in the middle of the sidewalk and turns to me. 'Harry did that? To you?' People are pushing past us and I carry on walking, bringing Lily with me through our linked arms.

'Yeah. Well, I mean, I'd had a few drinks. But I know for a fact I didn't have enough to black out. I woke up with my brain crashing around in my skull like a bloody earthquake.'

'Oh, Sally.'

'But could that have happened to you?' I ask. I'm deflecting, I know. But I don't think I can handle her sympathy.

'Fuck. I don't know. Perhaps it's possible. But are *you* OK?'

'Yeah. I'm fine. Nothing happened. Well, he cleaned out my bank account. But I don't think he touched me.'

'Jesus, Sally . . .'

'But anyway. Whether or not you were spiked, in some ways it's irrelevant. At least when it comes to the photos. You never gave consent to having those photos taken. Whether you chose to get wasted or not, you never gave him the right to violate you like that. And my guess is you never did get that wasted.'

Lily shudders. 'I guess so.'

'I *know* so,' I say. 'And Rachel. I mean, if he's done that to Rachel, then if we're honest, it's highly likely he slipped a little something extra in your drink too. He's clearly got form.'

Lily looks as though a lightbulb's just turned on in her head. 'What you were saying about ket, before when we were mucking around, coming up with ideas . . .'

'I wasn't mucking around, but go on . . .'

'What if something similar happened? It wasn't my coke. Not later on, anyway. He was giving it to me.'

'These fucking men.'

'I know. Jesus, though. What do I do?'

'We get him back.'

'We?'

'Yeah, you're not on your own.' I decide to broach the real reason I've brought her here. 'You know, there's this woman at work – her husband has been controlling all her money. And then Marie from the fruit and veg shop . . .'

'Who?'

We stop outside the church. 'Come and meet them.'

Lily looks at the religious building with horror.

'In a church?'

'Oh forget the religion. It's got walls, doors, a coffee machine. And it's private. You're not on your own, Lil.'

I walk up the steps and turn, holding out my hand. She takes it and follows me – albeit reluctantly.

'Fine. But if you think I'm gonna start heading to confession once a week.'

'Oh please!' I laugh. 'I'll be locked up if I head into the confessional. That's definitely not on the agenda.'

Chapter 26

Lily looks around her at the humble little room I've just deposited us in. It's a far cry from our usual glamorous hangouts. We're the first people here so I've got time to settle her in.

'Grab yourself a coffee,' I say, nodding towards the little machine. Lily looks unimpressed.

'But why does it need to be a *church*?'

'Don't sweat it,' I say. 'It's cool. Seriously. God's not gonna strike you down just because he can hear what we're all saying.'

Lily looks scandalised.

I giggle. She picks up the cups in the corner and eyeballs the coffee stains in the bottom. 'Well, if we're gonna meet here on the regular I think I'm gonna have to work some magic on it.'

'Sure,' I say. 'You can event-manage us. Spruce it up a bit. I'm sure the priest'll be over the moon with a font full of Aperol spritz and blow lined up on the pulpit.'

'Haha, very funny. But I'm definitely doing a makeover.'

'Fine,' I say. The door creaks open and Marie walks in with a young woman striding confidently by her side.

There's something different about Marie but I can't put my finger on it.

'Sally, this is Georgia.'

The woman steps forward and waves. She's wearing Nineties-style clothes – huge baggy jeans and trainers and one of those fitted cropped T-shirts with piped edges.

'Hi,' I say, looking her in the eye before remembering my manners. 'This is Lily. A friend of mine.'

They say hello and begin gathering around the mugs, waiting to get their caffeine fix. I chuck a few packets of cookies on the side from my bag, complimentary extras that I took from the Hamptons hotel I was staying at. Lily has decided against risking an intake of norovirus or whatever it is about the mugs that seems to be repelling her. Snobbishness, perhaps?

I make myself a cup of tea – I also made sure to bring my own teabags and milk. I can't abide those piddly little packets of UHT and you can't beat a proper cuppa. Georgia moves to talk to Lily so I see an opportunity to chat to Marie.

'What's different about you?' I say.

'My eyebrows.'

'Have you shaped them?' I ask, studying them more intently.

'No. It's just that you've never seen them before.'

I'm confused. But then it hits me. 'Your fringe! It's gone!'

'Well, not entirely. I've pinned it back. But yep. Time for the bangs to retire I think.'

I stand back and admire her. 'Your eyes are definitely brighter.'

'Well,' she leans in and whispers, 'they don't have to stare evil in the face every damn day anymore.'

We exchange a smile. Just then Shenika arrives and my

heart is full. I wasn't sure if she'd make it or not. Coming to meet a bunch of strangers because some random you've met on your cigarette break invited you along wasn't something I was banking on happening. But it seemed to have struck a chord because here she is.

'Everyone. This is Shenika,' I say.

'Hi, everyone!' Shenika goes to make herself a coffee.

'I think we're just waiting on one more,' I say, just as the door swings open again. 'Ah, here she is. You must be Terri?'

'I am!' Terri says, breezing in all girl-next-door, flowing wavy chestnut hair, denim maxi-skirt and chiffon top.

We all sit. Bags are placed by chairs; slurps of drinks are consumed.

I tap the side of my mug and grin ruefully as silence falls. 'I should really thank you all for coming. I'm not going to preamble too much. We know why we're here. Men. *Bad* men. Complete arseholes who think it's their right to take something from us. Our money, our dignity, our memory, our bodies, our *safety* . . .' There's a low rumble of muttered agreement. 'And now, we've had enough.'

'Hear, hear!' Terri calls.

I nod in her direction and carry on, enjoying making my little speech, riffing as I go. 'We all hear about the actions of men in the media. What they take from us. But why aren't we talking more about what that *does* to us? Why aren't we talking about the long-term impact that their actions have on us? What it makes us become? How it makes us live? How it impacts children?' The last word sticks in my throat before I almost spit it out like the hot, sizzling fat in the pan that day . . . I clear my throat.

'So what is this?' asks Georgia. 'Some kind of support group?'

Chapter 37

Finding intact morello cherries is a challenge. Most are pitted before you buy them, so I need to find somewhere organic that grows them and pick them myself.

In fact, I can make a day of it. Go late at night, steal them under the cover of darkness. In all honesty, it's probably just the sort of light relief I need right now. And terribly English. Like stealing strawberries at a 'pick your own'. I'm sure it could have been a favourite pastime of mine if I hadn't grown up in the city.

I'll take Rachel. It'll be fun, and mischievous, and a far cry from everything that's happened to her. Just what she needs.

I search online for nearby morello cherry farms. They're still in season so we're in luck, but most farms growing morello cherries are many miles north of Manhattan. I find a few located in the Hudson area and text Marie's burner phone.

Sally: Ask Rachel if she fancies getting out into the countryside this weekend. Fruit picking.

Then I move on to my other important mission – getting hold of one of Harry's rental apartments.

I know most of the names of the rental agencies in town because I work for one. And I'm sure Harry told me the name of the one that looks after his.

I pull up a search and scan the results, scrolling through the initial sponsored ads and some of the more downmarket websites that show up.

Then I see it. The name as familiar as my own. That's the one. 'Lloyds'. It feels familiar. Because I remember thinking about the British bank with the horse logo when he mentioned it. This doesn't have a horse logo, though it's rather swish. The site is incredibly professional, straight to the point but obviously delivering on luxury. Minimalist, contemporary apartments with outstanding views.

He's clearly rich, which makes cleaning me out even more brutal. I remember what Priya said: that he was proving he could take what he wanted. Needing it had nothing to do with it.

I flick through the property galleries on the site, wondering how the hell I'm going to work out which is his. I know he has two apartments, and I know one's a penthouse, but there's more than one penthouse on the site.

I'm scrolling through one of the penthouse galleries when something visible on the bathroom wall grabs my attention. Two large, moody black-and-white images of a woman that don't quite fit the otherwise sleek interiors. I zoom in on them and look at the woman's face. I recognise it, but where from? Then, it hits me. It's Harry's mum. It's sweet Caroline, from the photos in his wallet. This has to be his!

I look more closely at the images for confirmation but

nothing else stands out. Aside from a few large canvases on walls and bold ceramics it's pretty minimal – which I think suits the fact that he doesn't like to leave a stamp of his real personality anywhere. However, when I jump back to the property's home page it hits me. The property is called "Dulcet Whispers". I just know I've got the right one.

I send an online request to look around the penthouse, which is apparently available for a short-term let at the moment. It's pricey, but that suits me just fine. After all, I'm not paying.

I use a new name. Paula Halls. It seems inconspicuous enough. And I arrange a viewing.

When I arrive there the next day after work, I'm met at the reception by a snooty-looking concierge, her face a picture of someone highly inconvenienced. Talk about wrong job. The real estate guy, however, seems pleasant enough.

'Paula?' he asks, putting out his hand. I shake it, moderately firmly.

'Yes,' I say, using an Australian accent this time. Years of watching *Neighbours* as a kid has finally paid off. 'Thanks for arranging this so quickly.'

'And, with you wanting to make a quick decision, I take it you have . . .'

'References, yes. I've got two in my bag,' I say, tapping the side of my handbag. Of course, as somebody who has worked in lettings management since I moved to Manhattan, I know exactly what's needed, and what will be checked up on. So I mocked up two convincing-looking references, with contact details for Shenika and Terri. They know to expect a call. And they have the script.

'Excellent,' he says. 'Shall we?' He gestures towards the elevator and I walk in. He presses floor 42 and, when the lift doors open, we are greeted with just one door in the landing.

'Shall we take a look?' he says, leading me to the door.

I nod excitedly. 'I just know I'm going to fall in love with it,' I say. A look of triumph washes over his face. He thinks, because I told him so, that I'm the rich heiress of a wealthy Australian businessman. And I'm in town for at least three months. So he's pretty excited at the prospect of a substantial commission.

'Wow,' I say, as I walk inside. 'This place is just . . .'

'So it's a two-bed, two-bathroom apartment. As you can see, the open-plan area is extremely light and spacious, but there's also a separate snug, if you will, which makes use of the mezzanine design and opens out onto the balcony.'

'It's just perfect,' I say.

Part of me seethes that Harry is able to afford something like this. I wonder how many other wronged women have inadvertently contributed to his property portfolio?

The bedroom is equally luxurious, a super king-sized bed with beige linen sheets, a TV built into the wall that can be camouflaged away at the click of a remote-controlled button. There are fresh flowers on the bedside table, which I'm not a fan of especially, but I can appreciate the thought that's gone in.

After lots of ooh-ing and ahh-ing, we have a deal. I hand over cash for the deposit and the first month's rent. Harry's cash.

And now, I have the keys to Harry's biggest income stream – his penthouse apartment. Marie's gonna love it here.

But at that moment it hits me. I've seen one of his rentals, but I have absolutely no idea where Harry himself lives.

Where does he sit as he plans his vicious, appalling acts? He could be anywhere in this town. He could literally be a few blocks away from me right now. He could have been living round the corner from me all this time. He knows where I live, and yet, I have no idea where he calls home. No idea if he lives alone, or with someone else. Whether he's married. He might be living in a large apartment with three kids and a dog for all I know.

Harry manufactured a big gap in my memory, a black hole, by pumping me with a date-rape drug. But even before that there was an undeniably big black hole. Why didn't I question it?

How the hell could I fall for someone without knowing them?

Chapter 38

I meet Rachel at the Port Authority and we board a Greyhound bus with our backpacks. We've booked a hotel so we can wait until nightfall to raid the morello cherries, and we're due back in town at midday tomorrow.

In reality, we could probably have gone during opening hours. But there were a few things about that option that made me nervous. Firstly, the risk of us both being seen, potentially on CCTV, picking cherries just a few days prior to a man being poisoned probably wasn't a good look. And secondly, using false names to book in could have certainly sparked suspicion if the police were poking around.

The other reason I decided we should go under the cover of darkness and steal them was for the pure joy of it.

Besides, it's a chance for me to get to know Rachel a little better, and try to understand just how she's coping with everything. I can't pretend to know exactly how she feels, but I can be there for her at least.

After a four-hour drive where we've skirted around the big issues and instead chatted mainly about the latest Netflix show or which Manhattan restaurant deserves the Michelin star, we finally arrive in Hudson. I put the zip code for the hotel into my iPhone and we're guided through quaint streets and towards the cutest hotel. It looks like somebody's house, with a lawned front garden and mailbox, and sea green exterior with panelling, cream wooden window frames and a veranda with a hanging basket bursting with pink, white and green flowers.

We walk up the steps and check into a twin room, decorated with patterned wallpaper and heavy curtains.

'Reminds me of my childhood home,' Rachel says.

'Are you not from Manhattan originally then?'

'No. Grew up in the sticks. Tiny place called Cold Spring in Putnam. I left for college when I was young, wanted the big city, bright lights, all that. You've got to be careful what you wish for, I guess.'

Rachel stops talking and sits on her bed, opening her rucksack. She takes out her toiletries bag and places it on the wooden bedside table.

'You know, if you ever need to talk. Like, *really* talk? I'm here for you.'

She looks at me. 'Thanks. But I'm doing OK. Especially now I don't have to face him every damn day.' She hasn't especially convinced me, but I don't push it and leave her to unpack her things. She places her pyjamas under her pillows and it reminds me how young she is. Or perhaps it's a comfort thing.

We change into our trainers, jeans and T-shirts before heading downstairs to eat some food in the small dining area.

I order a wild mushroom risotto and Rachel orders the rigatoni bolognaise. We are surrounded by mostly older couples, and the room is almost silent other than the odd mumble and scraping of cutlery on ceramic plates. But the food is delicious and sets us up for the night.

When we've finished, the skies have darkened nicely to a moody blue. As we walk down the road towards the farm, sat nav mutely guiding us, we notice just how clear the skies are.

'It's so nice to be able to see above the buildings,' Rachel says. 'I mean, I know we're not above them but it's less . . .'

'Claustrophobic?'

'Yeah. I guess I'll always be a country girl at heart.'

'Think you'll move back home?'

'After . . .' she pauses '. . . you know. I did think about it.'

'Have you told your parents?'

'God no. I couldn't. They warned me about moving to the city. And they're so traditional. Old-school. We've never really had open conversations. You know, I think they relied on my school to teach me what I needed to know about sex.'

'But you would consider it?' I ask. 'Moving back?'

'Maybe. It's the prospects though, there's just not as many options for someone who wants to work in PR. Saying that, I'm not sure I even want to do this forever now.'

'It'll get easier, now he's gone. I mean, like you said, the other grads who report to the other directors aren't subject to what you were.'

'True. I just . . .' She trails off and I can see her fidget as she walks, her hands clamping and unclamping nervously.

'What is it?'

'I thought it'd be enough, you know, to get him out of the company. To not have to deal with him. But I don't know if it's *enough*.'

'You could have a point. But it's also about balancing the risk, the possible outcome, and how you'll feel longer term. I mean, so far, you've got rid of him, you're safer, and you won't have to live with doing anything criminal.'

She laughs. 'Apart from stealing fruit.'

'Apart from stealing fruit.' I smile back. 'But you know what I mean. You won't have to live with any regrets.'

'I think it might just be a deep regret though. Stopping there. Shaming him. I think I want more, Sally.'

'That's totally understandable. But put your own wellbeing first. And then, if you still think it'll be good for you, well, that's when you'll know what to do.'

After a couple of miles walking along an increasingly dark road, we approach the farm. We stop and I turn off the sat nav and pull a couple of balaclavas from my bag. I thought we should have them in case of CCTV, but also because I've never had need to wear one before and it feels kind of fun.

We walk a few more steps ahead and arrive at the farm, pausing by the gates. A white sign bearing a huge painted cherry and the words *Rose Valley Farm* squeaks quietly in the gentle breeze. The cherry beams down at us with what, in the daylight, is probably quite a cheery grin. At night, the broad smiling face looks almost sinister.

'Sure. Shall we get started then?' She smiles.

'Absolutely!'

The farm is surrounded by a low fence, which we clamber over with ease.

As Rachel's feet land safely on the ground next to mine, we turn and look ahead of us. I stick the torch on my phone and can make out tantalising bunches of sour cherries all within reach.

I take my lunchbox from my bag and we both fill it with shiny red balls of innocent-looking poison, humming along to "Whistle While You Work" under our breaths as we go.

Chapter 39

Wednesday night comes around far too slowly. It's like waiting for Christmas.

I meet Georgia at Harry's penthouse apartment to get ready. Marie has moved some things in and is living the life she deserves – for a few weeks at least. Sugar's over the moon too with all the extra space and has dismissed her usual bed in favour of stretching out next to Marie in the super king in the main bedroom.

She still hisses at me though.

'How are you feeling, Georgia?' Marie asks.

'No second thoughts if that's what you're asking.'

'I wasn't expecting you to back out. I just imagine it must be a big deal, you know, killing your own father.'

Georgia considers this for a moment and shrugs. 'No. Not really. He's never cared about me. He's never cared about Mom. And, if anything, the part of me that wants to do this is the part of me that's just like him. *He's* made me who I am. Anyway, I have to do it. He'll end up killing her if I do nothing.'

'Well,' Marie says. 'Don't forget there are some wonderful parts to your personality too. The parts your mom passed down.'

'Yeah,' Georgia says. 'I just wish we could bring them back out in her again.'

Georgia's already told me about her upbringing. She was never good enough, her grades never high enough, her face never pretty enough. Oh yeah, he told her that. Said she had a hard face that boys wouldn't like. He slapped her across it, sometimes. But years of living with a narcissistic father hardened her. She always loved her mum though – and she felt worse than guilty leaving home to live with her aunt when she was fifteen, but she couldn't hack it any longer. And every time she went back to visit, her mum became smaller, quieter and hid an increasingly large patchwork of bruising under her clothes.

I go into the kitchen and place the coffee grinder in front of me on the work surface, unlocking it and splitting it into two parts. I take the small bag of morello cherry pits from my pocket and tip them inside the machine. Then I place the parts back together, turn it on its head and hit the on button. It whirs and buzzes and eventually crumbly brown granules drop into the clear plastic base.

'It's working,' I holler. 'No need to break out the hammer and gloves!'

Once the machine's finished, I carefully tip the contents back into the little bag and seal it. Then I place everything I've just infected with pre-cyanide into a carrier bag, tie it tightly and stick it in the bin. There's no way Marie can risk using that again – not even after a good clean.

I wash my hands thoroughly and walk back through to the huge living area, merrily waving the bag of poison in the air. 'Here's our cheeky little murder weapon, ladies.'

'Looks like brown sugar,' Marie says, taking it from me to look.

'Careful not to open it,' I say. 'I don't want any of that getting on our fingers.'

I leave them chatting as I change into my disguise for the night. I have a chestnut brown bobbed wig with bangs that curls underneath slightly, a mid-calf-length skirt and a blouse with a scalloped-edged collar. I'm dressed as the daughter of one of the church's long-time helpers: Elaine. Tonight I am Chloe.

Chloe moved away when she was eighteen for college and they haven't really seen her since, but Georgia's dad still talks about her. She's the girl Georgia *should* have been, apparently. The role model Georgia failed to emulate when they were growing up and attending church together.

Elaine won't be at the church tonight though, because Terri sent her a message from a fake email – masquerading as Georgia's dad. Fake Pastor George sent Elaine to a Bible study uptown, said he'd get someone in to cover. Except actual Pastor George doesn't know any of this.

So I'll be turning up dressed as Elaine's doting daughter who has returned to town to help out, just as she did when she was little, because Elaine's taken ill.

Genius!

We leave Marie in the penthouse, Sugar settled on her knee purring, and we head downstairs in the elevator.

We get to the church in plenty of time before the service is to start, to make sure Georgia's dad isn't alerted to Elaine's absence before 'Chloe' arrives to explain the situation. We don't want him calling Elaine after all.

We stand on the sidewalk scouting out the building. There are three entrances to the church, the main one in the middle, which is where the churchgoers come and go, and two either side.

'The door to the left leads directly to the back of the building,' Georgia advises. 'And the one on the right leads you into the main hall, and the rooms leading off it. The CCTV is in the office upstairs. It doesn't cover all the rooms, like in our church, but it covers quite a few.'

The plan is for me to go in first and occupy Georgia's dad explaining Elaine's illness. Meanwhile, Georgia will let herself into his office with the spare key that he keeps at home. From there, she'll disconnect the CCTV.

We walk towards the church and I go in first, with Georgia diving into a nearby coffee shop to give me time to ingratiate myself.

I walk in the main doors and can see Georgia's dad stood by the pulpit, looking through his paper. I move towards him.

'Pastor George. I can't believe it! It's been too long!' I beam, speaking in a sickly voice with my now well-rehearsed American accent. I hold out my hand and he looks confused but his politeness forces him to take it.

'Sorry, do I—'

'It's me, Chloe. Elaine's Chloe.'

He immediately breaks into a smile. He's not exactly as I imagined. He seems small and neatly presented and, well, certainly not intimidating. I think that's what makes men like this even more dangerous. His true self is so well hidden.

He hugs me gently.

'Well, I never. Look at you! What are you doing back here?'

'Ah. That's the not-so-good news. Mom's taken ill.' His smile immediately drops, concern flashing across his face. I hold my hands out. 'Please don't panic – it's nothing to worry about. She'll be OK. But I came back for a few nights and, well, she's come down with the stomach flu. She can't come in tonight.'

'Oh no that is a shame.' He looks around him, clearly wondering who's going to help him out for service.

'So that's why I'm here. I'm going to help you. It'll take me back to when me and Georgia were kids, helping out.'

'Chloe that's so kind of you. But you must have better things to do.'

'Honestly. I'll enjoy it.' I look around me, taking in the building, the artwork on the ceiling, the windows. The brass figures. 'This place still feels like home.'

He smiles at me. 'If you're absolutely sure, I can't pretend I couldn't do with the help.'

I give him a quick cute smile and shrug of the shoulders. 'Of course. Now then, where are the service sheets?'

I begin placing the sheets in the pews, periodically smiling over at him with a cute scrunch of the shoulders.

Once the service is over, I help Pastor George with the goodbyes as the congregation disperses into the night.

'Well, thank you so much,' he says to me.

'I haven't finished yet,' I say. 'Mom said you have paperwork to get through on a Wednesday. So I'll make you a coffee, to keep you going.'

'No, really, you don't need to stay behind. Honestly. You've done enough. Go, really. I'm so grateful.'

'Don't be silly,' I say, wondering why he seems so keen to get me out of the place. 'I'll just make you a coffee, get some snacks, then I'll leave you in peace to catch up on your paperwork.'

He checks his watch, frowning slightly, but he smiles at me. 'OK, sure. That would be great.'

I head into the church kitchen, having received full

directions on where everything should be from Georgia, and I take my phone out from my pocket. There's a text.

Georgia: *All done. See you back at Marie's.*

Sally: *Noted.*

I place my phone back in my pocket and start making a coffee for Georgia's dad. As the percolator hisses and bubbles, I find a carton of creamer in the fridge, and grab a mug and a bowl from the cupboard.

I place everything on the pastel-coloured patterned tray that was propped up behind the sink and take the little baggie out of my pocket.

I tip the lot into the mug. Just to be safe.

Then I top up the mug of cherry pit cyanide with fresh coffee, a little brown sugar and some creamer, giving it a good stir. Then I pop a bunch of standard cherries in the bowl. He'll like those.

I stand back and admire my work.

A feast fit for a bastard.

Chapter 40

I walk up the stairs at the back of the church to the landing on the first floor. I struggle to balance the tray as I navigate the uneven, creaky steps, but, thankfully, I emerge at the top with no spillage.

Not one drop of wasted poison.

'Here you go,' I say as I enter the room. Georgia's dad is seated at his desk, staring at a spreadsheet on screen, reading glasses propped on his nose.

'You're an angel,' he says. 'And cherries too?'

'Yes, Mom had a bowlful, so I thought I'd bring some in for you.'

'Great,' he says, picking one up and eating it. 'Delicious.'

Of course, the cherries in the bowl are your everyday variety that I picked up at a bodega on the way. They're more a form of insurance. If he's poisoned by cherry stones, and his stomach contents show he's been eating cherries, well, it all makes sense, doesn't it? All adds up to misadventure . . . accidental death.

It seems accidental deaths might start becoming more commonplace round these parts.

I sit down on the chair in the office, determined to watch him finish his coffee before I leave.

It's a neat and tidy room, with books stacked on shelves. They're, unsurprisingly, mainly religious ones judging by titles such as *Confessions of the Soul* and *Know God, Know Yourself*.

I notice a framed photo on his desk – it's him, albeit looking a good few years younger, with a woman and a young girl. That must be Georgia as a kid. All part of his act – his phoney family-man act.

'How's the coffee?' I ask. 'Mom said you liked regular creamer, not any of those flavoured ones.' He picks it up and takes a slurp.

'Also delicious,' he says. He checks his watch again. I can't figure out why he seems so impatient. Perhaps there's another game on tonight? Maybe he's keen to make it to that bar downtown.

'How has Georgia been?' I ask.

'She's. Well.' He pauses, taking his glasses off his face and rubbing his eyes. 'She's a worry if I'm honest, Chloe. Deep down she's a good girl, but she's never been as ambitious, as committed as you. Never been able to apply herself in the same way.'

'But she's doing OK?' I ask.

'So-so. I don't see her that much to be honest. She doesn't come over so much to see me or Gloria these days, now that she's moved out.'

I feel a tsunami of anger rising up in my gut. He's blatantly lying to me. Georgia's *always* going round to see her mum. She's always checking in on her. So not only is he pretending to be the doting father and husband right now, but he's added some rather nasty badmouthing into the mix. And it rolls off his tongue as if he truly believes it.

'She doesn't see her mom?' I ask.

'Oh rarely, Chloe. And when she does, if I'm honest, she treats her terribly. She's so short with her. So cruel and cutting. It's had a really bad effect on Gloria. She hides it, of course.'

I strain to maintain my friendly exterior, but inside I am raging. For the briefest moment, I see myself throwing my hands around his neck and squeezing all the toxic life out of him once and for all.

But then I remember, death by poison might not give the poisoner that kind of instant gratification, but this is the plan. And it's working.

He takes another slurp of his coffee.

'Maybe Georgia's having a bad time herself?' I say, testing him to see if there's any compassion at all in there.

'She's got no feelings that one. It hurts me. Having brought her up in a good Christian household. She's had every opportunity. But she just doesn't *feel*. She lacks empathy, Chloe. It's heartbreaking that she's turned out this way. It's killing her mom.'

I wonder how many people he's told these lies to. I wonder how many people have distanced themselves from Georgia because of him. The extent of her anger is more than wholly justified. I've sat here listening to him spout his lies for all of five minutes and I would be more than happy to slash his dog-collared neck with a knife.

I take a deep breath as he picks his mug up again and takes another sip. It must be nearly empty by now.

'Well,' I say standing, 'I suppose I better let you get on. It was really nice to see you. Say hi to Georgia and Gloria from me.'

'Of course,' he says, standing himself and moving towards

me. He holds his arms out and embraces me tightly – and for a bit too long.

'Bye then,' I say, as I leave the room. He smiles back at me.

I walk out along the hallway towards the stairs and, just before I head down, I pause and look back over my shoulder. I see him draining the last of his coffee.

'Thank you God,' I mouth to the ceiling.

Chapter 41

I walk into the air-conditioned office building and head towards my desk. It's 9.10 a.m. I'm late. Again. Fuck's sake.

I've had another sleepless night – much to Priya's chagrin – so my eyes are red and I can't stop yawning. I hope to God there are no meetings in the diary.

I ended up going for a run really late, at 11.34 p.m. to be precise. I wanted to tire my body and my brain out – but it kind of had the opposite effect on my brain. My body was exhausted, legs and arms heavy as lead, but my brain was all fired up. So I had a drink about 3 a.m. – a straight vodka. Well, it was *a* drink in *a* glass – but I'm not sure a tumblerfull constitutes a single shot.

I still feel a little woozy from it, but needs must.

Thankfully, I didn't wake up with mystery grazes on my hands and knees this time, but the nights are becoming unbearable. It's as though all my energy saves itself for lights out, and I can't kick my legs hard enough to shake it off. It buzzes through my system like a bluebottle racing around under my skin.

I look at my hands. They are starting to heal, my skin bumpy and dry where grit pummelled its way underneath.

I hang my coat up on the hooks near Gilly on reception. 'Psst, Gilly,' I whisper, 'is David in today?'

'No, you're fine,' she says. 'You do, however, seem to have an admirer.'

'Sorry?'

She nods in the direction of my desk, and I see a huge bunch of brightly coloured flowers standing tall in an unassuming vase.

'Who brought those?'

'They were delivered this morning. I'm not sure who actually got them for you. Go look, there'll be a card I'm sure.'

I frown, confused. It's not my birthday and it's not like I have loads of anniversaries I want to remember in my life. Or anyone who would remember them for me.

I head over to my desk and pick up the biggest bunch of flowers I've ever seen. There's a rainbow of roses, pom-pom-like dahlias, big frothy peonies, trumpeting lilies, and delicate white baby's breath contrasted by spiky green leafy stems. I pick them up and remove the small white envelope. After placing the flowers back down on my desk I open the envelope.

Congratulations on the new apartment. C.

C? Who's C?

It's fucking Harry! As Connor. How the actual fuck did he know? How could he have possibly worked it out? I used an Australian accent, false references, a fake name. I paid cash.

Oh my God, Marie's there.

Did he see me visit the other night? I think back. I was so careful. And I left the penthouse in disguise as Chloe. I looked completely unrecognisable. I'd never wear a scalloped collar.

I'll admit, this is unnerving. He's too close. I look over my shoulder in a kind of knee-jerk reaction. Has he been watching me? Following me?

I pick my phone up, not quite sure what I'm looking for, but I scroll back through the onscreen notifications I haven't yet opened, all from different apps.

There's an untouched text from Amanda, and various alerts from my bank account for every time I used my card this morning – coffee, the subway to work because I was running late. But then there's one that makes me stop and scroll back . . .

Flora and Fauna. $129.99.

How has he done it? He doesn't have my bank card. It's in my handbag. I used it this morning. It's been weeks since he made that big transfer. He shouldn't have access to any of my accounts.

He must have taken a photo of my card when he drugged me. A token of his evil genius. I call my bank, put a block on my card and order a new one so he can't play this game again. I can't let him clean me out a second time. But when I think about it, I'm not sure he wants to. This is obviously more about the control than the cash. About the attention. Otherwise, he'd have spent a lot more than $129.99.

He's clearly toying with me, trying to get my attention. Showing me what he's capable of.

Even so, I think I'm still one step ahead. He got my money – but I got it back and then some. And now, we have the keys to his apartment for at least a month – paid for with his own money. Marie's moved in. I better check she's OK. Thank fuck we were sensible enough to change the locks on it straight away.

I text Marie, just to check in and make sure she hasn't run

into him. I don't want to worry her by raising the possibility when I'm not there to do anything about it, so I just ask how her day's going. She replies immediately, all is fine, she's at work at the shop, and the group cell phone's been quiet.

That's one less thing to worry about.

But I need to come up with a plan. I take a step back. If this was someone from the group, what would I tell them? To get my hands on his cell phone. He could have my bank details saved in there. He could have input my account details into different shopping apps, ready to spend all my money. Who knows. He's clearly up to something – and I can't see him stopping at flowers.

It's not quite a plan, but I'm on the right track. I pick the flowers up and take them over to Gilly on reception. 'Here you go, brighten the place up with them.'

'But they're yours?'

'I'd rather you have them,' I say. 'Turns out my admirer is someone I'm not too keen on.'

'Thanks, Sally.' She places them neatly to the side of the desk and sits back to admire them.

I go back to my desk. A worrying thought has crossed my mind.

He's playing with me.

And I'm not entirely sure I want him to stop.

Chapter 42

Marie: *Bonus Feminist Book Club Meeting. Today. 7pm.* ***BE THERE!***

It's a text from Marie using the burner phone. Something's clearly gone wrong.

I arrive just after Marie and Georgia, who's fidgeting wildly, her face looking haunted.

'What's happened?' I ask.

'You might want to sit down,' Marie says. Georgia simply stares into space.

Lily and Rachel burst in together, questions silenced at the sight of Georgia pacing the room. She is refusing to look at me.

It must be something to do with her dad. Does she regret it? Is she mad at me? Has she only just felt the gravity of it?

Finally Shenika and Terri arrive and we all sit.

'Georgia's dad's in the hospital,' Marie says.

'You were meant to fucking kill him,' Georgia shouts at me. 'You said it was a sure shot.'

'Whoa hang on. Marie, can you bring us all up to speed before Georgia fucking implodes?'

Georgia huffs at me and continues pacing frantically.

'Pastor George didn't die. He's in the hospital with cyanide poisoning. Georgia's mom is with him. He's very sick, vomiting, diarrhoea, his temperature's been raging. But they say he'll pull through.'

'But. He drank it all.' I'm completely baffled. 'I don't understand how he can have survived it.'

'It's a sweet fucking miracle!' Georgia belts out. 'Either that, or you don't know your cyanide from your cherryade.'

'Don't fucking talk to me like that.' I can feel the rage building inside me. 'It should have worked. I can't—'

'Georgia, sit down. You can be mad at Sally all you like, but it's not her fault.' Georgia looks like she might throw something but she doesn't know which of us to aim at. 'Somebody found him before he got too sick,' Marie explains.

'What?' I ask.

'Seems there's another reason Daddy dearest stays late on a Wednesday,' Georgia fumes. 'And it's not to do the fucking finances.'

'His mistress,' Marie says. 'You mentioned he kept looking at his watch. He was waiting for his mistress. She arrived just in the nick of time. He was starting to feel unwell; she called 911.'

'They got him to the ER, asked what he'd been eating or drinking, and the paramedics mentioned that they'd seen the cherries and coffee. The doctor realised the cherries could be a factor in his mystery sickness,' Georgia says. 'Pumped him full of hydro-something or other. Some antidote. Loads of oxygen. The works. Long story short, they saved him.'

'Oh my God. Fuck. Georgia. Do you think he knows?'

I feel like the worst kind of failure. I want the ground to swallow me up. Not only have I let myself be duped by

Harry, I've failed the group now too. How could I have fucked this up so bad?

'He's gotta know *something*,' Shenika says rationally. 'He'll put two and two together when he works out Elaine got a fake email. He'll realise that Chloe wasn't Chloe.'

Marie frowns. 'Yeah, but weird thing is, so far he hasn't said anything to show he's suspicious.'

'He's kind of just gone along with it all,' Georgia says. 'What's his fucking game?'

'What are we going to do?' Lily asks, ever practical. She might not like that we're trying to kill someone, but she's always been one to see things through.

'How does this man just keep slipping the net?' Shenika says. I can tell she's baffled too.

'Maybe God exists after all,' Georgia shouts. 'And maybe he's a bastard too!'

She storms over to the corner of the room and I can tell she's crying. I haven't seen her cry before. I move towards her, but Marie puts her arm out in front of me and shakes her head. She heads over instead.

'So he's been saved by his mistress,' I say out loud. 'And now his wife's by his bedside. This fucking man.'

'I wonder why he hasn't said anything?' Rachel asks. 'I mean, if he knows he's been purposely poisoned.'

'That's the bit that's worrying me,' Shenika says. 'He clearly wants to deal with this himself.'

Rachel's face darkens and she looks distant as she speaks. 'I'm so sick of them. I'm so, *so* sick of them getting away with murder and abuse and rape.'

Her use of the word isn't lost on any of us. She's been there. And perhaps her self-defence mechanisms, the emotional denial she's protected herself with for the last few weeks, is making way for something more reactive. Something more vengeful.

Marie walks Georgia back towards the group, her arm around her waist. They sit back down in the circle, Georgia next to me.

'Sorry,' she says. 'It's not your fault. I just want him gone.'

I place my hand on her shoulder and she just about manages not to shrug away from me. 'I know. We'll find a way. And I know this is going to be really difficult, but I think we might need to give it a while. He'll be on high alert right now.'

'But the longer we leave it . . .'

'We won't wait too long. Don't worry. But he'll be under supervision in hospital. We can't do anything until he's discharged. Anyway, at least he can't hurt your mom while he's in there.'

Georgia nods, swiping at her eyes with a tissue.

'Anyway,' Marie says. 'I was going to save this until our next meeting but, since we're all together, I might as well let you in on our plan to get Shenika's money back.'

We all gather round and listen, the intention to go out and do more damage lifting Georgia's mood a little.

'It's a good one!' Shenika says, before Marie fills us in on her upcoming character role.

Chapter 43

Text messages are pinging on my phone as I enjoy my evening run, desperately trying to burn off my angsty energy before attempting to sleep tonight. I ignore the messages, instead continuing to pound the pavement, music blasting in my ears. I am running back from the Hudson, playing dodgems with people on the sidewalk. I run a little further. My phone goes off again. Jesus Christ.

I stop, remove my phone from my running belt and press pause on my playlist. It's Rachel. Three texts.

Rachel: *You're going to be so impressed*

Rachel: *I've got him on a date. Harry*

Rachel: *I'm going to swipe his phone for you. Xoxoxox*

The first message was sent twenty-one minutes ago. Shit.

The thought of Rachel spending an evening with Harry makes my skin tingle with jealousy and crawl with fear. After everything she's already been through.

Sally: *Where are you?*

I stand in the middle of the sidewalk, waiting for a reply. It doesn't take long for the three grey dots to appear.

Rachel: *That rooftop restaurant he took you to. Fiesta. Gotta go! It's on!*

Fuck. She's there with him right now. At the same place he took me to the night the bastard spiked me! Has he got a fucking deal with management? I'll splurge on food and cocktails if you let me drug my dates?

I flag down a yellow cab and jump in, still sweaty from running, flyaways escaping my ponytail and sticking to the side of my face. We pull up outside the building and I race to the lift, pressing the 'up' button over and over, knowing full well it won't make it arrive any more quickly but I can't help myself. The lift finally arrives and I storm inside and stand next to a very smartly dressed couple. The sweat is starting to cool on my skin but I am radiating heat. It's not just the run that's making me feel like this.

The lift stops and I push past the couple into the restaurant. A polite, if wary waiter asks if he can help me and I bat him off with my arm. I've no time for pleasantries. There's no way Rachel's coming out of this unscathed unless I can get to her, like, now.

I scan the room. There's so much colour and music and decor, waiting staff racing around, it's hard to see – but also hard to be seen. Then I spot him, at a table. On his own. Where's Rachel? She must be in the loo. Hang on, what's he doing?

Shit!

I take my phone back out of my running belt and point it to the table just in time. He takes something from his pocket, conceals it in his palm and then, smooth as anything, reaches over towards her drink, grabbing the menu at the same time to cover up his actions.

Fuck.

I stop filming and rush to the bathroom to find Rachel before she can head back to the table, getting stopped by confused staff wondering what the hell a jogger is doing racing around their rooftop restaurant.

'Excuse me, ma'am, can I—'

I ignore them again, bursting into the restroom at high speed. 'Rachel? Rachel!'

I push on empty cubicle doors, bang on others. She is not here. How is she not here? Where else can she be?

I rush back out onto the main floor of the restaurant and whirl around, looking for her. And then my heart drops into my stomach. Somehow, she is back at the table. Knocking back her drink. No! No, no, no!

I race over to the table, panting, my heart racing. 'Rachel!' I shout.

She looks up at me, a confused smile on her face. 'Oh, hi?'

'Where've you been?'

'I was just on a call on the patio.' She seems shocked to see me and unsure of what to say.

She doesn't say my name, but he does.

'Sally?' He looks genuinely unnerved by the sight of me but I can tell he's trying to keep a lid on it. His face is completely calm, but his eyes keep darting between me, Rachel and the waitstaff. I can practically see his brain ticking over.

I ignore him and shake Rachel's shoulder. 'We need to go, Rachel. Now.' But she just smiles vaguely at me.

'Hang on a moment, how do you two know each other?' he says. There is a slow dawning of realisation across his face. That he himself has been played. But he can't work out how.

'Rachel, come on, we have to go,' I say, gesturing for her to stand.

Rachel's eyes start to lose focus and her head nods in slow motion.

'What have you done with her?' I demand, as Harry leaps up out of his chair. 'What the fuck have you given her?'

By now the other diners around us are starting to whisper and stare. I have a horrible sense of déjà vu but shake it off.

A waiter comes over, holding a tray like a shield. 'Can I help you?'

'Yes,' Harry says, clearing his throat. He's leaning into that authority that only complete dickwipes seem to command when everything goes tits up and they want to shift blame to anyone but them. 'My crazy ex-girlfriend has just burst in on my date.'

'Oh, please!' I say. What is it about these men who think they can call women crazy as an excuse for *their* crazy behaviour? But then, I realise, if anyone looks out of place here it's me. Harry's dressed for a date. Rachel might be slumped in her chair, but she is also dressed to impress. I'm dressed for a run. *I* am the one everyone is looking at.

'Is she OK?' the waiter asks Harry, motioning towards Rachel.

'We've been celebrating; she's had a bit too much Champagne tonight I think.'

The waiter looks out of his depth. 'I'll just go and get her some water, perhaps?' He scurries away, obviously keen to speak to a manager or someone who knows what they're doing.

I pull Rachel to standing, but she can't hold her balance.

'This shouldn't be happening,' Harry mutters under his breath.

'Of course it shouldn't,' I hiss at him. 'What the fuck have you done?'

'I haven't done *this*.' He gestures frantically at Rachel. There's panic in his eyes. I focus back on Rachel, who I'm holding up by both shoulders trying to make eye contact, but her head is lolling and nodding. Surely that drug couldn't be working this quickly?

Then, suddenly she collapses onto the floor. And Harry legs it.

Chapter 44

I sit by her hospital bed, stroking her head. This place brings back terrible memories. The bleeping, the rushing around, curtains whipping open and closed on the rails. It's high-speed chaos.

I remember sitting in places like this with my mum, him by her side, making sure she didn't tell them anything he didn't want her to. Her busted-up eye, her bloody nose, her broken wrist. She would tell them she took a fall down the stairs, that she tripped over one of my toys and went flying. He would make a point of telling me off for leaving my toys lying around, even though I knew I hadn't.

He once even went as far as to confiscate one of them, a big blue furry gorilla that we won at the fair. It was almost as though he was trying to get us all to believe that's what had really happened, never mind the doctors.

Gaslighting bastard. It got to the point that I was constantly questioning my memories.

Had I actually left an obstacle course lying around the house?

Did I really not see what I thought I saw?

I try to wipe my memories from my mind and focus

on the woman in front of me. Rachel's breathing is slow and laboured. I sit with her for ages thinking the same two thoughts over and over again.

He must have given her a huge dose. He could have killed her.

Her eyes gradually start to open, blinking as if in slow motion and looking around the room, trying to focus. Then she sees me and tries to sit up in bed. 'Sally? What happened?'

'Try not to move too much – just get some rest. You landed pretty hard on that floor.' She looks so confused and uncomfortable. 'Can I adjust your pillows for you?'

She shakes her head. 'What happened?'

'He spiked you, Rachel,' I say, stroking her arm gently. She closes her eyes again and breathes in. Everything about her is slow. We sit like this for a long time before a doctor comes in to check on her.

'Family?' she asks me.

'Friend.'

'Are you happy with your friend staying while we talk about what's happened?' she asks Rachel.

Rachel nods, wincing a little at the effort.

'She hit her shoulder on the side of the table when she collapsed,' I say. I've explained this so many times to so many people at this hospital already.

'I'm afraid we can't provide any strong painkillers at the moment, not with what we've found in your system,' the doctor explains. 'Does it hurt a lot?'

'I'll manage,' Rachel says. Her eyes are squinting. 'My contact lenses. They're drying out. Can I take them out?'

'Of course,' the doctor says.

'I have a mirror in my bag,' Rachel says. 'And my glasses.'

I look around on the floor and reach for Rachel's

handbag. I spot her house keys and a smiley little avocado key ring attached to them. I forget just how young she is. It makes me feel even worse for dragging her into all of this. She should never have come to the meetings. We should have sorted Ethan out for her. Left her out of it. Let her heal from the darkness he introduced into her world – not drag her further into it. I hand over her compact and glasses case and she balances the little mirror on the bedside table.

Rachel removes her lenses and turns back to face us with her glasses on, looking more like the Rachel I first met.

'Better?' the doctor asks. Rachel nods. 'OK, so we've found a few different things in your bloodstream that will have contributed to what happened. Alcohol, pregabalin and GHB. Did you put any of these things in your system voluntarily?'

Rachel nods wearily. 'I had Champagne.'

I jump in, saving her from trying to speak. 'The alcohol, but there wasn't much of that, right?'

'Well, there was enough to intoxicate. But it's the mix of these drugs that's the bigger problem. Could somebody have spiked your drink?'

Rachel nods. Then she starts to speak again, slowly. 'I was in a really busy bar,' she says, and I realise straightaway that I haven't given her enough credit. She's not naive. She doesn't want the police to go after Harry. She still wants us to finish the job. She's just been through all this – twice now – and she still wants us to deal with him in our own way.

'That's a strange mix of drugs to find in a spiking incident,' the doctor says.

'The pregabalin is mine.' I look over at Rachel, shocked.

'OK.' The doctor starts noting something down. 'What was that prescribed for?'

'Anxiety.'

A new wave of guilt crashes over me. How could I have let her get into this awful situation? How could I have done that? She's clearly already struggling.

The doctor nods. 'OK, well, if we're being honest, you shouldn't really be drinking on pregabalin.'

'Whoa, hang on a minute,' I say. 'You can't blame her for being spiked.'

'Of course, not. Sorry,' the doctor says. 'This isn't your fault. Not at all. I just want you to know, in future, to try not to drink on the pregabalin. Basically, what's happened in your system is a mass overload of downers, suppressing your respiratory system. Put simply, if you hadn't got here when you did, it could have killed you.'

Rachel takes a sharp breath in.

'And will she be OK?' I ask.

'We'd like to keep you in for observation, overnight. Just to make sure everything's OK. Is there anyone else you need us to call?'

'No, I'm just glad to have Sally here.'

'OK. Well, try to get some rest while you're here. We'll be back to check on you in an hour.' The doctor turns to me. 'Sally? If you're concerned about anything while you're here, the nurse's station is just to the left.'

'Thank you,' I say, and the doctor leaves the room.

'Rachel . . .' I trail off. I don't even know where to begin. 'I'm so sorry.'

'No, don't apologise to me. Just, please, don't put yourself in danger. Harry's a . . . Harry is well versed in this game. He's dangerous. Fuck, Rachel, he almost killed you.'

I see her shudder.

'I didn't know you struggled with anxiety,' I say softly.

'I didn't. Not until Ethan . . .' She looks down. 'I've just let men fuck me up.' Tears are wobbling on top of her bottom lid, threatening to spill over.

'You haven't let men do anything. They've just done what they wanted regardless. This is not about you. It's about them.' The tears spill down her soft cheeks. She already has black make-up streaked down her face. 'Please, Rachel,' I say. 'You don't need to prove anything to anyone. Just, be a part of our group, but do what you're comfortable doing. Just come for support. To vent. I mean, men have made us feel uncomfortable for long enough. We shouldn't be doing it to each other.'

She lets out a glimpse of a smile.

'Stay with us,' I say. 'But maybe you could use your intelligence in an advisory capacity. That is worth more than you can imagine.'

'Don't you understand though, Sally?' she says, her voice, although quiet, becoming more forceful. 'I want to get these men back. I *have* to get these men back. I'm not going to sit back and watch while you lot have all the fun.'

That's when it clicks. All these personalities that make up Some Women – there's more than meets the eye. The things they've been through have brought their rage to the surface in very different ways. Rachel has a hunger for this to rival my own. Of course, why else was she going all out on her own arranging dates with Harry? Why else did she and Lily decide to take on Ethan themselves? Rachel's been keen as mustard from day one.

'The pregabalin, is that because of what Ethan did to you?' I ask.

'I hate him, Sally. How *dare* he.' Tears start to well up and she sniffles. 'I've never had sex before. Never. I don't even like men. Never have. I've always known that. My first was supposed to be some goddess.'

Her tears roll faster and I find a tissue on the bedside table and hand it to her. 'He took your virginity?'

'Yep. And he never even asked.'

Chapter 45

'Sally! Oh my God. I was worried sick.'

I stand in the doorway to the apartment. Priya is fluttering around me but her words are low and muffled, like I'm underwater. So I just stand, unable to move, unable to compute why my best friend is so completely alert. I feel as though I'm on pause in my own world while everything else is silently racing around me.

I'm vaguely conscious of being guided to sit down on the sofa. I look at Priya and wonder if I know her. *How* I know her. She looks so familiar and yet so strangely unfamiliar all at once.

'Sally? Are you OK?' her voice echoes. The words mean nothing to me. But then fear rises in my gut, bubbling into my brain.

'Where is he?' I suddenly snap, twisting violently around. Suddenly I can hear the outside, the sounds of the city pressing in, loud and terrible. 'Where is he!?' I stare frantically all around. There's nobody here that I can see. But I can sense him. I can smell him. I can smell burnt, fried meat. I can feel him behind me. I jolt forward and try to stand but Priya gently sits me back down again, using firm hands against my struggles.

'Shhh, shhh, Sally . . . Try to relax.'

I'm fighting against her but her arms feel comforting. At last I collapse into them. Huge sobs force their way out of my chest, my eyes streaming and misty.

The next thing I know I wake up on the sofa in my pyjamas, a blanket over me.

The sun is pointing its rays in through our kitchen window, across into the living room area. I wince and rub my eyes. My head feels strange and floating.

I sit myself up and stretch my legs out in front of me. My knees are still red raw from whatever I did to them the other week, and my feet feel heavy. I look down at them. I am wearing my running shoes.

Not again. Not this again.

I can hear Priya in the bathroom. The door opens and she walks down the hall into the open-plan area and sits next to me. 'Sally. How are you?'

'I've done it again, haven't I?'

She nods. 'You were dissociating. It's like you weren't present in your own body. Like your consciousness was somewhere else. I haven't seen you that bad since . . .'

I flinch at the memory, pinching my eyes tight shut. I can't bear to think of myself out of control like that. Lost in bad memories, pictures, feelings.

It used to happen a lot when he was around. I'd hear the noises, the shouting. The thwack against my mother's body or the smash of glass. I couldn't bear hearing her cry out in pain. I couldn't do anything. Pillows, duvets, pressing my hands against my ears, closing my eyes tight shut, none of it worked. *Pretend you're asleep*, she used to say. Because if

I cried, he got worse. I had to stifle everything. Every bit of surging energy that was desperate to leave my body I had to snuff out. It felt like I was suffocating myself.

Then one day, without even thinking about it, I just ran. I opened the front door and ran down the road barefoot, pyjamas on. The lights in people's windows were just starting to flicker on. It must have been early morning. I could hear birds tweeting, starting to wake up, but they sounded like they were on another plane. Like I was stuck in between two sheets of glass. My body was wide awake but my brain was shutting down, and all I could hear was my own breath, hard and fast, as I pelted down our street.

It became a thing. The noises would set me off. The fear would jump-start my body and I would race out the house. I don't think he cared. My mum *did* care, but I think she thought I was safer on the streets than I was in our house. Our family home.

I was skinny and pale. And I just kept doing it. Teachers began to comment that I was turning up late to school. Often I was too exhausted to concentrate. But who was going to get me out of bed to show up on time? My own mother couldn't get out of bed half the time.

And then, after it happened, after that Boxing Day night, the night I didn't run, I was moved to foster care. And sleep-running became a regular thing. The memories of that night . . . those sounds must have haunted my sleep, because I would wake up in the park, or hiding behind a letterbox, or standing with my face against the glass door of the newsagent's. Panting. No idea how I'd got there.

It only stopped when I was placed in a permanent foster home. They paid more attention, I guess. I liked them, but they were never my parents. Cassie and Phil. They were sweet, and they really tried. I'm so grateful for the life they tried to give me – the cosy home, the clothes, the hobbies, the birthday parties. But when I turned eighteen, I left and I just never really looked back. I appreciate all they did, but they didn't need me. They didn't need someone like me. No matter what they said. I was doing them a favour.

They must have been so disappointed when I threw it all back in their faces the moment I found booze. Fifteen years old and getting wasted. They tried to be supportive. Even when the late-night excursions, the weird sleep-running, started all over again. They found me a therapist, they made sure my school understood. They set boundaries that almost worked. Mostly didn't. They fought for me when I needed it most and gave me the unconditional love I craved but didn't know what to do with. They were good people who ended up with a foster kid who had already lost herself.

I can't afford to lose myself again. Not now.

I get up.

'You should rest today, Sally,' Priya says, putting a hand on my knee.

'Fuck that. I'm not wallowing,' I say, with as much certainty as I can muster. 'Besides, I've been put on a warning thing at work.'

'Ah. Maybe you can explain to them, tell them that you're having trouble sleeping?'

I shrug, I don't think that's going to go down well. It's a crap excuse at the best of times, and I obviously can't go into detail. They'll think I'm crazy for starters.

'Is it Harry?' Priya says. 'Is this because of what he did?'

'I think it's because of what he did, but I don't think it's him, per se. I think, it's just brought it all back.'

'You need a trained therapist, someone specially trained in managing trauma.'

I shake my head. 'No, Priya.'

'Just trying to help.'

'Yeah but I don't want to go naming it. Dissociation, whatever. It's a distraction.'

'That's exactly what it is. It's serving a purpose. It's distracting you from something you don't want to deal with.'

'Then it's making things worse,' I say.

'Look, Sally. We know what can happen when you're in that state. It's not safe.'

'Can we just forget about it?'

'What happened yesterday anyway? You never came home the night before either.'

'Harry spiked Rachel. From the group. She almost fucking died, Priya. I was at the hospital with her.'

'Oh my God. Which one?'

'Which one?'

'Hospital?'

I realise immediately what she's worried about. 'It was Lower Manhattan, OK.'

'But that's where . . .' She trails off.

'I know! But I didn't have much choice. I couldn't leave her.'

'You need to be careful, Sally. For all our sakes.'

'That's not all.' I show her my hands and knees. The scars are healing but you can still make out the damage. 'I woke up like this the other day. I don't know what's going on with me. Everything seems to be getting worse not better.'

She leans over to me and hugs me tight. 'But all those times you thought you could smell fried food. Sally, like I said before, I genuinely couldn't smell anything. All that stuff, about your mom. I think you really do need to talk to someone. Not just me, a trauma specialist. It's not going to be easy, but I think maybe now's the time. Or it will just keep getting worse.'

I know she's right. I've been dodging this one for years. Dodging it so hard I'm literally on the other side of the world. But the fact remains he's still out there.

I light a cigarette, inhaling deeply into my lungs, and know immediately what I have to do.

I need to give the young me closure.

Chapter 46

I'm sitting in the back of a taxi. I'm too exhausted to walk anywhere after last night's escapades. Sunday mornings used to be reserved for recovering from boozy hangovers, now I'm recovering from a late-night sprint.

I'm picking Marie up first from Harry's plush penthouse where she's still staying, then we're going on to the church for a meeting of Some Women. I'm not sure how much longer she'll be able to stay at his place. The lease runs out in three weeks, but he might not want anyone associated with me staying there. Besides, he'll discover the locks have been changed eventually and do something about it. But for now, she's safe. I just wanted to give her a little space.

With Harry in mind, I take out my phone and review the footage I captured of him spiking Rachel's drink one more time. It's not one hundred per cent clear, but you can just make out what he's doing to her drink. That, coupled with her hospital stay, would totally nail him.

Seeing him mid-act unnerves me. It's as though there are two different Harrys. The one I loved spending time with, the one I was falling for. And this vile, vindictive man. A man who disregards women. Was the other Harry just a figment of his imagination? Some character he decided to play to get me into bed, to get me to open up to him?

Worse still – to get me to trust him?

Was there anything real about the time we spent together?

I find the mobile number he shares with his tenants and open WhatsApp.

Sally: *She almost died.*

The two ticks turn blue immediately. He's seen the message. He's clearly been wondering what happened. Keen to know whether he's a murderer or just a piece of shit con man and abuser of women. I instantly regret not stringing him along. I could have pretended he killed her. But I don't know this man at all. What if he gets a kick out of the thought of killing someone? What if he's done it before? I don't want to give him the pleasure.

And yet I'm hit by how pleasurable it feels to be in touch with him again. Talk about a bad drug.

I can see him begin typing back but then he stops again. I don't give him a chance to say anything, I just send my footage. He looks at it immediately. I give him a moment to digest what I'm saying. Then I spell it out.

Sally: *You need to do something for me, or this little movie could put you away for a very long time . . .*

I realised last night that Harry could be useful to me. He's rich, he's unemployed, he's flexible. And he knows how to con people.

Don't get me wrong, I hate him.

Truly, I hate him.

Don't I?

Of course I do. But he *is* useful. There's no denying it. Because my biggest mission of all has to take place back home, thousands of miles from New York. All the time I've spent focusing on paying Harry back has just been a distraction. Playing stupid games. There's something much more important I need to do in order to finally move on with my life. And he's the perfect person to help me do it.

He has to. He's no choice. And I'd rather drag him into my plans than risk incriminating any of the women.

That's precisely why it has to be him. There's no other reason.

I go to message Marie as I'm approaching her block but, as usual, she's already there and waiting for me. And, once again, she looks amazing.

She climbs into the cab beside me and we drive a few blocks, all around us horns blaring, bikes weaving in and out and pedestrians making a dash for it.

We get out of the cab beside the church entrance and walk in together.

Everyone gathers in their chairs.

'Where's Rachel?' Shenika asks.

'We need to talk about that,' I say, feeling uncomfortable about the level of responsibility I have in the whole sorry saga.

I talk everyone through what happened. Lily, of course, was already aware. I called her from the hospital. I knew she would feel a tug of responsibility and guilt too. And Lily's offered her spare room. After all, Rachel's family live miles away.

But really, this is on me. And I am sure to make that clear

to the group. I haven't been as responsible as I should have been.

'It's time I paid my dues,' I say. 'I need to make up for my fuck-ups. Terri, I've managed to fix up a date with that godawful catfisher this coming Friday.'

'Really?' Terri says. 'He's dangerous. Do you want one of us . . .'

'No,' I say firmly. 'This one will definitely work better if I go it alone.' I have to do this alone. I have so much anger building inside of me, and I need to unleash it in any way I see fit. I almost need the thrill of the danger, the risk, of confronting this monster.

'OK. If you're sure,' Terri says. She doesn't look convinced when I nod but doesn't pursue it.

'Anyway,' Marie says. 'We have something to report back to you all. We've got Shenika's money back.'

'Really?' I say impressed. 'Do tell all.'

'Honestly, I've never had so much fun.' Marie beams. 'I'm thinking of joining Barb's amateur theatre group now.'

'Go on,' I laugh. 'Just tell us what happened first. Then we can discuss your dream role in *Les Mis*.'

Marie grins. I haven't seen her look so self-assured since I first met her. Not in a positive, happy way anyway.

'OK, so I dressed up in a new outfit – Shenika and I went to Bloomingdales, so even the prep was fun. Shenika knew where her husband, Paul, was going to be, so I got there early, sat alone at the bar, and conjured a few tears.'

'Wow, can you actually do that?' Lily says excitedly. 'I mean, not even all professional actors can do that.'

'I know, right! Anyway, I sat there, playing with a martini, pretending to drown my sorrows and, just as Shenika said, he pulled up a seat along the bar. He was a bit far away at first, but the bar was quiet, and he noticed me sitting there sniffling.'

'He always did like to play the hero,' Shenika says, a look of disgust on her face.

'So he comes over and asks what's up. And I tell him, my husband's been emotionally abusing me. Controlling me. And, then I hit him with it – he's taken all my money. I can see a flicker of realisation cross his face, but I keep on talking. I tell him I've had legal advice, banking advice, et cetera, et cetera and that nobody can do anything about it. Because he's very cleverly put everything in his own name over the last few years and then, as I had just found out that afternoon, transferred all my money to an offshore account where I can no longer gain access to it or indeed start legal proceedings. I said it was practically untraceable. That not even the legal experts could work out how to get it back.'

'And? Then what?' Georgia asks.

'Then, he's asking me, without trying to sound too interested, how he did it and I'm like, I don't know, some financial adviser or something. And I dive into my handbag and pull out a card and I tell him, I found this in my husband's suit pocket. I hand it to him, then I excuse myself, saying I need the ladies' room, but I "accidentally" leave the card there. When I get back, he hands me the card back, but I know he'll have photographed it on his phone.'

'He absolutely did,' Shenika says. 'Because my money all came back to me. Every single penny. And then some. He reached out to the guy – one of Terri's skint digital forensics grad friends . . .'

Terri sits up straight in her chair. 'Oh, they're such good value.'

'Yeah, and they took the call from the number on the

card, and obviously sounded like they knew what they were talking about because, well, they did. He fell for it hook, line and sinker.'

'Yeah and the greedy prick sent some of his money too, didn't he, Shenika? To keep it from the IRS,' Marie says.

'Yep. About $5,000. Guess he thought it was a good tax loophole.'

'So you going to have a spending spree down 5th Avenue then?' Lily asks.

'Nope. Made a donation – $5,000 to a women's refuge.'

'Oh, that is just delicious!' Lily gleams.

We're still going over the details when we hear a door slam from beyond the corridor outside. Everyone sits to attention.

'That's weird. I'm sure the other group cancelled their session today,' Marie says, her face pinched. She stands up and moves to the door.

'Wait,' I say. 'I'll come with you.'

We all go, rising as one. There's safety in numbers. Each of us is more spooked than we'd admit out loud. We follow Marie out, past the empty room where the other groups usually meet, the twelve-step groups and the refugee support group. Then we continue into the main area of the church. It's dark and empty.

'Could it have been the priest?' Terri whispers.

'No,' Marie says. She checks her watch. 'He's usually at the soup kitchen down the block at this time. Besides, why would he be sneaking around in the dark?'

Marie finds a light switch and turns it on. There's a collective exhalation as we can all see again. The place appears to be empty. But even from this distance, Marie notices that the fire door used by all the groups that meet here hasn't been closed properly.

'This door shouldn't be open,' she says, pulling it closed. 'Someone's been in here.'

'Do you think they've been listening in?' Lily looks alarmed.

That thought is the first to cross my mind too, but I can't let everyone panic. If we panic, we lose control.

'It's probably just coincidence,' I say. 'Probably someone from the other group didn't get the message it was cancelled.' I try to placate them but I'm not even convincing myself.

I think back to the flowers that Harry sent me. To the fact that he knew about the lease on his penthouse.

Has he been watching me all this time?

Is he watching me now?

Chapter 47

I haven't told Priya about my plan to meet the catfisher. And I certainly haven't told her how excited it makes me. I felt almost calm after Marie and I dealt with Frankie at her apartment. Calm and relieved. Fuck the beta blockers, turns out you just need to accidentally murder a bad man to reset your emotions.

Sadly, it didn't last long. And Harry's treatment of Rachel got me more riled up than ever. But my focus on the catfisher is definitely helping.

I used my Lisa profile to snare this man. Lisa is a bit more outgoing than Alison. If I really want to bait a violent woman-hater that's exactly what I need to be. Confident and assertive. I can't afford for him to feel anything gentle towards me. I need this guy's hate. And, given his track record with women, I know it won't be hard.

I'm leaving Manhattan for this one. The bar Terri met him in was in Queens and as it happens the creep suggests the very same one. (It's almost as though men follow predictable patterns. They must have the same playbook.) So I head up north in a cab, blonde wig in situ. There's a bad smell in the taxi – has the driver been eating in here?

It's rank. I open a window and he eyes me through the mirror. 'Smells a bit in here,' I say unapologetically. 'Like fast food.'

'Lady, if you don't like it . . .'

'Can we just drive, please?' I say. I notice his eyes fix on me for a few seconds longer. Then I remember what Priya said. Can I really smell it? Is it like some kind of hallucination? Some awful throwback? The idea that my brain is shifting from states of reality to states of fiction makes me feel woozy.

We pull up outside the bar and I get out, paying with my phone. I take in a big breath of air and am overwhelmed by the smell again. Fucking hell. It's following me.

As I look across the road at the bar I notice the neon-lit sign, Tony's Whiskey Bar . It's as bright as can be. I cross the road, the cars whizzing by. I feel as though I've turned the volume up in my ears, everything is so loud. I walk through the door and it's as though I can hear the electronics in the signage buzzing. It shakes my skull, and it takes a while for it to leave my ears.

Terri described the man to me in detail. She won't, can't forget the sight or smell of him. I arranged to meet him in the same way Terri did. Now I just need to follow the rule book – by taking a seat, being stood up, then being attacked on my way out.

But, in my case, I'm fully expecting this to happen. I'm prepared to deal with it.

I order a drink, then gingerly sit at a table, trying not to touch the sticky surface. I wonder how long to give him before I walk out, and realise I have to stay at least half an hour to make it look real. I imagine him watching me now; that's clearly part of his M.O. I wonder where he is waiting. Is he here in this room or is he in the bathroom itself? Or maybe the cleaning cupboard? Terri said he was adamant they met at this bar the first time around, and he was ridiculously keen that we had to meet here too. He must know this place like the back of his hand.

I actually wonder if he's working in cahoots with someone who works here. There's the barman polishing glasses by the bar. He keeps glancing at me. Maybe he'll be lining up to get in on the action?

I give it twenty-six minutes. By that point I'm sufficiently bored and, to anyone watching, I have clearly been stood up. As expected. I stand and follow the signs down a side corridor to the bathroom. There's a door to what I'm guessing is a back alley towards the end. I have my bag over my shoulder and my spidey senses are on high alert. I walk past the bathroom and pause, for a moment debating how armed I should be when I go in. But then, suddenly a door on the other side of the corridor opens and I'm grabbed by my neck, a hand over my mouth.

I'm thrown into the room and the door locks behind me. And then I see him. I am slumped on the floor and he towers in front of me, making it crystal clear that he's in control. He sneers down at me. His certainty that he has the upper hand has clearly affected every muscle in his face, tightening them like guitar strings. For the briefest of moments I feel a frisson of fear inside my stomach, but it is swiftly replaced by sheer fury.

I tamp it down. I play the game. I plead with him desperately.

'What do you want? Please don't hurt me.'

I don't want to alert him to what I'm about to do. To the fact that I knew that this was coming – even though the way he threw me so quickly to the floor has rather hurt my hip.

He just grins, his face contorting even further. There aren't many people who look worse when they smile but this dude has mastered it. He jumps on top of me and I struggle, one arm trying to push him off, the poor defenceless woman. The other frantically feeling around in my pocket – which is hard to get to because his weight is keeping me from moving. I pull the material hard from underneath my hips, freeing my pocket. In one move, I pull out the syringe and plunge it into his neck.

He lets out a yelp, but it doesn't incapacitate him quickly enough. He knows what I've done and he's angry as hell. He puts his hands around my throat, both of them, holding me there, squeezing hard. My breath is stuck somewhere between my mouth and my lungs, and I can't get any more oxygen inside of me. I feel my eyes widening, the only things I can possibly move. My chest is heavy; he is like a boulder on top of me. And I start to panic.

Why hasn't he passed out yet?

He grasps my neck more tightly and I feel myself losing consciousness. I am in and out of the room. I open my eyes, trying to maintain a focus, but then I go again. And I am in the kitchen. And I can smell our paltry dinner frying in a pan on the stove. I can taste it in my mouth. I see him, flinching away from me in pain, his hands covering his face. That man who ruined my life. I see my mum, a tangle of limbs on the floor. Then I see her back on the bed, her hands flailing around her as she struggles to breathe, feebly slapping at his arms. Then I'm back in the room, and the dirty catfisher suddenly slumps, his hands releasing the pressure from my neck. I gasp, bringing oxygen back into my lungs, feeling returning to my head, and I manage to roll sideways from underneath him.

I sit up a little and look at him. He's out for the count. This guy isn't just a con man. This guy is a rapist and a murderer. He has to be. If he hasn't managed it yet, then he's certainly going to try again. I could see the hatred. I could see the expectancy of raping me. I could feel his dick against my body, pushed hard into me, even while he was strangling me.

I stand up and look down at him.

Pathetic cunt. I pick up my bag and remove the knife from it. I straddle him.

'Oh, you were really hoping for a scene like this weren't you,' I say. 'Shame you're not awake to see it.'

I think about waiting for him to come around a bit, so he can experience his own death – otherwise I'm just putting him down gently, like a pet dog. But the bar has people in and time is not on my side. Fuck it. I might be giving him the easy way out, but at least he won't be able to hurt anyone else.

For a moment, I think about how else I can shame him. I undo his belt, unzip his fly and let his now flaccid dick flop out, all stumpy and grey. Gross. I leave it there, and place his hand on top of it, wrapping his fingers around it while they still have heat. I chuckle at my little scene. But it needs something else now.

I take my knife high above my head, and I pound it into his neck. His blood spatters all over me.

All I have to do now is get the hell out of here.

I take off my top and replace it with the one I've packed in my bag, then I unlock the door and walk as casually as I can out the back door and into the alleyway. Then, standing underneath a street light, I take out my compact and a few cotton pads, and carefully remove his blood from my face.

Suddenly I feel more alive than ever.
Recalibrated.
Released.
Normal.

Chapter 48

If anything that was a rehearsal. Preparations for the main event. But my God, do I feel good. It's as though I'm purging history. Resetting it. Redressing the balance.

But there's one act that needs to be complete before that can ever be addressed fully. It's my therapy. Not Priya's recommended type of therapy, but I know my own mind, and I know what I need.

I arranged to meet Harry as me again – as Sally this time. After all, he's going to be hard pushed to say no to my little request for a favour. There's that little matter of the footage I shot in the rooftop restaurant last week.

He's sitting in the corner of a quiet café that I suggested. It's a dingy little place that I knew he would hate. Making him feel out of place and on the back foot is, of course, helpful.

I have dressed as I would always dress. Bright, stylish, a multitude of patterns. But I do not feel out of my depth here because I grew up haunting cafés like this. Harry, meanwhile, has tried to dress for the occasion – and if there's one man who simply can't carry off grunge it's Harry. He's too. . . clean-cut.

I can't deny, though, he is simply beautiful. I guess if you had to choose a pastime, and you had the looks and the charm, why not become a con man? You're more likely to succeed in conning women than most other men. Maybe he just wanted to be at the top of his game. Well he's not going to stay there. I'm going to make sure of that.

'Harry,' I say as I slide into the seat opposite him. 'She survived. Rachel, I mean. I'm assuming there could be a few corpses lying around as a result of your little chemistry expeditions.'

He leans forward, placing the tips of his fingers on the table between us. 'You know I never intended—'

'Sweet Harry, you intended to cause harm, however you look at it. And you know, GBH, well, if it goes wrong, it's murder.'

'But, as you say, she's alive, so . . .' His eyes pierce into my own and we hold them on each other in a battle of wills.

A waitress walks over. 'Can I take your order?'

'Two coffees, black please,' I say, ordering for him. She scribbles it on her pad and walks away, leaving us to talk.

'I have footage,' I say, not taking my eyes off him.

'And what's it going to prove? That I put something in her drink – it could have been sugar.'

'Into Champagne? She went to hospital. She had blood tests. The things in her system are on record. And I have footage, so, really, sweetie, you're one hundred per cent in the shit.'

He leans back, leaving his arm lying stretched out across the seat next to him. This is his nonchalant look. But I know, deep down, he's bricking it. His fingers start tapping on the table.

'So, to keep me on side,' I say, 'I need you to do something for me.'

He laughs, his eyes sparkling and his white teeth beaming out from between his lips. Those lips . . . those plump, kissable lips . . . I dig my nail into my palm to stop myself fantasising about him. Part of me wants to give myself over to him. I wonder if this is something I've inherited from seeing my mum treated so badly over the years. This man is a monster, just like all the rest. Other than his looks, there are no redeeming features in Harry. He's shown his true colours. Yet I can't help but yearn for him.

In a funny way, my burning desire to feel those lips glide across my naked flesh for him makes me hate him even more. I guess seeing fucked-up relationships as a kid has created some kind of masochistic drive in me.

'Go on then,' he says cautiously. 'Tell me what you want.'

Those words dance in my head and my breath catches involuntarily. He said that to me in bed on our second date. He must remember it. He smirks, eyes still holding mine. And he knows what happened not long after I told him what I wanted.

I clear my throat and I am irritated with myself for letting him catch me off guard.

'I need you to come to London with me,' I say. 'This weekend.'

'Oh, Sally, if you wanted a dirty weekend you should have just said. You know I'd happily oblige.'

I ignore him. 'I want you to come to London with me and do your thing. The things you've obviously had so much practice at.'

'What, charming women?' The waitress brings our drinks

over and Harry grins at her. Her cheeks flush slightly. I hate how he fucking knows he can turn it on any time.

'I want you to charm a man. Then I want you to drug him.'

'Not part of my repertoire I'm afraid.'

'It is now,' I say. 'Because otherwise . . .'

'Why can't you do it? You seem to be pretty good at dealing with men yourself.'

He disarms me again. Does he know about Some Women? Does he know what I've been doing? I explain: 'I can't do this one on my own. We have history, me and the guy.'

'Aw, what happened? Did he make you come a thousand ways and then steal your money?'

'No,' I say. 'He killed my mother.'

He looks down. There's something about the mention of my mother that makes him think twice. That makes him drop the front, if only for a moment. He looks back up at me. 'I'm sorry.'

'Whatever,' I say, pouring sugar into my coffee. I need as much buzz as I can get. 'It's done, and you're going to help me make it right.'

'It must have hit you hard. Being so young when your mom passed.'

'Don't pretend you care.'

But there is a different look in his eyes. He is reflecting. On his own mum perhaps. If indeed he really did lose her too. But I'm not wasting my time trying to counsel him. I've my own shit to deal with.

'I really did like you, you know. I'd already planned it before I realised.' I sip my coffee, saying nothing. 'Aren't you going to say anything?' he says.

'No,' I say, even though there's a warm feeling spreading

through my core like heroin. 'All I want is for you to track down the man with a burnt face. Drug him. And I'll do the rest.'

'And the rest is?'

'Shaming him. I'm going to shame him.' It's the truth. But it's not the whole truth.

Chapter 49

I handed the reins of Some Women over to Marie. She's in the best place I've ever seen her. A whole new outlook on life. Although her whole new outlook has also given her the ability to see inside my soul. She knows what I'm planning. She told me I didn't need Harry to carry out my task for me, and that if I was truly honest with myself, I'd see that. I told her that was bullshit – and I almost believed myself – then booked two seats on a flight to Heathrow with Harry's money.

I took the window seat, and Harry is sitting in the middle, next to a boy of about thirteen or fourteen who won't stop farting.

For every whiff of fart I make sure to look dramatically at Harry and tell him off in a firm whisper, like we're a long-married couple who deal with each other's bodily functions on a daily basis. I giggle to myself every time it happens, and Harry, for once, is lost for words.

We have about seven hours of our knees touching. Of our arms brushing against each other's. I can't work out if we're even-stevens yet, or if that's just some form of denial. I need to be near him. It's like a compulsion, and I feel strangely safe with him. It's not just that he is practically under contract with me. Although there is a certain comfort knowing that he has to do as I ask otherwise face the music – a cacophony of screaming inmates and banging jail cell doors. As much as he's a confident fucker on the outside, I can't see him surviving behind bars. Biscuits and gravy for dinner, a strictly limited wardrobe . . .

It's something deeper than that. We get each other, Harry and me, on a fundamental level.

Which is why I have to keep reminding myself that said contract doesn't just include this trip and his fun little mission. It includes not conning any more women. Period. I'm not one hundred per cent sure how I'm going to make sure he holds up that end of the bargain yet, but I'll figure out something.

He sits back with his headphones in, his eyes shut. So I read my book, *Madame Bovary*, a man's take on a woman's adventure. I like the character. Deeply flawed and deeply bored. Resonates. But it feels weird, written by a man. It's like Harry writing about my glorious revenge. Although saying that, I'm sure he'd enjoy ending that with my untimely death.

Reader: just because a woman decides she lacks a bit of excitement in her life doesn't mean she should end up unalived.

As we touch down and taxi to the terminal the sound of seatbelts unclicking and phones being turned back on makes us all sound like strange little insects taking part in some kind of confined dawn chorus. Harry stands to get his bag out of the overhead locker and drops his phone in the seat between me and the teenager he had to squeeze past to get out. It is face up. And then it lights up. I lean in. It's a dating app message.

Celeste: *Wednesday would be perfect* ♥

Celeste? He's still doing it. He's still arranging to meet more women. Bastard! How big a threat does he need to face before stopping? It's like an addiction.

My chest feels trampled on. How can he still be doing this? And I don't just mean thinking about conning women – but thinking about conning women while he's *with me*. I feel fury simmering in my blood but then remember, he doesn't know what my actual plan is yet. Just the half of it. If he did, he'd be on the next flight home. I'm still one step ahead.

Harry recovers his bag from the locker and quickly retrieves his phone from under my nose. We stand and wait in turn to leave the plane, neither talking about what I obviously just saw, my frustration levels rising as people stand in the middle of the aisle like some kind of human dam as they slowly remove their overhead bags. Eventually, we are moving.

We both thank the air hostess waving us all off at the open door and walk through the bridge into the terminal. There's no need for sunglasses here. And, as far as Harry's concerned, things are going to get even darker.

Chapter 50

We walk from the Tube to the hotel I've booked. Well, hotel is pushing it. But at the very least we get a bed for the night and some form of breakfast.

It's a whitish building in need of a lick of paint with a great big white-and-red sign saying *HOTEL* on it. Harry looks unsure as I walk up the steps and stand underneath the small red awning. 'You coming?'

He looks around him and follows me in. I can sense the distaste in his mouth as we walk in, greeted by an Axminster carpet, and mismatched furniture. (But not in a good way, we're talking Formica, darling.)

I can scoff – I'm allowed. I grew up round here. At least, I did until I was about eight. Then I was whisked away to the West End. See, my story is so ridiculously *My Fair Lady* I really should have been named Eliza.

I check us in and we climb a narrow staircase to the room. It's a double bed. Because I like a challenge. Playing on the edge of a cliff is always entertaining.

'I see what you did here,' Harry says as we walk in.

'Who says I want to fuck you,' I say. 'Besides, this is purely business. And I need to keep an eye on you.'

I put my bags down by the side of the bed, and he places his on the other side. He walks around the room, lifting the tired voile curtain up from the window and peeking outside, watching people walking by. The view is of a newsagent's, the Tube station and a vape shop. He stands, quietly, still unsure as to why he is here, what his role is going to be. Aside from spiking the drink of a murderer, of course.

'Cuppa?' I ask. My voice becoming more East End than it usually is. There's something about being here, in this part of town, that takes me back to my roots. Takes me back to my mum.

'If you've got a coffee?' he says, then he looks over at the little milks. 'I'll take it black.'

I fill up the crappy little plastic kettle and let it boil, pouring us both a drink into small plain white cups and saucers. I open two small milks for my tea and chuck in half a sugar. I hand Harry his black instant coffee. He takes a sip and practically heaves. Then he lies back on the bed, his feet up. Clearly trying to assert his position. It's pointless.

'So, you better brief me on our *business* then,' he says. 'I mean, I didn't think it would be a good idea to try and get any supplies through customs.'

'We're in my town now. I know how to get it. I'm not as sweet and innocent as you might imagine.'

He raises an eyebrow. 'Whatever made you think that's what I'd imagined?' He laughs.

'Well, you did try to con me.'

'No, Sally. I *did* con you.' He looks hard at me, as though challenging me.

'Whatever. At the end of the day, it's not how it starts that determines the winner, it's how it ends.'

He laughs mockingly. 'Go on then. Because I want to get the hell out of this dump as soon as possible.'

'My stepdad. He's your target.'

'Your stepdad? So why couldn't you deal with him?'

'Because the last time I saw him I chucked a pan of hot fat over him. Because he knows that there is no way I would ever go near him other than to . . .' I pause.

'Get revenge.'

'Precisely,' I say, shaking the memories from my head. I need to keep my cool. I can smell that smell again. Even though I've come to realise it's probably all in my head, I still open a window. It sticks and I have to push it hard and get it on a latch.

I explain the plan. He's to find Martin at the Royal Oak pub.

'I take it there's nothing royal about it,' Harry says.

'No,' I say. 'But he will be there. He's been going there since he came back.'

'Back from where?'

'Wherever the hell he disappeared to after he murdered my mum,' I say.

Harry sips his black coffee, clearly not enjoying it. He mulls over what I am asking him to do. 'And how will I know it's him?'

I pick my handbag up from the floor, unzip it, then open the inner pocket. I take out an old photo. 'It's an oldie this one, but you can't miss him,' I say.

'Jesus, Sally. When was this taken? It's like thirty years old or something. How am I supposed to recognise him from that?'

'Because there aren't many men frequenting the same pub

with burns all over their face,' I say. 'So you can't miss him. His face is badly scarred, mainly down one side. He lost a bit of hair that's never grown back. His hair is a gingery blonde and grey. And balding. Except he refuses to shave it, so he just looks like a tit.'

'Is that what's under your tattoo?' he asks, his voice softening. 'A burn?'

'Splashback, yes. But what's on my skin isn't important.'

He sighs. 'OK, so what? I spike his drink and then what?'

'No, you spike his drink and get him back home.'

'How the fuck am I gonna get away with that?'

I roll my eyes. 'You get away with it with women. Women who have become so accustomed to the fact that there are abusive men and date-rape drugs everywhere. Women who are constantly on high alert, knowing it could happen to them. And yet you still manage to do it. Some arrogant bastard who thinks he can't be touched? That'll be a doddle. Some old fucker with a drink problem isn't going to think for one second you're in the game of spiking him.'

'Except I am.'

'Except you are. And you're bloody good at it. I should know.' I feel a wave of disappointment rise up in me. I left London because of my stepdad. I started a new life. Then Harry rocks up and reminds me that you can't outrun bad men. They infect every city or town or village. Make it their hunting ground. And there's always one just around the corner . . . 'So you need to charm him like you charmed me.'

'What, is he? I don't swing that way.'

'No. Listen, Harry, it's not hard. Charm him like a mate. He can't have many of them. He'll welcome you with open arms. Especially if you get the rounds in. Which also, incidentally, gives you the opportunity to pop something in his drink. But like I need to tell you that. Fuck's sake, Harry, I thought you were a pro at this.'

'OK. So why? What's the endgame here?'

'He has some stuff of mine. I need to get it back.' This is a lie of course. But what's the harm in a little white lie? Harry tells them daily.

My plan is much grander than this. But Harry doesn't need to know that yet, because if all goes well, the only person who's going to be implicated is him.

Harry looks at the time on his phone. 'I take it this is going to happen tomorrow. I've hardly got enough time to find what I'll need.'

'Don't worry about that, I told you: I'll get the GHB, or whatever's on offer tomorrow daytime. You'll stay here.' He glances at the door. 'Yeah,' I say. 'Old-school. I can lock you in while I nip out. You can watch *EastEnders* or something.'

'What?'

'Ha, nothing,' I say.

I open my bag and remove the duty-free vodka I bought. 'Fancy a top-up? Otherwise this evening is going to get very boring.'

Chapter 51

I pour us another vodka. The bottle is more than half empty now, and my brain is starting to relax a little. I need to be on the ball for tomorrow, but in order to do that, I also need to keep the shakes at bay.

They've been coming for me lately. It's not a fact I've shared with Priya. She's been on my case about booze long enough.

'So are you going to tell me why then?' I say, necking another vodka from the coffee cup.

'Why what?'

'Why a man, apparently as rich as you are, feels the need to con women. I mean, bit extreme. Can't you bet on the horses or something instead?'

Harry sighs, and necks what's left in his cup. I pour us another, the sound of the bottle glugging filling my chest with glee. 'My parents divorced,' he says.

'Boo hoo! Happens to most.'

'Are you going to let me finish? My parents divorced and my dad played dirty. My mom ended up with very little, so she had to find her own ways and means of surviving.'

'Such as?'

'Mainly through finding rich men, getting them to fall for her, and then rinsing them. I was kind of an accessory to it. I had a script, a sad story to tell. They would fall for us both, take us both in, and we'd be able to continue living the life that we were already accustomed to, before my dad elbowed us out of it, that is. So, I became good at it, and when she died, I had to survive.'

'You couldn't just get a job like normal people?'

'I thought it was a job. That's what she always taught me. It was pretty much all I knew. And before that, well, my dad really did work in advertising. Scamming people out of money is in the blood.'

I let out a laugh, and it almost feels as though we are back on one of our dates, opening up to one another.

'Doesn't explain why you're conning women,' I say. 'I mean, if it was your dad who was the villain of the piece, then how the hell have you ended up having such disdain for women?'

'I can't get away from the fact that I'm my father's son as well as my mother's.'

'That's not an excuse,' I say. 'I lost my mum, had an abusive stepdad. I still went to uni.' I don't tell him I didn't finish. 'I still found the wherewithal to move continents and start a new life. You had choices, Harry. You're just choosing to pretend otherwise.'

'OK, OK. Look, I'm sorry for what I did. That's what you're aiming for, right? To get me to apologise?'

'No point unless you mean it. No point unless you stop fucking doing it.' I feel wounded. It's as though I need him to stop doing it for *me*. *I* want to be the reason he stops. What does that make me? One of those women who thinks they can change the 'bad boy'. God, I hate myself sometimes.

'I do mean it, though,' Harry pleads. 'And you're right, I don't know if I can stop doing it. But I'm sorry I did it to you. You were different.'

'Oh please. You don't think I've heard that line before?' I'm immediately defensive but part of me wants to believe it.

He sighs. 'What do you want me to say? I'm a bad guy. I really liked you. But I couldn't get into a serious relationship. Never have. Never will. It's a pact I've made. To myself.'

For some reason those last words hit me harder than anything he's said. You always think you could be the one, don't you? We all talk about it, we all know it's bullshit, but there's still a nugget of hope inside of us. A little narcissistic seed that makes us believe that it might just happen. We might just be the one.

I want to be the one. And then I want to reject him.

'And I suppose your brother never existed?' I ask.

'Nope. Made him up. Only child.'

I feel as connected to him now as I did before he conned me. We are similar – our awful pasts make us similar. We just have different endgames. I'm fighting for good; he's just fighting for himself. At least, that's how I spin it to myself. I've been enjoying putting an end to this motley collection of vile men, sure, but the outcome of my actions is always beneficial to society. Taking a bad guy off the streets. Debilitating him. Disarming him. We might have been born of chaotic parenting, we might be full of rage, but that's where it ends. We're like yin and yang. Like Spider-Woman and the Green Goblin.

I pour us some more vodka. We might as well finish it. It's not as though drug dealers are early risers – I can track down what we need after lunch. It's hardly going to be difficult round here.

'So how come, if this guy killed your mom, he never went to jail?' Harry ventures.

I scoff. 'She was a single mum with a history of drink and drug taking. She wasn't important. I don't think the cops tried all that hard.'

'But if he was your stepdad, and then he disappeared? That's suspicious as hell. Besides, you saw it happen, didn't you?'

'I had a lot of stepdads. Anyway, I was a kid. A traumatised kid.' I realise the defensive way I am explaining this to him is precisely the way I should be talking to myself – instead of blaming myself for all the things I thought I should have done growing up. 'After seeing all that violence, I refused to speak.'

'Why?'

'Why? Jesus fucking Christ, I don't know. It wasn't a conscious decision. I just stopped speaking. They shoved me in a kids' psych unit for a while. Apparently they investigated, but couldn't find anything. Of course his fingerprints were all over our house, because he bloody lived there – on and off. And I think that's what got him off to be honest. The fact that he was a consistently transient feature in our lives – and consistently violent. Because there were other men. I don't know if they were boyfriends, or if they were means to an end, but the neighbours saw different people coming and going, so they weren't prioritising Martin. And without me speaking, they had no witness. So they decided, for a while anyway, that it was me. Locked me up in that psych ward for a couple of years.'

'What was you?'

'That I killed her.' I swallow hard, desperate to knock any welling tears away.

'But how could anyone think that? You were so young.'

'I was the only person there. My fingerprints were on the knife, because I pulled it out of her. I thought I was helping her.'

'Oh, Sally.' He reaches for my hand but I pull it away.

'You must be furious,' he adds, more coldly, clearly aggrieved at my rejection.

'You think?'

The vodka bottle is nearly empty and I decide I need to close my eyes. He's riled me, which is probably a good thing, seeing as how I have to sleep next to him in this tiny excuse for a double bed. I find a spare blanket in the wardrobe and throw it at him. 'Here, you sleep on top of the duvet with this; I'll sleep under it.'

He laughs.

'What's so fucking funny?' I snap.

'You're scared of being close to me,' he says. He unbuttons his trousers and steps out of them, all the while keeping his gaze locked on mine.

I immediately realise that my body wants something my mind wished it didn't. But I refuse to be taken in by him again. I think of Some Women. I'm here for them as much as I am for me.

'I can't believe, after what I've just told you, that you've the fucking audacity to move straight on to sex.'

'Face it, we're the same.'

I shake my head. 'You men'll try anything, won't you.' I climb into bed under the duvet still dressed in my clothes, while he strips down to his underwear. I can't bear to admit he's right, but I can't risk having sex with him again. Not after everything.

He gets under the blanket, the duvet separating our

skin, but the heat of his body penetrates the thin layers. He switches off the light and lays his head on the pillow next to mine. I can feel his breath on the back of my neck and its unbearable. He leans closer and whispers to me, 'You're not like the others. I'm sorry.' I ignore what he's said and squeeze my eyes shut tighter. I can hear his heart beating, almost feel it in my back. It's not relaxed. If anything, it's speeding up.

He wants me too.

I take a deep breath and try to will myself to sleep.

Chapter 52

It was Boxing Day night. I was eight years old.

I always made the most of Christmas. We never had much, but she tried, my mum. To be honest, I'd have much rather sat and had a nice Christmas dinner with her – fish finger sandwiches, whatever, just some time where I could sit with her, wearing a party hat, grumbling about the Queen's speech, desperate for it to end so we could watch *EastEnders*. My mum telling me off for being 'unpatriotic'.

I imagine that's what she'd say, anyway. I have these fantasies, you see, about how things could have been. I sometimes forget that they're not real; I've relived them so many times.

Christmas Day 2004 was nothing like the fantasy. And on Boxing Day, things went from bad to worse.

I hated him. He made me call him 'dad', but he wasn't. He'd brag about fights with snooker cues, breaking them into two, 'carving up' some fella's face. All part of a normal night out for him. He would smile at me when he said it, his cracked teeth turning his smile into a sneer.

I don't know how she ended up with men like him.

He wasn't the first – but he was the worst, and he was, of course, the last.

She always said I should make myself scarce when he was around, entertain myself, hang out with my mates. She did her best, trying to protect me from him. But she couldn't do it all the time. To protect herself, she used cheap vodka. It cushioned the bruises and the sickening emotional blows he chucked at her. I hated it when she drank, but at least she smiled for longer. Before she blacked out, that is.

Once, I tried to stand up to him. He laughed it off, holding me at arm's length. I must've looked like something off of *Scooby-Doo*. I was furious. Raging. And that night he came to my room, and he hit me so hard I was off school for over a week. We couldn't risk them finding out, because if they found out, he'd be even more angry. And he'd do it again.

So that Boxing Day, I did as my mum suggested and I went out. Knocked on my friend Holly's door.

Their house was decorated with the full works: Christmas tree, tinsel, snow globes and fairy lights everywhere. A far cry from our house. All we had was a sparsely decorated fibre-optic monstrosity that was supposed to be a tree. They offered me a warm mince pie, which I devoured in mere seconds. I think that was when Holly's mum realised I was hungry, because she plated me up some leftovers – a bit of cold turkey and a few roast potatoes. I ate them on the sofa while Holly picked at chocolates. *The Royle Family* sitcom was on TV and Holly's mum and dad sat laughing while drinking Baileys liqueur.

But soon it was time to go. Time for Holly to get in her pyjamas and settle for the night.

So, I said my goodbyes and walked back out into the night, traipsing around the park, stalling for time. But that

Boxing Day was particularly cold, and I worried about my mum. I hated leaving her alone with him. And I hated being in the house, too.

Sometimes, I didn't want to be anywhere.

I got to the front door and the lights were on but the curtains were open. There was nobody in the living room, but I could hear shouting and crashing. I scrabbled frantically to get my key in the lock as the voices got louder. Something smashed. At last the key scraped through the lock and I pushed the door open, flying through the hallway and into the kitchen.

She was already on the floor, blood everywhere. She was clutching her stomach where a knife was sticking out. And he was standing over her. I went to scream but he grabbed me and we struggled and I couldn't get a sound out. I couldn't make a noise.

He kept telling me if I knew what was good for me I'd shut up. But I looked at her, slumped, in her dressing gown, blood from her guts seeping out, the puddle getting bigger. She was holding the wound, her hands sticky and red, but she was fading. I grabbed my phone from my pocket to call 999 and he came at me again, snatching the phone from me and throwing it out the back door.

The whole place stank of fried, burning food, and I looked to my left and there was a pan on the hob, and the hob was still on. It was spitting. She was cooking for him. I knew she would be because he always demanded food when he got back from the pub. He was blind drunk. He was wearing that horrible, cheap black leather jacket that looked like plastic. He loved that jacket. He spent our money on it. I remember looking at it, repulsed. But then I saw her go. Like, just go. One minute there was a glimpse of her;

the next . . . gone. I screamed and he lunged at me again, pushing me against the kitchen workbench and trying to stick his hand over my mouth. I reached to the side and picked up the pan and hurled it at him. Burning-hot fat and bacon and charred bits of meat splattered across his face. I immediately felt pain on my collarbone. I'd sprayed myself with it too. But I couldn't look; I couldn't take my eyes off him. He was standing there, yowling like an animal, hands over his face. I just stood, paralysed.

He ran to the sink, and he put the tap on so fast it was splashing everywhere. He stuck his face in it and I could almost hear his skin sizzling.

Then he left. He ran out the door.

And the next thing I remember is the loud pummelling at the back door and window. It was so, *so* loud. I opened my eyes and I had my mum's arm wrapped around me but I couldn't move it. She felt cold and, when I wriggled around trying to escape, I could see her eyes were staring with such big pupils it looked as though you could see into her mind. But there was nothing there. She wasn't there. It was like seeing a monster. It was no longer my mum.

I began screaming. No words just screaming. Screaming. Screaming.

The glass shattered at the door. Loud, heavy thuds. And I was wriggling and screaming and I couldn't move, then the door burst open and there were people everywhere, some in uniform; others were familiar – a neighbour, I think. She began wailing and I wanted her to just stop. To shut up.

It took them a long time to free me from my mum's death hug. They couldn't take her arm away completely – they could only create enough room that I could wriggle out.

They assumed I must have crawled in moments after her death, when she was still warm and pliable.

They took photos of me as I stood there, in our kitchen, burning smells, fat, and weird, awful smells too. I could feel wet patches in my clothes, blood and fluids soaked through my T-shirt and jeans, and blood matted into my hair.

I don't remember all of it exactly, but I read the news reports. I found them online, years later. The headlines were devastating:

Girl lies with dead mum like cub in wild

A cub unable to leave its dead mother. Which was true – because I had nothing else. Nowhere to go. No family outside of her. My mother was my everything.

And Martin, my stepdad, my evil, grotesque stepdad – he'd long gone. He was never on the tenancy. He never married her. The estate we lived on was so transient nobody really took any notice.

Nobody followed up about him.

I was in so much shock I didn't speak for months. Completely catatonic. As rigid as she was. But even when I started to get better, nothing of any sense came out of me.

And the only conclusion they could come to was that I had done it. I had killed my beautiful mum.

Chapter 53

I hand Harry the GHB.

'Where did you get it?' he asks, slipping the baggie into his jeans pocket.

'I know this place.' I shrug. 'So, you know what you're doing? You've got the address?'

He taps his other pocket. 'Yep. Businessman from America, landing in a part of London I wasn't expecting to. Desperately trying to fit in. Letting them fleece me for free drinks because I'm a bit scared of them.'

'Excellent,' I say. 'This absolutely cannot go wrong, OK? This goes wrong, that film's going to the cops.'

'I get it. Jesus. I know what I'm doing.'

'I know,' I say, eyeballing him.

I leave the hotel first, and find myself a base nearby. A pub not directly opposite the Royal Oak, Martin's favourite haunt, but one that's en route to the house.

My old house.

The bastard's so fucking arrogant, so fucking evil, that he moved back into the same street.

I didn't know that he had moved back into the area until recently. I had plucked up the courage to go back – to visit the scene of the crime. Face my demons, I guess. And guess who I saw in the local shop buying beer and cigarettes? I couldn't believe it.

That's when I bought the plane ticket – with the compensation money I got for all the trauma I went through, for being wrongly accused as a young girl. It was something my foster parents fought for and put in trust for me until I turned eighteen. I'm still not sure I thanked them properly for all they did for me. Setting me off onto a good track, getting me through school, into uni. But my anger turned everything on its head. It distracted me.

And Martin doesn't have a clue how much rage I've carried around with me for nearly two decades. But he's about to find out.

I walk into the Queen's Head and immediately feel at home with its old-school London pub vibes – all red patterned carpets and wallpaper, dark mahogany wood and brass fittings. There are a couple of old guys in here, sitting alone, and a group of women who look like this isn't going to be their final stop judging by the high heels and plush-looking satin they're wrapped up in.

I get myself a pint, enjoying the cool bubbles as they hit my mouth. I've missed beer. I rarely drink it in New York. I needed to be someone else, someone far removed from the Sally who downed eight pints after lectures at uni and missed the next day. The Sally who enjoyed doing a few lines and getting into fights in bars. The Sally who was so haunted by her past that she just couldn't move forward.

I *needed* to move forward. I needed to be someone else.

I sit on a stool by the window where I have a good view of the road outside, and continue reading my book, wondering how long it's going to take. Some bloke offers me a drink and I decline, politely, pretending to be shy and awkward, and I stick my nose back into my book.

Eventually, I get a text.

Harry: *ETA approx ten minutes.*

My heart kicks into gear. This is it. I'm about to come face to face with him. With Martin. Although, by the time I get there, he'll be half asleep.

I see them wander past the pub and notice they're doing the classic drunken walk, with Harry trying to hold Martin up as they zigzag across the pavement. I give them a few minutes' grace then finish my drink, grab my coat and follow them back to the house.

I need to wait until he's out cold before I go in, so I circle the block a few times just as cold drops of rain start to trickle onto my head and into my eyes. But I don't care – inside I'm on fire. Finally, my phone lights up.

Harry: *He's out.*

I turn around and walk back to the house, pushing the front door open. The house is almost exactly the same layout as the one I grew up in. I feel dizzy with the memory of it and have to steady myself before I move further into the hallway.

Harry walks towards me. 'It's done. He's in there.' He points to the lounge.

I start to walk in and Harry grabs my arm. 'So what now? You're just taking some stuff? So why not just grab it and we'll leave together.'

'No. This is personal. I need to take some time here on my own. I won't be long.'

'But you're just—'

'Stop worrying. I just need to do this on my own.'

Harry's face drops. 'Jesus, Sally. You sure you don't want me with you?

'What difference would it make? And remind me again, why would I think it's a good idea to confide in you?'

'Fair play.'

'So can you just leave me to it?' I hand him the key to the hotel room. 'I'll meet you back there in about an hour.'

Harry takes the key, moves towards me as if to hug me, then backs off again. He turns, then closes the door. And suddenly, I am alone in this house. With him.

Chapter 54

It's all I can smell. Everywhere. Hanging in the air like fat. Suffocating me. My skin prickles with the memory of it as I place a foot inside the kitchen.

I stand still, taking it all in, and retrieve a pair of disposable gloves from my pocket. I'm glad I brought them. The place is a tip. Plastic bags on the side, empty beer cans, plates stacked high with the odd piece of cutlery between them. There's some terrible pale blue cord carpet tiles that are threadbare and spoiled with bits of food. I look at the hob, which sits in the same part of the kitchen as my mum's did. The same part of the kitchen where I grabbed the pan of burning fat and crunchy blackened bacon. I feel vomit rising up and swallow hard. Then I spit into the sink and turn on the tap, glugging water directly from it to cleanse my palate, washing away any trace of me.

I walk into the living room where Harry has left the TV still on, making colours flash and intermittently light up the room. A black and glass coffee table covered in ash and pooled beer sits in front of the TV, and there's a grotty old tabloid creased up between the arm and the cushion of the beige leather sofa.

I delay moving around to the front of the sofa for a moment to take the place in. To understand how he's been living all these years. But as I walk over to the fireplace I see a framed picture that stops me in my tracks. It's a photo of my mum and me. I run my fingers lightly over her image and feel as though my breath has been knocked out of me. I haven't seen this photo in years. We're smiling on it, standing in front of the water sprinkler in the back garden – literally just a few doors down from where I am now. I remember that day. It was a brief moment of calm, of fun and laughter. But that night was like all the others. He put a stop to it. And I hid under my duvet.

Jesus, why did he keep it? Is it some kind of trophy? The lives he's fucked up? Or is he so far in denial he genuinely believes we were once a happy family? Whatever his reason, he's revised my entire history and turned himself into this sad, bereaved man deserving of pity. Hideous.

I look away, keen to keep my wits about me – and conscious that they are fading in and out with all the ghostly memories of this place.

I take a breath then walk towards the sofa where Harry's left Martin unconscious. The sight of him almost winds me. As I look at his face, it seems to contort with rage and expand with laughter as the past plays out in front of my eyes.

He is on his side, breathing heavily and slowly. He's bloated from years of drinking too heavily, stretching his T-shirt tight around his back.

I roll him onto his back, his belly eventually following the rest of him, and his mouth gapes open, making him snore loudly, albeit inconsistently. The sound blankets me in a familiar feeling of comfort – the only time I felt safe was when he was out for the count.

His facial scarring is still very apparent, hard and shiny, even in the dimmed light. I'm sure he played the victim card on that one too.

I grab my bag from the floor next to the sofa and take out the bottle of vodka I brought with me. It's a cheap, non-brand bottle from the offie. I need it to look as though he bought it himself. His mouth still open, I hold the bottle high above his head and theatrically pour the vodka into it, seeing how far away from his mouth I can direct the flow.

It lands mostly inside his horrible mouth and he splutters on it but he can't move. He can't get up or swallow or help himself in any way. He is spluttering and inhaling it further and deeper into his lungs. I watch in awe, wishing only that I could have seen him consciously panic. But I need him to go, and I can't take any chances. This was the only way.

If the police do happen to dig a bit further though, *I* wasn't the one seen leaving the pub with him. *I* wasn't the one who spiked his drink. *I* wasn't the one operating without gloves thinking that the worst that could happen to this wank-stain of a man is that he'd wake up with a bad head and a load of shit missing from his house.

The noises continue, and I notice something coming out of his mouth. Vomit perhaps? It seeps out and runs slowly down the side of his face, coating him in white liquid with bits in it. And yet still he inhales, spluttering and coughing because he isn't conscious enough to swallow it all down. His body starts convulsing a little, and more vomit runs from his mouth, but the damage is done. Eventually, the gasps slow and the chest stops moving.

He is gone. But the relief doesn't hit me yet.

I think about Ethan. About Georgia's dad. These vile, abusive men still walking around, still breathing. I know I've killed Martin. I know it. But it's no way near enough. I want people to see him in all his ugly glory. Stripped back to the monster he really is.

My gloves still on, I undo his fly and wrench his boxer shorts down, wincing at the sight of what lies beneath. I have to hold my breath and look away for a moment to compose myself.

And I thought working an admin role in real estate was far from glamorous. Jeez.

I tug his jeans down as far as I can under the heavy weight of him, and leave them loose around his ankles, one of which is resting up on the arm of the sofa. He looks a fucking sight, vomit seeping from the corner of his mouth, his tackle hanging out for the world to see, but this *still* doesn't tell the whole story.

I open my bag and pull out a full-head furry teddy mask and a small bathroom mirror. I feel like Mary Poppins with so many useful items stowed away in my little rucksack.

It's a bit of a struggle to get it over his head, but I manage to manoeuvre it just enough to waggle it into place.

Then I position the mirror on the carpet near to where his arm has flopped down, as though he dropped it with his last breath.

I stand back, appraising my work, and giggle. Something akin to jubilation balloons in me. These violent men are just *so* clumsy, aren't they?

I pick up my now empty rucksack and walk back to the other side of the living room where the photo is. I scoop it up and place it in my bag. Then I turn off the TV, turn out the lights and pull open the curtains, setting the stage for his gruesome discovery once the morning light hits.

Just imagine the fun the sub-editors are going to have with this one down the local paper.

I giggle again.

He stole my childhood and silenced me for years. But I know eight-year-old Sally would have approved that this is how he'll be remembered.

It's about time she had the last laugh.

Chapter 55

The rain is coming down heavy by the time I leave the house and my flared jeans trail in the puddles despite the fact I'm wearing heeled boots. As much as my woollen coat is soaking up the relentless rain nothing can weigh me down after tonight.

He's gone. I've seen it with my own eyes. No more running.

I walk back into the hotel reception and up to the second floor where our room is. I knock at the door, but Harry doesn't answer so I push down on the handle. It opens. He hasn't locked it. He must be asleep.

I walk in and switch on the light. But there is nobody there. The bed is made, and his bag has gone. He's even washed up our two mugs.

Bastard!

I walk over to the bedside table and find a note folded in two.

When Sally fucked Harry

Does he know I did more than I said I was going to? Has he realised he's been implicated in a murder? He never wore gloves, didn't bother to disguise himself because he didn't think he needed to. After all, he was drugging someone – a thing he's done multiple times to multiple women – in a country, in a place, where he has zero connection. But now that man is dead. And if anyone's tied to it, it's Harry.

No doubt he's at Heathrow already, buying a ticket for the next flight out.

It's all too predictable, him running like this. But it's left me feeling shallow. I've just committed the most important murder in my life, and there's nobody here to celebrate with, nobody to clink glasses with, nobody to . . .

I look over at the empty bed, the blanket that he slept beneath last night. I wanted to fuck Harry. And not just in the way he thinks I have.

I have to admit it. And I hate myself for it. A huge weight has been lifted, but has anything else changed? How can I move on if these men keep holding me back? How can I move forward if stupid fucking feelings keep getting in the way?

Chapter 56

It's always a bonus having an empty seat next to you on a long flight. I'm glad he left early. Although he's going to feel stupid for allowing me to play him like a fucking fiddle this time.

I land back at JFK and grab a taxi, messaging him as we pull out of the airport. I tell him to meet me at his penthouse at 8 p.m. Friday night. Marie is moving back into her sister's, so I tell him I'll hand the keys back and then we're done. He's all paid up. And his career of conning women is well and truly over. It's time he put some proper graft in to earn his money. Maybe he can retrain and become a plumber. Or a dental assistant. Something he actually has to work for, anyway.

I race home for a quick shower before our next meeting of Some Women.

'Jesus, Sally, can't you just sit down for two minutes?' Priya is putting on her lipstick by the mirror near the door. 'You've literally just landed. Aren't you jet-lagged?'

'I'm pushing through it. If I don't, my sleep will go proper tits up.'

'Fine,' she says.

'You look nice anyway. Off to see Steve?'

'Yeah, and off to his mom's place later. There's a big Steve-related question I believe I'm going to need to answer tonight.'

'Oh. My. God. Seriously!?' I clap my hands together in genuine excitement. We've been talking about this for months. I know his family's a pain in the arse, but if all goes to plan, Priya will be over the moon. So will I. It's about bloody time to be honest.

'Yeah, well.' She slips her feet into a pair of heels that stand neatly on the floor. 'Don't bank on it yet.'

'I'll keep everything crossed for you.'

'OK. Love ya!'

'Laters!' I blow her a theatrical big kiss and she leaves the apartment full of anticipation. It's then that I realise I'm running late. Again. I squeeze the remaining water from my hair and chuck on a pair of jeans, white T-shirt, tailored dark green coat and brown heeled boots. The sun is starting to fade and the leaves are beginning to turn. This is my second autumn in New York. I never fully appreciated it first time around. But I know that New York is simply stunning this time of year and now, it feels like something really exciting is just around the corner. Change is coming – in me, in Priya, and in the women.

I leave the apartment just as my phone pings. It's a work email. Subject: *Disciplinary*.

I'm clearly about to get the sack for skipping work. But I had far more important things to do. And now, I've got my money back in my account, plus a bit of extra cash from cleaning out Harry's account too. Fuck David and his boring job. I couldn't care less.

I walk into the church with a peach iced tea and a half-wrapped, half-eaten bacon buttie in hand.

'Whoa, Sally Parker! What the hell is that?' Lily greets me, pointing incredulously at my sandwich. '*You* don't eat bacon.'

'Things change,' I say, taking another bite and realising just how much I missed smoky bacon. My mum didn't just make it for my awful stepdad. But I could never enjoy it after Boxing Day night. That was another thing he stole from me – but now I've got it back. I finish it off and lick my lips, savouring every last bit.

Rachel's back in the group. She's physically better, but I'm not convinced she's mentally strong enough yet. She's been staying at Lily's who's been giving her as much TLC as she can handle.

It feels like, as much as we've got to celebrate, as much as we've achieved so far, there's definitely unfinished business with Rachel.

And there's *definitely* unfinished business with Georgia's dad.

'I'm just going to do it myself,' Georgia says. 'I want to do it myself.'

'But it's too risky,' I say. 'Something happens to him at home, or in the church, you're one of the first people they'll be questioning.'

'Sally's right,' Marie says. 'They always question close family first. And if you don't have an alibi . . .'

'I don't care. I'll go to prison. I don't give a shit.' Georgia jumps up from her seat. 'I've had it.'

'Georgia, please,' Marie yells after her. But she's already stormed out of the room and slammed the door behind her.

'Oh God. What are we going to do?' Lily says.

'There's no stopping someone when they're that wound up,' I say, resigned. I know how she feels. I just don't believe she'll take the time to plan anything, to consider evidence or alibis. She's raging, and she's desperate.

Everyone's face is full of concern. For Georgia, for all of us. After all, there's the risk of her leading the police back to our group if she does something sloppy.

'We're so close,' I say. 'Marie's husband is dead, the catfisher's dead, we've got all our money back from Harry and from Shenika's husband. Ethan's been shamed out of his job.'

'Yeah,' Lily says, 'and the funny thing is, he hasn't popped up anywhere else, either. I mean, the agency world's pretty tight, but nobody's heard of him getting appointed anywhere. There's been no mention in *PR Month*'s "Movers and Shakers" column. Not a whisper.'

'Maybe he's left town,' Rachel says. 'Maybe he can't work in PR anymore.'

I watch her face as she says it and there's something I can't put my finger on. Did she just wink at me?

'Wait!' Shenika says. 'Did you all hear that?'

Everyone looks around them. 'What?'

'Shh!' she whispers. 'Listen.'

We sit in silence, straining to hear whatever it is that Shenika heard.

'Hear that?' she says.

'Footsteps,' Marie says. 'Yes.'

'Fuck,' Lily says. 'Someone really is watching us aren't they? Oh my God, we're gonna be in so much—'

'Shh!' I say.

We all listen silently a little longer, and we can just make out shuffling, and a door opening.

'It's got to be the same person as last time,' Terri whispers. 'Too much of a coincidence.'

My heart is pounding. It's Harry. I just know it. Is he one step ahead of me again? Is he planning on taking revenge for being compromised in London like that?

'Perhaps we should close the meeting early,' I say. 'In fact we definitely should.' I'm already picking up my bag and jacket, desperate to get outside and have a scout around.

'Let's leave the building together though,' Marie says. 'Strength in numbers and all that.'

Everyone gathers their things and we all walk anxiously into the main church area. Marie switches on the light so we can see our way through to the door.

'There's nobody here,' Shenika says. 'It could just be building noises. You know, like the creaks and shifts of a house?'

'What if it was just Georgia?' Lily asks hopefully. 'What if she was just hanging around. Wanting to come back in?'

'Let's just all get home,' I say, feeling increasingly paranoid. Ironic really – Lily's usually the one who panics, not me. 'We'll reconvene Friday.'

'I'll text a reminder out,' Marie says. 'We need to try and get Georgia back into the group. Stop her doing anything stupid.'

Everyone says their goodbyes and walks off in different directions.

'I'm afraid I can't walk with you tonight, Sal,' Marie says as we reach the corner. 'Me and Barb are off to burlesque class.'

'No way!' I say. 'Oh my God, that's just brilliant. Have you got a stage name?'

'Of course.'

'Well don't keep me in suspense.'

'Meet Nancy de'Vil.'

'Love it!' I say, hugging her. 'Have the best time.'

'Oh we will!'

I watch as Marie crosses the road and heads down the steps to the subway. I take my phone from my pocket to see if Harry's replied. He has.

Harry: *Fine. Friday at the Penthouse.*

It's on. I smile and place my phone back in my pocket. Then I set off towards home, turning left to cross 8th Avenue in a crowd of people. I can feel someone pressing behind me too close and shift away as the light changes and we cross as one. But someone is cutting into my space. I refuse to look around, and instead surge forward, trying hard to maintain a steady and confident stride. I break free of the crowd and dart up the pavement towards an alleyway that leads to my building, but the footsteps become louder and faster and my heart jumps up and down in my chest.

I turn around and, within a split second, hands are grasping my neck. My back is pushed hard forcing me into the alleyway and I'm winded, struggling to catch my breath.

My vision is blurring but one thing is clear in my sight.

A pastor's dog collar.

I scrabble at my throat, trying to pull away his hands.

I can't hear.

I can't see.

I can't breathe.

I feel it more than hear it. A scuffle. Something whipping through the air. A shout?

Then his hands unlock from my neck and I slump down the wall, gasping for breath. I cough, trying to get as much air as I can into my lungs, and then I see him on the ground next to me. From elsewhere, I hear a woman's voice.

'Sally? Sally, you OK?' I try to focus my vision and I realise I recognise her. It's Georgia.

I nod, still holding my neck, still trying to get more oxygen circulating around my body.

'It was him, in the church. Watching us,' Georgia says, scrambling to get something into a plastic bag. Is it a knife? Has she stabbed him? I glance back to my right and can see blood pooling out from under his body.

'He's dead, Sal. He's finally dead.'

She holds out her hand and I stand, grabbing the wall to steady myself. And then we run. And I'm flooded with déjà vu.

Chapter 57

I'm almost ready to leave for the group meeting – my last group meeting – when the door flies open at warp speed nearly knocking me sideways.

'Fucking hell, Priya. You trying to take me out?'

She practically falls in through the door, bottle of Champagne in hand. 'Get the flutes out, girl, we've got some celebrating to do.'

'You said yes then?'

'Course I fucking did.'

She pops the cork, letting Champagne bubbles shoot up over the rim of the bottle. 'Oops.' She laughs.

'You already had one?' I say, grabbing two Champagne glasses from the kitchen cupboard.

'Course I have. Had to pretend, didn't I?'

I leap towards her with a flute held out in front of me, catching as much overflowing Champagne as possible. I hand her the fizzing glass and take the bottle from her to fill up another one.

'So when's it going to be? How did they all take it?'

'Well, the funny thing was, they thought it was going to be hardest for me. And they let me go last. You know, like it's a big family meeting with a big family decision. So they all said their answer first. I guess they were trying to soften the blow for me.'

'And I take it they all said yes.'

'Of course. When it got to me, I let the tears come, played the dutiful partner, then I took a deep breath and said, *Yes. It's what he would have wanted.* And I cried, actual real tears. Fuck me, Sally, the relief felt so good. And his mom's like, *Well, that's that then. We'll inform the doctors. We'll do it right away.* So we all climbed in a couple of executive cars, headed down to see him, all solemn and everything. They knew already that we were having the meeting, they were prepared for us. And, well, given how rich they are, it's in the private wing of the hospital. So we walked into the room, and eventually the doctor came in, and she said, *Who wants to be here.* And I said, *I do.* But Steve's mom and sister left. They couldn't do it. His dad asked if I needed company and I sniffled and said, *No, I'm fine. I need to do this for me.* And one by one they left. And I held Steve's hand, in the same position it's been in for months, and then they did it. Switched the machine off. Fuck, it was weird, Sally. Watching him go. But oh my God, the relief.'

'And that's it then,' I say, taking a sip of the Champagne. 'He's gone?'

'Yep, we don't need to worry about that fucker waking up and ruining our lives anymore. He's gone. Here's to you running into us that night.' She clinks glasses with me.

'So can you stop being a royal pain in the arse and freaking out about everything now then?'

'Yep. I couldn't give a fuck if you go running at night in your pyjamas.' She laughs, and we clink glasses again. 'Oh my God, Sally. I've been having nightmares for months.

I kept thinking, *He'll wake up. He'll tell the police what happened.*'

'I know,' I say. 'It's been hell.'

We take a beat, finish the last of our Champagne.

'I'm so gonna miss you,' Priya says, her eyes welling.

We hug, and Priya spills Champagne down my top.

'Clumsy cow!' I say and she laughs. Great big laughs full of relief.

'Finally.' Priya throws her head back and exhales. 'Your horrible stepdad's gone; Steve's gone. We're free. And nobody's gonna open their eyes and land us in it.' Then she pauses, her mind appearing to wander elsewhere. 'I fucking hated him, Sally.'

A tear wobbles in the corner of Priya's eye. I hold her tightly.

'I know.'

'It's just weird, isn't it. Before that night, I spent every single day walking on eggshells. Waiting for him to do something even worse than the last time. Then after, we spent every single day waiting for him to wake up and fuck *our* lives up. I just can't believe it's over.'

We sit for a moment in silence. Then she looks up at me, giggling. 'I'm so glad you got chucked out of that bar that night, Sally. But I can't believe you're going.'

'I'll be back later though. And we've got breakfast tomorrow.'

Priya looks confused.

'You promised me you'd make your famous waffles, remember?' I say.

She smiles. 'Sure thing!'

* * *

'Look,' I say to the group as we all sit, glasses in hand, celebrating the completion of our work. 'I've got something to tell you.' I take a breath. 'I'm going to be leaving soon.'

'What?'

'No!'

'Sally, why?'

I can't work out who's said what as they're all speaking over each other, but I get the general vibe of disappointment.

'It's just time. New York's helped me to face something I needed to face. It's done its job. I just think it's time for a change – that's all.'

The room looks solemn. 'Oh, come on, don't be so miserable about it,' I say.

'But we've all got so close,' Terri says.

'Well, keep on coming back then. You don't need me.'

'I'm in!' Georgia says.

'Me too!' Lily adds.

'There you go then,' I say.

Rachel looks up. 'I've a friend from college. She's having some trouble with her boyfriend. I've already said I'll help her.'

There's something in Rachel's demeanour today. It's almost as if I'm meeting her for the first time. There's a sparkle in her eyes.

'Bring her to the group!' Shenika says and Rachel grins.

'Same time, same place next week then, ladies,' Marie says. And I feel as though I've handed over the baton. And it's in very good hands.

We say our goodbyes and I'm surprised at how emotional I feel.

'Are you crying, Sally Parker?' Marie says.

'Looks that way. I'm really going to miss you all.'

Marie lingers behind after everyone else has left. 'It won't be the same without you.'

'Ah course it won't.' I laugh. We hug, tightly. 'Partners in crime you and me,' I say.

'I know. I can't believe how much my life has changed since we met.'

'Same.' I smile.

Chapter 58

I leave Marie in the doorway to the church and jump in a cab. It drops me off outside Harry's penthouse building and I go up in the lift to drop off his keys and have one final moment with him. I can at least allow myself that. A fifth date so to speak. And then that's it.

I let myself in and walk towards the kitchen, still feeling a bit tipsy from the Champagne. I open the fridge and grab a bottle of one of Marie's Budweisers, opening it on the built-in bottle opener under the sideboard.

It's strange being in here with no Marie. It had started to feel like her new life belonged here, but it was just the stepping stone into it. I'm pleased she's back at her sister's with Sugar, a whole new wardrobe and a place at the local am-dram society just waiting for her. And she's looking for a new place too. A whole new start.

I take a swig of the beer and wander about the apartment. He's late. Just what I need when I've a big road trip to get on.

I walk into the main bedroom to take in the view of the Manhattan skyline one more time. Then I hear a knock at the door.

I walk past the mirror, shaking out my hair. This is precisely the reason that it has to be the last time. I'm far too bothered.

I go to the door and open it. He's standing there, a wrapped present in his hands. He passes it to me and kisses me on the cheek. I don't flinch; it feels natural. He walks into the penthouse – his penthouse – and I can feel myself melting. Losing all sense of rationality.

Just one last time. It's what I always told God when I discovered masturbation as a kid. It felt dirty and wrong and I promised and promised but I did it again and again. But dirty and wrong feels less powerful than this. Whatever this is. Is it love? A warped, fucked-up kind of love? I'm starting to wonder if I know myself at all. If I met another version of me at a support group, I'd probably give her a slap.

'There's beer in the fridge. From when Marie was here,' I say, sitting down on the sofa and placing the wrapped gift next to me along with my bag. I've no idea how he thinks he's going to win me over with a bottle of perfume or piece of jewellery. Although, it's a bit too big and a bit too heavy to be either.

He walks over to his own fridge, the one I've just given him permission to open.

'Marie?' he says.

'A friend of mine.'

'But why did she live here?'

'Why do you think, Harry? I don't think I've met a single woman who hasn't been fucked over by a bloke. It wasn't hard to find others.'

He opens a beer. 'So what? You were using this as some kind of refuge? I guess I can't criticise you for that.'

'No, not really.'

'And Rachel?'

'Fine. No thanks to you. As fine as can be anyway. It's not just the physical effects, you know.'

He hangs his head. 'I know. I'm sorry.'

'But you're still doing it?'

He looks at me. A look that neither confirms nor denies. We're on two different paths that, if they meet, can only cause friction. And no, I'm not talking frottage. It could never work. Never.

'Are you going to open it then?' He nods towards the present. I pick it up and place it on my knee, opening the plain silver wrapping paper to reveal a gift box.

I open it up and there's some kind of silver vase inside. I place my hands inside around it and pull it out.

It can't be.

'How did you get this?' I ask, my heart pounding, feeling both completely freaked out and comforted by what's inside.

The object is engraved.

Connie Parker. 1977–2004

It's my mother.

I pick the urn up and hold it in my arms. That bastard kept her. He had control of her even after her death. I feel like I might faint.

'I found it in the house. I took it. I was going to give it to you at the hotel, then I saw what you did to him.'

'What do you mean?'

'Jesus Christ, Sally. Don't pretend I'm stupid. I mean, you opened the curtains for the whole neighbourhood to see. I had to get out of there.'

'He deserved it.'

'But you implicated me.'

'You nearly killed my friend. You wiped me out. I mean, for fuck's sake, you could have killed *me*. You didn't give a shit.'

'But I did.' He looks me in the eye and I'm conflicted – angry and disgusted and wanting him all at once. He did this for me. He reunited me with my mum. I waver, wondering if I'm doing the right thing. But that's precisely why I need to do it. He knows how to crack me.

'This is no good,' I say. 'Whatever the fuck this is.' I wave my hand between the two of us, then look back at the urn. I hold it close to me. 'I never got to say goodbye to her. I was too ill. They kept me in that hospital for years. Like I was some kind of evil, callous kid who'd lost the plot.'

He sits next to me. 'We're the same, you know, in lots of ways.'

'No,' I say firmly. 'We're nothing like each other.'

Then he kisses me – taking us back to the beginning of the story. I kiss him back, feeling myself sinking into it. Wanting so much more. I know, if I let him, he will just keep going.

'And you're never going to stop,' I say, my hot breath in his ear. He moves his mouth back to mine.

'Neither are you,' he says, mouth pressed against mine, pulling me into him. I am caving, bit by bit, giving in to the one thing I want more than anything.

With an effort, I remember that I have a purpose – and it isn't falling in love. It's much bigger than that.

I push myself into his lap and allow him to thread his fingers through my hair against the back of my head. I find my bag at my hip and feel around until I find it between key rings and compacts and perfume bottles.

'No,' I whisper back to him, still kissing him. 'I'm *never* going to stop.'

I grasp it tightly in my fist, and then I plunge the steak knife into his neck. Directly into his carotid artery. Blood hits me instantly and he pulls away, holding his neck, his face contorting.

He pushes me away, staring at me, fear in his eyes. Real fear. God, this is the real him. I'm finally getting to meet him – no mask, no veil. I'm meeting the real him. For the first and last time.

He tries to stand and pull the knife out, but I guide his hand away and gently sit him back on the sofa. 'You don't want to do that,' I say, holding him as he slumps next to me. 'You only get to do this once. You need to do it well.'

He can barely speak, but he's trying. 'You. Stabbed—'

'I know,' I say. 'I'm sorry about that.' I hold him, stroking his arm. There's so much blood. His arm is slick with it. He begins panting rapidly. Little shallow puppy breaths.

I'm covered in his blood. I can feel it all over my face, trickling down onto my cheeks, my lips, and into my eyes from my forehead above. I lick the blood from my top lip, tasting metal and cocoa butter lip balm, and I scrunch my left eye shut to stop any more of his blood obscuring my vision. I wipe it clean with the back of my hand.

I'm glad I wore my new waterproof mascara today.

He holds the hilt of the knife in vain. I move both my hands to his neck, cupping his hand as it weakens its grip. 'There,' I say, applying pressure to the wound. 'That should help you hang on a little bit longer. I mean, we'll be lucky to get fifteen minutes out of it.'

This is without doubt the closest I have ever got to a man.

It's the closest I'll ever allow myself to get.

Eventually his breathing becomes slow, as if he's missing beats, and his eyes shut. There's a small raspy intake and then . . . nothing. Silence. Muscles heavy as lead.

I kiss his forehead gently. 'Goodbye, Harry,' I say.

Chapter 59

Priya's cooking her signature waffles while I fanny around on my iPad looking at photos of the campus I'll soon be studying at in Seattle – a place for a different kind of unfinished business.

As the smell of Priya's cooking comforts my nostrils I realise that this is probably the closest to 'home' I've ever been. I feel deeply sad, but I've got so much more to see and do.

I'm just clicking out of the university website and back into my home screen when a headline on the 'Top Stories' panel leaps out at me and I inhale sharply.

'What is it?' Priya says, placing a plate of warm waffles and cinnamon under my nose.

I direct her eyes to the headline.

**Award-Winning PR Director
Found Dead in Hudson**

Police recovered the body of a man from the Hudson Friday morning after a passer-by saw a human hand floating in the water and alerted authorities at around 7.30.

The hand had been amputated from the body, which divers discovered several hours later, 200 yards from where the hand was found. Both hands had been removed, but one is still missing.

The body has been identified as that of Ethan Taylor, a 39-year-old award-winning PR director who hasn't been seen since early last month.

Investigators say they are unable to determine the exact cause of death until a full autopsy takes place due to decomposition and damage from the busy waterway.

The city Medical Examiner's Office will officially determine the man's cause of death in due course.

'Oh my God!' Priya says. 'Isn't that the handsy guy from Lily's work?'

'Not anymore.' I laugh.

'Bit of a coincidence, don't you think?' she says, forking a mouthful of waffle, her appetite undeterred.

'Maybe.' I smile. I thought Rachel had been looking brighter of late.

I look up at Priya and she grins widely, then puts her plate down on the bench and hugs me tight. 'I'm going to really miss you, Sally Parker.'

'I'm gonna miss you too,' I say. And I mean it. It's funny, isn't it, that you go around desperately looking for the love of your life, jumping on dating apps, thinking it's got to be all about sex and romance. But in reality, you find the loves of your life in the form of other women. Women who have been where you have. Women who keep on keeping on.

Women who hold each other up.

'What will you do now?' I look around at the place one last time. We both grab a suitcase and head to the lifts.

'What, now I don't have to go to any more of Steve's miserable family gatherings? I don't know, chill the fuck out perhaps?' We both laugh. The lift doors sweep open. We ram the cases inside and are taken down to the lobby.

'He was a dangerous fucker,' I say, as we step into the sunshine. I'm parked just down the road. 'I mean, does it really not bother you that they'll never know what he did to you?'

'Ah fuck 'em. I've had to deal with his beatings, his put-downs. They weren't there for me. Let them mourn their imaginary son. At least we know you killed the real one.' It's a secret that's been hanging over us for nine long months. A secret that kept us tightly bonded. And I don't think it matters where in the world I am – nothing can break that bond. Not now Harry's gone.

'Anyway, you got everything?'

'Sure have!' I say, and I get into the car and turn the engine on, winding the window down on Priya's side. My mother's ashes are in the footwell next to me, and I can't wait to take her to see the Atlantic Ocean. We always dreamed about doing this together one day. Now, finally, we are.

I smile, and give Priya another wave. She's promised to check in on Some Women next week, offering her therapy services now she's no longer having to dodge justice. Whatever that means. Justice is never really justice in its truest sense, is it?

I turn the stereo on. 'White Boy' by Bikini Kill blares out and I smile. My mum loved that band. And, as I listen to the lyrics, I know I've got more to do. I need to honour her memory.

Because there's one pandemic that never made the news. And it's been raging since the dawn of time.

Epilogue: Three months later

Fairy lights are still wrapped around city-centre trees and a gigantic bauble made of a tangle of twinkly lights sits proudly in the middle of the shopping district. I've always found January particularly bleak, and, even though it isn't raining over Seattle today, the sky has been fifty shades of grey all afternoon. Now, with dusk hitting, the sparkle of the lights and glare of the shopfronts add some much-needed contrast against the almost-night sky.

There's always more magic to be found in darkness.

And I do like it here. I was able to transfer the two and a half years of biochemistry I'd done back in London to the university here. Two more semesters and I'll be finished. Maybe I'll do a postgrad. There's nothing to stop me. I'm free as a bird. It's the perfect tonic and a way to move forward.

I'm walking down the sidewalk away from campus after my last lecture of the day when I hear something smash. I pause and realise I'm standing next to a narrow alley, one of those narrow causeways that run along the backside of restaurants and shops, lined with huge skips and discarded cardboard boxes.

Then I hear it again. Glass, smashing against concrete.

But I can't see anything. And then I hear a shout, and shoes hitting the pavement, people running.

I feel frozen in place, standing right on the edge of the alley, consumed by a memory of my first night in New York. The night I met Priya.

I'm being manhandled out of the bar by a doorman, his grasp firm on my arm.

'Right. You've had enough. Time to go.'

I am breathless and angry. And memories from England keep flashing through my mind. My mum, being marched home from the pub. Him shouting at her.

I shake my head slowly from side to side. The dizziness, the chaos of racing thoughts. People passing me in all directions. Car horns blasting.

What just happened?

I set off down unfamiliar Manhattan streets, putting distance between me and the bar.

Just. Keep. Walking.

I see more faces passing me in the street, getting close up, leering. Patronising. 'Watch out, lady.' 'Fucking drunk.' 'You want some?' I stop, swaying slightly, and a man catches my arm. 'You OK? Do you need to sit down?'

'Fuck off,' I sneer, my words not coming out clearly. He shakes his head, raising his hands in submission, and walks on. I keep going.

I turn a corner, to get out the way of all the people. It's dark. But I feel safer with nobody around. Then I hear shouting. Arguing. Getting louder and louder as I stumble down the alley.

The back entrance to some bar. Two people are there. A man and a woman. The man's huge frame towering over her.

'You fucking bitch!'

The woman cowers beneath him. Priya.

As Priya cowers, I see in her my mum. My earliest memory is of her shaking in the corner of the room, looking at me, her face all black and puffy. 'It's all right, love. Everything's OK. You just get yourself to bed now. Pretend to be asleep, won't you.'

It wasn't OK. It was never OK.

I shake my head. I try to focus on what's in front of me.

Priya is begging. Pleading. 'Please, not now. Look, I promise. Tomorrow, we'll sort it. I'm sorry. I'm sorry.'

He's holding her by the throat. Steve.

They haven't seen me where I'm crouched. My hand brushes over something. Glass. A bottle. I look back up. Tears are streaming down Priya's cheeks as she bats uselessly at his hands.

I grab the bottle and lurch at him from behind. Hitting the back of his head as hard as I possibly can. All my rage unleashed. He lets go and she stumbles sideways, holding her throat. He falls, slamming hard on the pavement. Thwack.

The sound pulls me back into myself. I look at the bottle in my hand and hurl it at the wall, smashing it into pieces.

Priya goes to him. On the ground she's panicking. She checks his pulse. 'Oh God. Oh God.'

I stand confused. My vision blurs over and everything is in twos, threes, jerking in front of my eyes like a static television. I stagger, my feet all clumsy. I try really, really hard to be normal as I sink to my knees.

'He's not moving. He needs an ambulance. He's alive.' Her eyes are streaming. Is she crying for him? She picks up her phone and begins punching into it.

But she stops, holds it away from her and looks at him. Her fingers touch her neck where he gripped her.

Then she grabs me by the arm, shaking me, pulling me up.

And we run. Feet fast and hard on concrete. And we leave him there, unconscious, where he will be found moments later and blue-lighted to hospital.

The Seattle alleyway swims back into view, along with it a terrified young woman, pressed up against the bricks. A man looms over her, unbuckling his belt. Neither of them has seen me.

I never set out to kill anyone. But needs must – back in New York, it was him, or her. And once you've taken a life, well, it really does get easier. Especially when you're doing the world a favour.

There's a length of pipe leaning against a box nearby. Its weight is solid in my hand.

Dear reader, it appears I still have work to do.

Acknowledgements

Huge thanks to everyone who's helped Sally find her way into the world. Thanks especially to Emma and Elisha whose editorial guidance has been invaluable (and whose document comments have often had me giggling aloud) and to my ever patient and hugely supportive therapist (did I say therapist? Sorry, I meant agent) Jo. Thanks also to the wider Avon team who have helped on editorial (Maddie and Jess), marketing and publicity (Emily and Becky) and sales (Katie and Hannah). Also big thanks to Sarah who came up with the wonderful title, and Rebekah who designed the most gorgeous cover any author could wish for. As ever I'm eternally grateful to my husband Chris for helping me kick around new and increasingly visceral kill methods, to Sam for putting up with a stepmam who publicly uses the word 'trendy' in trendy coffee shops, and to my mum, family and friends who are eternally cheering me on from the sidelines (even though I never stop wanging on about my books). And finally I should thank my burning inner rage - together we created something good for a change.

Fern Britton
Picks
Exclusively for
TESCO

EXCLUSIVE ADDITIONAL CONTENT

Includes an author Q&A and details
of how to get involved in *Fern's Picks*

Fern's Picks

Dear lovely readers,

This month's pick is a deliciously dark revenge story with a villainous female anti-hero you'll find yourself rooting for from the very first page.

As the title suggests, *When Sally Killed Harry* is no love story: it's a hilariously twisted serial killer thriller set in modern-day New York. Sally, our heroine, is sick of dating apps – she's had enough bad first dates with arrogant men to last her a lifetime and only agrees to one final match to appease her housemate. Enter Harry, very much not our hero, who seems like the perfect catch.

Harry is charming, smart, funny attractive and even humble and they hit it off right away – but as Sally realises when she wakes up after a date without Harry or her life savings, when something seems to good to be true, it's usually because it is. When Sally gets over the shock, she realises she's not Harry's only victim she teams up with her fellow women scorned to exact their revenge on Harry, and all the men who wronged them…

This book is filled with gallows humour and plot twists to die for coupled with compelling emotional depth and depictions of female friendship that will resonate on so many levels. This is a gripping rollercoaster of a book, perfect for anyone who wants to see the tables turned on *The Tinder Swindler* or *Sweet Bobby*.

I do hope you enjoy it, and I can't wait to hear what you think!

With love
Fern x

Fern Britton Picks

Exclusively for TESCO

Fern's Picks

Look out for more books, coming soon!

For more information on the book club, exclusive Q&As with the authors and reading group questions, visit Fern's website **www.fern-britton.com/ferns-picks**

We'd love you to join in the conversation, so don't forget to share your thoughts using **#FernsPicks**

Fern's Picks

A Q&A with Lucy Roth (a.k.a. Lucy Nichol)

Warning: contains spoilers

The heroine in revenge thrillers are often morally ambiguous. How did you approach Sally, so that audiences could empathize with her while challenging their moral boundaries?

I think morally ambiguous characters in this genre need to have a blend of two things. Firstly, they need a very real and justifiable reason for their anger – something that will propel them to act on whatever they've faced. When it comes to Sally, Harry's treatment of her triggers many years of past trauma, so she definitely has good reason to go after him. Secondly, I think these characters' actions need to be fantastical and pretty 'out there' – after all, we're not seriously saying wronged women should become serial killers, but it's fiction! And we've all fantasised scenarios about 'getting our own back' without worrying about what that makes us in reality – because fantasy is fantasy. It's a cathartic release. So, in fiction, why not have some fun with it?!

What do you see as the broader cultural significance of feminist revenge thrillers, and how does *When Sally Killed Harry* contribute to the evolution of the genre?

We've grown up with so many news headlines about women being murdered or abused, and had to live our lives so carefully, meticulously planning running or walking routes. Women have shouldered the responsibility of bad men's actions for so long, that, when it comes to fiction, we need an escape. We need a way to acknowledge the reality, but to enjoy a different ending. It's important in society that perpetrators are held to account, that progress is made to positively influence how young boys and men relate to women and to continue to acknowledge the many women fighting back in positive ways – campaigning, speaking out, facilitating support. But fiction has a different purpose. And a bit of fantastical revenge is, as I say above, cathartic. I think that's why this genre has become so popular and why I don't think it's ready to go away any time soon. *When Sally Killed Harry* adds to this, and I absolutely don't think it'll be the last!

When Sally Killed Harry is a funny story with a lot of moments where the reader laughs out loud. What role does humour play in your story, and how did you use it to navigate the tension between empowerment and the darker aspects of revenge?

The genre already provides some light relief through fantastical revenge, and humour only adds to this. But it does need to be balanced sensitively. In *When Sally Killed Harry*, humour is never used when the women are discussing their experiences at the hands of abusive men, because there's simply nothing funny about that and it happens in reality every single day. But when it comes to the fantasy revenge aspects, that's when I felt free to chuck in a few laughs – a revenge plot going wrong and becoming a bit farcical, for example. There's also lots of relatable humour in there – after all, we've all had a bad date that we can look back on with equal parts laughter and cringe.

Tell us about the role of friendship and female bonds in the novel. Why were these important in your storytelling?

I'm such a big believer in women lifting up other women. Watching programmes like *Bad Sisters* where the main focus is on the relationships between the women rather than the women and their partners is joyous – and something most of us wholly relate to. As someone who has a relatively small and fractured family, I remember that my side of the hall on my wedding day was mostly made up of my closest girlfriends, compared to my husband's side that was jam-packed with loads of aunts and uncles and cousins. So, my girlfriends mean the absolute world to me – they are my family. So, it was completely natural for me to focus on female friendship in the book.

Fem's Picks

I love the idea of your girlfriends as your chosen family! In a similar vein, there's a trend in content online about female friendships serving as free therapy, much like Priya and Sally's dynamic throughout the book – was this an intentional nod the online world, or an organic representation of the dynamics in your own life?

I think it was probably more an organic representation than anything else – it came easily because it does represent reality. My girlfriends are always there for me, and I hope they feel I'm there for them, too. In fact, once a year, six of us get together to decompress and recalibrate in a woodland lodge with a hot tub, tons of food, bubbly and beer to sing along to Neneh Cherry and pick out our Eurovision favourites. We've done it every May since lockdown rules were lifted and it's become the one calendar event, we all stick to because we all need it so much. Girlfriends are without doubt the perfect tonic.

Have your own experiences of misogyny and violence against women shaped your writing?

Firstly, I need to say that I feel lucky to have got through life without anything seriously bad happening to me. That said, I've had my top grabbed at on the street, I've been flashed at from the bushes, I've been harassed by a supervisor on work experience as a teenager, I've been bullied and gaslighted by male business leaders, I've had my arse grabbed when I was minding my own business. And I have to think carefully about where or what time of day I go for a walk or a run. I'm no man-hater – I am married to a wonderful man and have a fabulous stepson in his mid-twenties and I can confidently say both are feminists. I know it's not all men – but how am I to know which are the bad ones? Every woman is affected by the actions of bad men, whether they've been directly harmed by them or not, because they limit how we life our daily life. That is always at the back of my mind, and I have more than one book either in print, in the proverbial drawer or itching to get out of my head that addresses this.

Fem's Picks

Building on your own experiences, you mention a lot of <u>female</u> musicians throughout the book – and give particular mention to riot girl band Bikini Kill at a poignant moment. So, Sally is clearly a fan, but what about you – is this book a nod to 'riot girl feminism'?

Music is featured in some way in literally everything I write, because it's so, so important to me. I think because I grew up listening to bands like Hole, Babes in Toyland and Bikini Kill (who I was lucky to see play live!) and they all introduced me to the fact that women can be snarly and angry and say things out loud in ways we were always taught that, as girls and women, we shouldn't. I loved that and it had a huge impact on me growing up. And I think Sally is representative of that idea too – that, when she's had enough, the world's going to know about it. She's not the most palatable person, she would no doubt hate the word 'nice' and she's no people pleaser, but just because she's a woman, does she really need to be nice and conforming and gentle and liked by everyone? Hell, no!

I always create playlists for my books too because songs often set the scene for me. I was out running before I got into the full swing of writing *When Sally Killed Harry* and 'You're a Germ' by Wolf Alice came on and I was like – that's it. That's the vibe. It became my 'theme tune' when I was writing the book. It's angry and talks about a horrible, toxic man who seems to be preying on an impressionable younger girl, but there's a kind of cheerleader vibe to it as well when she's sending him to hell. And that cheerleader vibe to me represents the women supporting each other.

I'm always fascinated by how different authors approach their writing – can you tell us a little bit about your process and routine?

I think I approach it depending on which way the wind's blowing. The quote from Alice in Wonderland – *I knew who I was this morning, but I've changed a few times since then* – definitely epitomises me. My moods swing, my ideas come thick and fast (or sometimes they vanish entirely), I change my mind (and hair colour) a lot, and my energy levels are up and down. So, I write what I feel like writing at the time – and whether that's jumping headfirst into a scene and seeing where it takes me, or carefully plotting a synopsis because I've got a hook and some twisty ideas, really depends on the day. One thing I will say though, is that often I've written most of a book when a brand-new idea for a twist suddenly takes me and I have to go back over it all from the beginning to drip feed it in. But it never feels laborious, because these are the bits that make writing the book exciting to me.

You obviously deal with a lot of darker themes in the relationship between Sally and Harry – and whilst I think we can all agree this isn't a rom-com – do you think it could be classified as a romance in any way?

I think we can call it a *toxic* romance! The thing is, if we look back at past dates or relationships, there will often be some very bad examples and experiences in our own romantic history. Things that feel exciting at the time but also make you feel sick or angry or insecure. Or someone you can't stop thinking about who you know is definitely *not* good partner material. Harry takes that to another level – and Sally's response is also pretty wild. Sally, in spite of her trust issues because she's making such a big effort in trying to open up more to people, is taken in by him on a romantic level. But then, probably also due to her past and having no reference point for what healthy love should be, she develops a kind of animalistic attraction to him that she can't explain. And I think we've all been there – but Sally, being the extreme character that she is, takes it to the max!

Questions for your Book Club

Warning: contains spoilers

- Do you think Sally's actions, and those of the women in her group, were justified?

- Who in Sally's group, Some Women, did you relate to the most and why?

- The book deals a lot with misogyny and the different ways in which women have to navigate risks in their daily lives – for example being conned when using a dating app or attacked while walking alone. There is a huge pressure on women to take responsibility for themselves – but is there a way in which men can play a more proactive role?

- If you met your own Harry Collins, what would you do? Where would you turn to for support?

- Sally is both driven both by impulsive and planned actions – which do you find resonate with you the most, and why?

- Sally can sometimes come across as narcissistic. How much of her character do you think is pure narcissism (and why might she have developed in this way) and how much of it is simply out of sync with how women are expected to behave?

- Sally undergoes some deeply traumatic events, both throughout the novel and in her past (which we slowly learn more about throughout) – to what extent do you thinks Sally's past trauma dictates what she does next?

Fem's Picks

Fem's Picks

- If you met your own Harry Collins, what would you do? Where would you turn to for support?

- Why do you think feminist revenge thrillers are so popular these days? Can you recall any books or movies from the past that explored a similar revenge theme?

- Any dating horror stories or cringey tales of your own?

- And just for fun, if you had to cast the movie of the book – who would be your dream Sally and Harry?

An exclusive extract from Fern's new novel

The Good Servant

March 1932

Marion Crawford was not able to sleep on the train, or to eat the carefully packed sandwiches her mother had insisted on giving her. Anxiety, and a sudden bout of homesickness, prohibited both.

What on earth was she doing? Leaving Scotland, leaving everything she knew? And all on the whim of the Duchess of York, who had decided that her two girls needed a governess exactly like Miss Crawford.

Marion couldn't quite remember how or when she had agreed to the sudden change. Before she knew it, it was all arranged. The Duchess of York was hardly a woman you said no to.

Once her mother came round to the idea, she was in a state of high excitement and condemnation. 'Why would they want *you*?' she had asked, 'A girl from a good, working class family? What do you know about how these people live?' She had stared at Marion, almost in reverence. 'Working for the royal family... They must have seen something in you. My daughter.'

On arrival at King's Cross, Marion took the underground to Paddington. She found the right platform for the Windsor train and, as she had a little time to wait, ordered a cup of tea, a scone and a magazine from the station café.

She tried to imagine what her mother and stepfather were doing right now. They'd have eaten their tea and have the wireless on, tuned to news most likely. Her mother would have her mending basket by her side, telling her husband all about Marion's send off. She imagined her mother rambling on as the fire in the grate hissed and burned.

Fem's Picks

The train was rather full, but Marion found a seat and settled down to flick through her magazine. Her mind couldn't settle. Through the dusk she watched the alien landscape and houses spool out beside her. Dear God, what was she doing here, so far away from family and home? What was she walking into?

When the conductor walked through the carriage announcing that Windsor would be the next stop, she began to breathe deeply and calmly, as she had been taught to do before her exams. She took from her bag, for the umpteenth time, the letter from her new employers. The instructions were clear: she was to leave the station and look for a uniformed driver with a dark car.

She gazed out of the window as the train began to slow. She took a deep breath, stood up and collected her case and coat. *Come on, Marion. It's only for a few months. You can do this.*

Available now!

The No.1 Sunday Times bestselling author returns

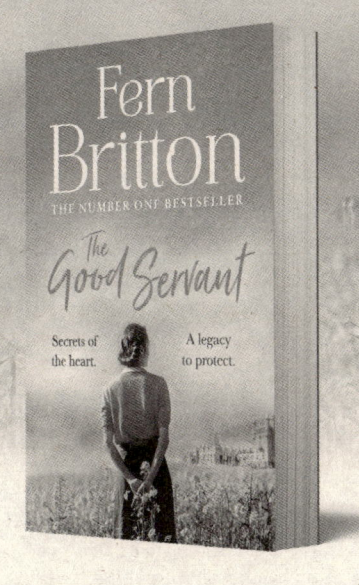

Fern's Picks

Balmoral, 1932

Marion Crawford, an ordinary but determined young woman, is given a chance to work at the big house as governess to two children, Lilibet and Margaret Rose.

Windsor Castle, 1936

As dramatic events sweep through the country and change all their lives in an extraordinary way, Marion loyally devotes herself to the family. But when love enters her life, she is faced with an unthinkable choice…

Available now!